ALLEN COUNTY

P9-BYY-882

3 1833 05797 7693

P[...]

DOMESTIC BLISS MYSTERY SERIES

POISONED BY GILT

"Fans of charming interior cozies and trips to Home Depot will appreciate this tragic twist on the challenges of eco-friendly innovations." —*Publishers Weekly*

"Erin Gilbert and her business partner Steve Sullivan are back in action. . . . With each installment, Caine devises the most charmingly written mystery filled with choice interior design morsels that make reading her books an absolute delight." —FreshFiction.com

FATAL FENG SHUI

"I love this series. Leslie Caine has a knack for cracking-good plotting and character development, with a touch of humor, and for giving readers something beyond standard cozy fare. She integrates the story with bits and pieces of design wisdom without getting the plot too far off-track. . . . All-in-all, it's a fun series cozy fans should give a whirl." —*Mystery News*

"This is Nancy Drew all grown up, armed with a tape measure and fabric swatches." —*Rocky Mountain News*

"Caine, a certified interior decorator, adds helpful decorating tips to her well-constructed mystery, making this a stylish, satisfying cozy." —*Publishers Weekly*

MYSTERY

NOV 1 3 2009

KILLED BY CLUTTER

"Sympathy for the hoarder's obsession and compassion for the elderly add appeal to the puzzle."
—*Booknews* from The Poisoned Pen

"Erin Gilbert is someone I'd like to hire." —*Deadly Pleasures*

MANOR OF DEATH

"A blueprint for murder." —*Mystery Scene*

"Caine delivers another top-notch Domestic Bliss whodunit. . . . Everyone in Maple Hills has something to hide, and that 'something' has to do with the decades-old death of Abby, the young girl who is rumored to haunt the Victorian mansion next door to interior designer Erin Gilbert. Can Erin unravel the truth before she becomes the next victim? Nifty decorating tips complete the package." —*Publishers Weekly*

"*Manor of Death* by Leslie Caine is a blueprint for murder as the third Domestic Bliss mystery unfolds. . . . Tips abound in this delightful package." —*Mystery Lovers Bookshop News*

FALSE PREMISES

"*False Premises* is a pleasant mystery that readers caught up in the current redecorating craze will not want to miss."
—*Mystery Reader*

"Replete with interior decorating, antique furnishings, not to mention floor plan and clothing critiques."
—*I Love a Mystery*

"Humor is never in short supply in this fun, engaging mystery, which is certain to delight fans of cozies."
—*Romantic Times*

DEATH BY INFERIOR DESIGN

"What a delight! A mystery within a mystery, a winning heroine, a yummy love interest, some laugh-out-loud lines ... and as if that weren't enough, some terrifically useful decorating tips."
—CYNTHIA BAXTER, author of *Dead Canaries Don't Sing*

"Mystery lovers who love *Trading Spaces* will adore *Death by Inferior Design*, a tale of dueling designers. In this stylish debut, Leslie Caine paints a winsome heroine with family woes, furnishes a well-upholstered murder, and accessorizes with well-patterned wit and a finishing touch of romance. Open the door, step inside, and enjoy!"
—DEBORAH DONNELLY

"Leslie Caine deftly merges hate-fueled homicide with household hints in her 'how-to/whodunit' mystery."
—MARY DAHEIM

"Witty and smart, with home decorating tips to die for!"
—SARAH GRAVES, bestselling author of the Home Repair Is Homicide series

"Leslie Caine's *Death by Inferior Design* sparkles with charm, design lore, and a sleuth with a great mantra. Cozy fans will embrace the Domestic Bliss series."
—CAROLYN HART, Agatha, Anthony, and Macavity awards winner

"*Trading Spaces* meets *Murder, She Wrote*! Talk about extreme makeovers! Dueling designers Gilbert and Sullivan might want to kill each other, but no one expected anyone to try it. Who will hang the trendiest curtains? Who will choose the poshest paint? Who will come out alive? I'm not tellin'." —PARNELL HALL

"[An] appealing heroine and warm, genuinely winning voice." —*Publishers Weekly*

"Interior designer/sleuth Erin Gilbert is wonderfully appealing and reading all the lovely details of her latest decorating job will make you feel like you've stumbled across the deadly side of HGTV."
—JERRILYN FARMER, bestselling author of the Madeline Bean mysteries

"An elegant and witty mystery that satisfies in every way. A surefire winner!"
—TAMAR MYERS, author of *Statue of Limitations*

"Caine has created a cozy with an edge, and its twists and turns keep the reader guessing until the end."
—*Romantic Times* (3 stars)

"For killer decorating tips, pick up *Death by Inferior Design*, a murder mystery by decorator Leslie Caine. Advice is woven into this whodunit featuring rival designers as sleuths." —*House & Garden*

"An interesting book, with lots of insider information on the interior design business... I'll look forward to the next in the series." —MAGGIE MASON

"This story is delightful in every way, and author Leslie Caine packs a solid punch as a writer.... Entertaining, humorous, serious, and totally engrossing from the first page to last... This tidy murder mystery has everything, from witty repartee to sorrow, from strong characters to a thrilling plot." —*Midwest Book Review*

"A promising debut... Caine writes with a passion that reveals a vision and a sense of style that should attract readers the way HGTV attracts viewers."
—*Alfred Hitchcock Mystery Magazine*

"Caine puts her experience as a certified interior decorator to good use in her debut.... If only all professionals had her discerning eye and sense of humor, there'd be fewer crimes against fashion and fiction." —*Peninsula (CA) Post*

Also by Leslie Caine

a domestic
bliss mystery

HOLLY
AND
HOMICIDE

Leslie Caine

A DELL BOOK

Dell

Sale of this book without a front cover may be unauthorized. If this book is coverless, it may have been reported to the publisher as "unsold or destroyed" and neither the author nor the publisher may have received payment for it.

Holly and Homicide is a work of fiction. Names, characters, places, and incidents are the products of the author's imagination or are used fictitiously. Any resemblance to actual events, locales, or persons, living or dead, is entirely coincidental.

A Dell Mass Market Original

Copyright © 2009 by Leslie Caine

All rights reserved.

Published in the United States by Dell, an imprint of The Random House Publishing Group, a division of Random House, Inc., New York.

DELL is a registered trademark of Random House, Inc., and the colophon is a trademark of Random House, Inc.

ISBN 978-0-440-24503-2

Cover design: Jamie S. Warren
Cover art: Daniel Craig

Printed in the United States of America

www.bantamdell.com

2 4 6 8 9 7 5 3 1

For my fabulous agent, Nancy Yost, to whom I and every fictional character I've ever created give a resounding and much-deserved standing ovation

HOLLY
AND
HOMICIDE

Chapter 1

The article about a grave robbery caught my attention. It was a short piece, only three or four column inches, on the second page of the *Snowcap Village Gazette*, which quoted a haughty wisecrack made by the local sheriff: "Probably another case of yuppie skiers robbing us of our ancestry, like the way they're turning the Goodwin estate into the Wendell Barton B-and-B." My heart started racing, and I thought: *Here we go again*.

Sullivan handed me a cup of coffee. Although he'd pulled on a pair of jeans and a black T-shirt before heading downstairs to the kitchen of the aforementioned Goodwin estate, he slipped back under the covers beside me, his own cup in hand.

"Thanks, sweetie." I took a tentative sip. Perfection. "Did you see the story about the grave robbery in this week's *Gazette*?"

"Yeah. Annoying potshot about the inn. Sheriff Mackey sounds like a major jerk."

"No kidding." Wendell Barton, who owned the ski resort a few miles from here, was just *one* of the partners who'd purchased this fabulous Victorian mansion from Henry Goodwin, a direct descendent of its original owner. Steve's and my two-person company—Sullivan & Gilbert Designs—was in charge of the remodel. "I suppose by 'yuppie skiers' turning this place into a 'Wendell Barton B-and-B,' he means you and me."

"Not if he's ever seen you try to ski," Sullivan teased.

I considered swatting him, but didn't want to risk his spilling coffee on our divine gold-and-burgundy silk duvet. I settled for narrowing my eyes at him. He laughed and kissed my forehead.

I felt the warm glow that I'd grown so wonderfully accustomed to during the nine-plus months since we'd started dating in earnest. "I'm getting better at skiing, you know. You said so yourself."

"Yes, you are, Gilbert. If you make good use of our last three weeks here, you might even be able to stop without grabbing onto a tree."

His snide remark called for a comeback, but my worry about the grave robbery nagged at me. Why would somebody steal a person's bones? I took a couple of sips of coffee and reread the article.

"I'm sure the incident at the cemetery was just a prank," Sullivan said. "Drunken frat boys on a ski trip, blowing off some steam, maybe."

"Their timing's odd, if that's all it was. They had to dig through snow and frozen ground, just for a dumb joke. You'd think they'd get maybe two inches down and decide to go TP some trees instead."

"Yeah, but it *has* to be a prank. What *sensible* motive could there possibly be? It's idiotic to dig up a random fifty-year-old grave. Wasn't there a really common name on the tombstone?"

" 'R. Garcia,' and the cemetery records are inadequate, so they don't even know how to track down Garcia's relatives." My imagination started to run wild in spite of myself. "Maybe that's why this particular grave was chosen . . . so as to ruffle the fewest feathers. I hope I'm just being paranoid, but this could be the handiwork of one of the hundred or so townspeople trying to prevent the Snowcap Inn from opening."

Sullivan stared at me, his gorgeous hazel eyes incredulous. "Seriously, Erin? You think someone's going to . . . what? Plant a skeleton in a closet here? Stick some bones underneath the gazebo to freak out the building inspector this morning?"

"Yes. That's precisely what I'm afraid someone wants to do."

He took a sip of coffee, appearing to ponder my words. "No way."

"All I know is, every time Henry Goodwin, or anyone

else, puts up a sign about the Snowcap Inn, someone covers it in graffiti."

"Still, Erin. That's a gigantic leap...from scribbling four-letter words on a sign to digging up a grave and planting someone's remains here. Don't you think?"

How could I answer that? His point was valid, but my counterargument was a combination of women's intuition and past experience. A string of terrible past experiences, to be more precise. The police department in Crestview—our hometown some seventy miles away—had undoubtedly been on the verge of assigning a homicide task force to follow me around. In the last three years, client after client had dragged Designs by Gilbert into a string of luck so bad that Job himself might have offered me a sympathetic shoulder. My gloomy run of catastrophes had magically lifted on Valentine's Day, when Steve and I finally gave in to our mutual attraction. Since then, we'd become the proverbial happy couple. And yet, even as a young child, I'd known there was no such thing as happily *ever* after. We were long overdue for a stumbling block.

I tried to employ my "confidence and optimism" mantra, but it was too late. With my penchant for stumbling across dead bodies, I knew with unshakeable certainty that "R. Garcia" was sure to turn up in my van or my laundry basket. Our idyllic job would devolve into a disaster. This wonderful three-story house had been built eighty years ago, as commissioned by the current owner's grandfather—the founder of Snowcap Village—but in these last couple of months, it had come to represent how far I'd grown in my career and in my life. Now this grand home, with its cupolas, curved turrets, festive stained-glass accent sidelights and transoms, and all its countless hand-crafted details, was somehow going to turn dark and ugly. And so was my life.

"Erin? You're shaking. Are you cold?"

"A little."

He set down his cup and pulled me close. "Let me warm you up again." He kissed me, and for a time, my fears melted away.

An hour later, I trotted down the stairs. Our bedroom was on the third floor of Henry's house—soon to be the Snowcap Inn. When the inn officially opened on Christmas Eve, Henry, too, would live elsewhere; he planned to rent a condo in town and then, once his mayoral duties officially ended next November, to travel. As I entered the central hall, which we were converting into a hotel lobby, I spotted Sullivan's notepad on the newly built receptionist's desk. He'd probably left his pad there by mistake; it contained measurements for the perfect Christmas tree to grace this space. Sullivan and Henry had headed out several minutes ago to cut down one of the large spruce trees on Henry's enormous parcel of land.

When I entered the kitchen through the double doors, a tall, angular, fortyish woman was peering into the knotty-pine cabinets and compiling an inventory of kitchenware. I waited till she'd completed her count of serving spoons, then said, "Hi. I'm Erin Gilbert, an interior designer here at the inn."

She peered at me a little too imperiously for my liking.

I got the feeling that she was tabulating the cost of my Icelandic cardigan (a gift from Steve) and designer slacks. She was wearing a crisp white shirt with pleats and piping, black pants, and loafers. She had limp brown hair in a blunt cut just above the nape of her long neck. She would have been pretty, except for her permanent-looking scowl. "Mikara Woolf. Manager-to-be of the Snowcap Inn." Her voice was confident, yet flat.

"Nice to meet you. Henry Goodwin said that you'd be starting sometime this week. My partner, Steve Sullivan, is here, too, and he—"

"Yeah, he's out back with Henry. Something about Christmas decorations...chopping down a tree, I think. Quite a hunk, that Mr. Sullivan." She raised an eyebrow. "You two are sleeping together, right? And you're not married?"

"Um, much as I hate to get us off on the wrong foot, frankly, I don't see why you're asking, or why I should answer."

She gave me a slight smile. "Oh, I realize it's none of my business...even though you *did* give me my answer just now. I'm simply checking the accuracy of the local rumor mill. I'm a native...back from when everybody knew one another. The town went to pot ten years ago, when Snowcap Village was turned into the 'New Mini-Vail.' Back when Wendell Barton bought the mountain...along with every*thing* and every*one* else."

"If part of small-town life means everyone discussing who's sleeping with whom, there's something to be said for tourist towns and anonymity."

She crossed her arms and gave me another visual once-

over. "Spoken like a city girl. Where are you from originally? New York? Philadelphia?"

"No, I grew up in the suburbs. Of the Albany area."
She cocked an eyebrow as if she doubted me, and for the
purposes of full disclosure, I conceded, "But I went to college and trained in New York."

She smirked and nodded. "Another New Yorker.
Figured as much."

I bristled and found myself adding defensively, "Steve's
a native Coloradoan."

"Yeah, I figured that out, too."

"Huh. I'll have to remind him to stop wearing his
'Colorado Native' sweatshirt so often."

To her credit, she laughed. Maybe she wasn't quite as
standoffish as all that. "Guess I'm coming off as a little
judgmental. My apologies. It's been a rough week. You
wouldn't believe the flak I'm getting from my sister and
former neighbors for accepting this job. They think I've
sold my soul to the devil by agreeing to work here . . . considering it now belongs to Barton."

"Oh, for heaven's sake! *Henry Goodwin* has the final
say in everything regarding the remodel, *not* Wendell
Barton. Henry has control over just about everything for a
full year. Furthermore, the inn *doesn't* belong to Wendell.
He's just one of three partners, including Audrey Munroe,
my friend and landlady back in Crestview. She's got more
integrity than anyone I know. She's not about to cede full
control to Barton, or to anyone else, for that matter."

"I assume you mean Audrey Munroe of the *Domestic
Bliss* television show." Mikara gave me a smug smile.
"She's currently dating Wendell Barton."

"What?!" Apparently the Small-Town Gossip Express was way ahead of me.

"Angie, my sister, spotted them together at The Nines last Saturday night."

Much as I wanted to deny the accuracy of Mikara's information, it could very well be true; there'd been some sparks between Wendell and Audrey when I'd last seen them, at an inn meeting on Friday afternoon; Steve and I had gone back to Crestview immediately afterward. During the remodel, we had full use of any of the eight mostly completed guest bedrooms, which we'd designed ourselves. That allowed us to make the ninety-minute commute to Crestview only when we so chose, which generally meant on weekends, so that I could be with Hildi, my adorable black cat, who was happier at home.

Truth be told, I disliked Wendell Barton. He'd struck me as a blowhard. I'd yet to find a Snowcap resident who had a single nice thing to say about the man. Then again, from the sound of things, Mikara hadn't found any residents to say anything nice about *me*, either, so maybe this town was snooty about all nonnatives.

"In another week or two, Wendell's going to have Ms. Domestic Bliss in his sweaty palm," Mikara continued, "and next thing you know, he'll flatten that gazebo you just built out back and erect a half dozen condos in its place."

"If you're so negative about Snowcap Inn's future, why did you take this job?"

"I'm a pragmatist. The inn is paying me really well. Especially compared to the pittance I used to make at the art gallery."

I heard the back door open, followed by the stomping of snowboots on the mat and the rumbling tones of Steve's voice. I couldn't help but smile. All this beauty that surrounded us—the blanket of pure white snow, the glittering stars, the red sashes and green boughs on all the storefronts, the charming cabins, town homes, and quaint shops in Snowcap Village—was only encouraging my lovesickness.

The two men entered the kitchen. Henry, soon to be the former owner of this large estate, was a tall, lanky man in his mid-forties who looked like he'd stepped out of an L.L. Bean ad. He'd been born with a silver spoon in his mouth, although he'd apparently traded that spoon for a camper's spork. Aside from his current duties as mayor, he hadn't held an actual job in his life. He'd invested his father's sizable fortune well and spent his time pursuing women and the great outdoors.

Steve's face lit up when our eyes met (which made my day), and Henry smiled broadly at the sight of Mikara. "You've got perfect timing, Mikki, as usual," he said. "Just in time for you to butter up your sister." Henry waggled his thumb in the direction of the back door. "Angie's here now, doing the inspection on the new gazebo."

"Wait," I said to Mikara, instantly anxious. "Your *sister* is the building inspector?"

"It's a small town," she replied with a shrug.

"But you just told me she doesn't want the inn to open!"

"She'll be reasonable, though, won't she, Mikki?" Henry asked.

"Sure. She won't cause trouble . . . as long as you don't

have any violations. She'll be a total stickler for detail. Don't go expecting her to cut you any slack, is all I'm saying."

Henry stared at her. "But...the city codes are chockfull of minutiae that could be used to nitpick us indefinitely! You're her sister. She'll show some family loyalty, surely...right?"

"If that's why you hired me, Henry, you misjudged my sister by a mile!"

Henry massaged his forehead in a silent confirmation that he *did* hire Mikara for political reasons. "Good thing it's just the gazebo, then. We can tear it down if we have to. But she passed the inn's plumbing and electric work two weeks ago."

Sullivan grimaced. "If Angie already inspected the plumbing, why was she taking tap water samples last Friday?"

"She does some contract work for the health inspectors, too," Mikara replied.

Henry paled a little at this news, but seemed to visibly steel himself a moment later. "So, Mikki, you wanted to make this a live-in position, right? Did you pick out a bedroom yet?"

"Not yet. Why? Does my bedroom have to be located in the basement?"

He laughed heartily and winked in Sullivan's and my direction. "Such a kidder. No. Just not the master bedroom."

"Ah, yes," she said with a sigh. "I remember that room well."

Henry winced slightly at the remark, and I had to mask

my own reaction. Had Henry actually hired his former lover to manage their love-nest-cum-B&B? No chance of trouble *there*!

"I'm sure you plan on charging hundreds a night for that room," Mikara added.

"Absolutely. It's a huge space. Erin, Steve, and Audrey Munroe are using the third-floor bedrooms until we open on Christmas Eve. Gilbert and Sullivan Designs is refurbishing this place from top to bottom, literally."

I gave Sullivan a quick grin, which he answered with a wink; we were actually Sullivan and Gilbert Designs, but clients inevitably got it wrong.

"The bedrooms just need Christmas decorations and whatnot," Henry continued, "then they're all set to be rented out. So . . . I was hoping you'd consider moving into my old office on the main floor."

"Fine. That makes sense," Mikara said with a grim nod. "You don't want to confuse the paying guests by having them mingle upstairs with the hired help."

He clicked his tongue. "Come on! You're not the hired help. You're the *manager*. I need you to lead the troops. My contract only gives me control of the daily operations of this joint for another ten months. As of next October first, I'm entrusting the operations and procedures of the Snowcap Inn entirely to you. I wouldn't have sold if I hadn't always pictured you here, managing the inn."

Although I personally found his minispeech quite persuasive—so much so that my mind's eye was already envisioning a lovely transformation from home office to Mikara's bedroom—she glared at him and put her hands on her narrow hips. "You should never have sold this place, even so."

"We've been through this before," he snapped. "I'm a sworn bachelor. It was nuts, my having this huge place all to myself. Especially when I'd just as soon be backpacking across Europe. Besides, the Snowcap Ski Resort is never going away. This town has got to accept that fact . . . learn how to maintain its community ties even while embracing the seasonal tourist trade."

"So you sold to Wendell Barton and a couple of in-name-only partners."

"They're hardly puppets, Mikki. Audrey Munroe and Chiffon Walters each own thirty percent of the inn now."

"But Chiffon's just a mindless bimbo who happened to record a couple of hit pop songs some five years ago. And promptly bought a luxury condo next to Wendell's mountain. She's no match for Barton!"

"That's not true! Chiffon's got a great head on her shoulders. Barton's powerless unless she or Audrey sides with him. And I trust both of them implicitly." He added pointedly, "I set things up that way specifically so Barton could never tear down this house and put a hundred condos in its place."

"Better get ready for the bulldozer, then," Mikara said with a snort. "Your Ms. Munroe and Mr. Barton are the new hot couple. Or as hot as anyone in their sixties can be, that is. Angie saw them necking at The Nines."

Henry looked stricken.

"If Wendell's dating Audrey strictly to win her vote, his plan will backfire," I quickly interjected.

"Erin's right," Steve added. "Audrey has a mind of her own."

"So does *every* woman—" Mikara glanced at Henry, then added sadly, "—right up until she falls in love."

There was an uncomfortable amount of truth in Mikara's remark, which gave me pause; we women *do* have a tendency to adopt our lovers' viewpoints. Sullivan glanced at me, and I felt my cheeks grow warm.

"Erin, did you see where I left my notepad?" he whispered. "I measured the—"

"It's on the desk in the lobby."

He nodded.

The doorbell rang. "That's probably Angie," Henry said. "I asked her to give us the results of her inspection right away. Let's all treat her with respect, regardless of what she says."

"Oh, darn," Mikara muttered. "Now I won't be able to spit in my sister's eye, like usual."

Ignoring her, Henry strode into the lobby. Moments later, a blonder, younger version of Mikara entered the kitchen, followed by Henry. Mikara forced a smile. "Hey, Angie," she said. "You've got the work done already?"

"Yeah. But there's a big problem."

Why am I not surprised? I thought. Henry grimaced and did a double take, but Mikara merely sighed and introduced me to her sister.

"Nice to meet you, Angie," I said with a big smile.

"Hi, Angie," Sullivan said, giving her a charming smile. "Good to see you again." She barely looked at him, which to my mind was similar to the jury not looking at the defendant before they announced their guilty verdict.

"I can't believe there was anything wrong with the gazebo construction," Henry said. "You know what a great job Ben Orlin always does."

"There's nothing wrong with the gazebo. But there's too much lead in your tap water. I can't approve of this residence being converted into a motel."

"Fortunately," Henry promptly countered, "you don't *have* to. We intend to use the house as a small bed-and-breakfast *inn*."

"Right," Angie said with a sneer. "That's even worse. You'll have to get restaurant approval. Cooking meals and serving tap water rife with these poisons is out of the question."

"We use the city water here. Same as everyone else."

"It's got nothing to do with the water supply. You've got bad pipes. You'll have to replace them all."

Sullivan and I exchanged puzzled glances; contaminants could be removed with filters, which would be much easier and less expensive than replacing pipes. We needed to wait until Angie left to tell Henry that, though; my hunch was that otherwise Angie would find some arcane ruling that prohibited water filtering.

"Our pipes are copper, not lead!" Henry shouted.

"Must be the solder in all the joints," she said with a shrug. "Or else maybe they're copper-coated lead pipes."

"Oh, come off it!" Henry shouted. "You're making this stuff up, and we both know it! Now, what's it going to take to get you to give the water here a passing grade?"

"Are you offering me a bribe, Mr. Goodwin?"

"No, I'm just—"

"Good, because that would be a federal crime, and

you're in enough trouble already. What with your lead contaminants and your faulty front steps."

"Front steps?"

She gave him a sly grin. "I must have forgotten to tell you. They're too steep for a business...and particularly for a business that's going to have geriatrics and little children going up and down them all the time."

"Toddlers and geriatric guests can use the back door and our handicap access."

"*Or* you can follow the law, and rebuild to meet the city codes, so they can use your *front* steps."

"Angie!" Mikara cried. "Quit busting Henry's chops!"

She glowered at Mikara. "Hey, sis. You know, it's like what you said to me when you left the house this morning: 'I'm just trying to do my job.' " She used a lilting voice and flitted her eyes derisively, mocking her sister.

"You're being a brat, Angela!"

"And you're being a weasel!" Angie shot her sister a furious glare, then she softened her expression slightly and said to Henry, "The bottom line is there are unacceptable levels of lead in the water supply. Fix it, or else you're not going to be able to convert this place into a bed-and-breakfast."

"But we're opening on Christmas Eve! In three weeks!"

"Then you'd better *get the lead out,* hadn't you," she said. "Plus, have the entire concrete stoop demolished and rebuilt to code." She tore off a pink copy from her clipboard and handed it to him. "Here's your official notice. Pity your violations will probably delay your opening. But take heart, *Mayor Goodwin.* There's always *next* Christmas."

She strode toward the front door, glanced back over her shoulder, and said with a haughty smile, "Good seeing you, Henry."

"Be real careful on the steps," he snarled. "We wouldn't want you to fall and crack your head open."

Chapter 2

That went well," I said with a sigh.

"Yeah, it sure did," Henry said. "It's really touching to see how strong that sisterly bond is between you two, Mikki."

Mikara wore a pained expression as she stared at Henry, but she held her tongue.

"Angie's concerns are easy enough to resolve, Henry," Sullivan said. "It should take less than a week to remake the front steps and to fix the troubles with your water. We'll put in a rush order for a commercial-grade water filter. Then we'll hire a plumber, and with any luck at all, we can have Angie back out here for the retest in ten days."

Henry widened his eyes. "You're saying we can just filter out the lead from the water?"

"Yeah," Sullivan replied. "It'll cost a couple grand, but replacing all the pipes would be much more expensive."

Henry released a sigh of relief. "Great! Then we're still in business! Interesting that Angie didn't mention a simple water filter. No doubt she'll just drum up some more picayune nonsense in the code books to throw at us. But, at least for the time being, we're a step ahead of her."

"You can't expect my sister or anyone else to greet your inn with open arms, Henry," Mikara exclaimed. "We elected you as our mayor! Next thing we know, you're partnering up with Wendell Barton himself. It feels like you turned your back on Snowcap Village."

He looked stunned. "I did no such thing. I worked my ass off, trying to watch out for the future development of this town, and I turned down a small fortune by declining Wendell's bid for full ownership." He regarded her coolly and shook his head. "I'm surprised you agreed to come work for me in the first place, considering how you feel."

"I needed the money. Plus, I love this house. You know that. I love its history and what it means to this town. *Somebody* needs to treat this property with the respect it deserves. Eventually, the townies will embrace the Snowcap Inn and will proudly show it off to visitors. But for now, Henry, you should try looking at things from their perspective. Act like our forty-two-year-old mayor, not like a twenty-year-old kid who's dying to skip town and get back to nature."

Henry jabbed his index finger at her. "I'm your boss, Mikara! If you can't accept that and treat me with respect for the one lousy year, you should leave now!"

Not backing down, she took another step toward him. "Oh, for God's sake, Henry! Of course I respect you! But I'm here to get this place running smoothly, so I'm not about to sit back and watch you actively make enemies!" She pointed at the door to the main hall. "You need to get out there and shake some hands, brush some elbows, just like you did last year to win the election. Convince the townies you're not bailing on them. Remind everyone this house is converting to a B-and-B, not a BaseMart department store! Treat my *sister* with some respect!"

"Fine. I'm not going to argue with you." Henry stuck his hands in the pockets of his jeans. "I'll play the friendly politician again, for the sake of harmony."

"Good! Now everyone please excuse me and let me complete my inventory." She pivoted and marched back over to the drawer where she'd been counting serving spoons when we first met.

Steve, Henry, and I took the not-so-subtle hint and left the room in favor of the spacious lobby. Henry began to pace on the slate floor in front of the enormous moss-rock fireplace. Sullivan and I exchanged glances; his thoughts were no doubt similar to mine. Lovely as this town and this house were, we'd stepped into a hornet's nest—one with a formidable queen bee. I hoped Henry actually *was* weighing her excellent advice, and not just capitulating quickly as an aftereffect of their past history.

"I should've seen this coming," Henry said quietly. "I honestly thought Mikki would be the one lifelong Snowcap resident nobody would dare harangue."

"*And* you assumed you'd sail through Angie's final inspections with Mikara working here," I muttered.

"Yeah, of course I did," he snapped, pacing with increased fervor. "In theory, it seemed like the perfect move. But if anything, we're getting *more* guff from her sister, now that Mikara's officially manager. Looks like I'm going to have to outwit Wendell at his own game."

"*What* game? What does one-upping Wendell Barton have to do with appeasing the building inspector?"

Still marching back and forth across the hearth like an overwound toy soldier, Henry didn't answer. He popped a Tic Tac in his mouth. He'd once explained that he suffered from anxiety attacks but hated to take medication, so he'd managed to convince himself that breath mints were beta-blockers. "We have to show this town that Audrey Munroe and Chiffon Walters are the real owners of the Snowcap Inn."

"The thing is," Sullivan interjected, "they each own a smaller percentage of the inn than Wendell does."

"Just by a few percentage points," Henry grumbled.

Sullivan was clearly worried, which meant we were picking up on the same signals; Henry was now acting like a client on the verge of making an ill-timed decision. His bearing was eerily reminiscent of a homeowner we'd worked for just six months ago who suddenly insisted upon moving her recently completed marble fireplace to a different wall.

"Come on, Henry," Sullivan said. "Let's go chop down that tree we picked out."

Henry frowned. "In a minute." He squared his shoulders. "I'm going to have to take some action here. Especially since it looks like Audrey and Wendell are in bed together, or might be soon."

"In all honesty, Henry," I began, "Audrey's one of my favorite people, and she's not—"

He held up a hand. "Poor choice of wording. The point is, though, Chiffon and Audrey need to be kept happy and brought forward . . . front and center in everyone's mind. We need to publicly reveal that both women have a big role in this inn. You know what I'm saying? Plus, they both need to feel valued and needed. Otherwise, the minute my back is turned, they're going to let Wendell buy them out."

I shook my head. "Audrey's already wealthy, and she truly loves this house. In some ways, it's a larger version of her own house in Crestview. She just wants to have a hand in running a successful B-and-B in the mountains, I promise you. She isn't in it for the money."

"She *will* be, though, when Barton puts visions of dollar signs dancing in her head. But even if you're right about Audrey, Mikara made an excellent point earlier. We can't trust *Chiffon* not to let Barton pay her off. So I'm giving her a big, splashy ego boost by showing her off to this town. I'm calling Chiffon up, and I'm putting *her* in charge of the Christmas display outside. She already expressed interest in doing that for us. If you two could please help her with anything she asks, this will all turn out just great."

Precisely what the woman who wanted us to move her fireplace said. Immediately prior to the sinkhole that developed. "So...I should hold off on hanging the outside lights?" I asked.

"For now, yeah. Just till we see if they'll fit in with Chiffon's ideas. To keep Audrey from feeling left out, I'll put her in charge of dreaming up a theme for the interior Christmas decorations."

"Should *Audrey* pick out the tree with me?" Sullivan asked.

Henry was already saying, "Hello, Chiffon?" into his cell phone and didn't answer. Once again, Steve and I exchanged glances. Steve mimed having a noose tighten around his neck.

A few minutes later, while Sullivan and Henry engaged in the manly pursuit of chopping down a tree, I took it upon myself to order a top-of-the-line high-volume water filtration system. Even an inspector hell-bent on flunking this place would be unable to criticize our lead-contaminant levels once the filter was installed. The unit would be shipped immediately and would arrive on Friday.

Oddly, the plumbers in town seemed to have time available until I identified *where* the work was to be done, at which point they claimed to be booked solid till after Christmas. I blew up at the third plumber, who'd grumbled about "the Wendell Barton B-and-B," and I cried, "What is it with you people?! Don't you all take service calls at Barton's numerous *condos*?"

"Sure we do, lady. Just not at the mayor's house. He claimed to be one of us in order to get our vote, then the chump sold out to Barton!"

"Suit yourself. You're only depriving yourself of a nice paycheck. I'll get a plumber from out of town, or see if Ben Orlin can install it."

"Better to lose one customer than all of the local business. Or to get all my work flunked by the building inspector from here on out."

That captured my full attention. "You mean that Angie Woolf is coercing you into refusing to work for Henry?"

There was a pause. "Not exactly," he said. "I haven't talked to Angie in weeks. That's just the buzz around town. But you didn't hear it from me." He hung up.

Stunned, I mulled the situation and decided to discuss the townies with Ben Orlin, our contractor, who seemed to be one of the only local residents likely to be frank with me. Three months ago he'd forewarned that we were going to be run through the wringer before we'd be allowed to open our doors. At the time, that notion had seemed silly; who could possibly object to a tasteful B-and-B? Obviously we'd underestimated the widespread hostility toward Wendell.

I dialed Ben's cell phone and heard it ring nearby. It sounded like he was upstairs. I looked up and called out, "Ben?" from the middle of the hall.

"Yeah. Just a sec, Erin." He was leaning over the oak railing now, and waved to me. "There's someone on my phone."

"No, that's me, too. I didn't realize you were nearby."

"Just fixing the closet door that came off its tracks on the second floor. Be right there."

A moment later he came down the stairs. Ben was an unassuming man in his early forties. He always wore work boots, baggy jeans, a long-sleeved thermal, and a flannel shirt. He seemed to shave only on Sundays. This being Tuesday, he had a moderate stubble.

"Did Angie Woolf have problems with the gazebo?" he asked.

"No, with our concrete front steps. She says they're too steep."

He grimaced. "That's going to be a pain in the . . . neck to fix. Did she leave the specs?"

"I think so. She said the whole stoop would need to be demolished and rebuilt."

He scratched his head through his mop of brown hair. "That means I've got to go rent a bulldozer. And hire a demo crew. Might as well get right on it. We'll have to hope the weather forecast will cooperate for pouring new cement. If so, I might be able to do the job myself."

"Do you think you could also install a filtration system for the tap water? It's supposed to arrive on Friday."

He grimaced, but then replied, "Yeah, sure. No problem."

"Thank you. That's a relief. When it comes to construction, you're really a jack-of-all-trades."

He shrugged. "You kind of *have* to be in this business. Plus, I built my own house from the ground up. Gave me something to do during the construction slumps."

"Your skills are sure turning out to be helpful for our sake. Angie seems to have it in for us. The plumbers I spoke with wouldn't even come out for fear of losing customers in town and Angie flunking their future inspections." I paused, but he had no comment. Still hoping to get his perspective, I prompted, "Everyone in town calls this 'the Wendell Barton B-and-B.' I hope all the work we've given you here is a good thing for you, ultimately. It's more than clear that the old-time residents of Snowcap don't appreciate this project."

"It's no problem. Folks don't ever begrudge *my* working on the Goodwin estate. I took over this carpentry business from my father, who headed up many a renovation in this house." He grinned proudly and gestured at the steps. "He rebuilt this staircase himself, step by step, spindle by spindle."

"It's spectacular," I said honestly as I gazed at the stunning creation. It was one of the grandest staircases I'd ever seen, suitable for Rhett to ascend with Scarlett in his arms. This was actually the second time that Ben had told me about his father's handiwork, but it displayed such fine craftsmanship that the story bore repeating.

"I think I already told you that my grandfather was one of the chief carpenters who built this house for Henry Goodwin's grandfather, some eighty years ago. So this old house and me have got a bond. Not even Wendell Barton can take that away from me."

"It sounds like you don't like him, either."

He squirmed but then answered affably, "He came in and changed the whole nature of this town. I got the same old gripe everyone's got with him." He chuckled. "I'm sure Mikara gave you an earful. She's been catching quite a bit of criticism around town for coming to work here."

A drawer slammed in the kitchen behind us. Ben winced. "Oops. *That* ain't gonna sit well. I'm gonna catch holy hell myself for talking about her behind her back."

"Sorry about that," I answered quietly. "And for your needing to rebuild the front porch steps, too."

"That's all right. 'Twasn't your fault." He started to head toward the front door, then stopped. "Hey, I almost forgot to ask. Where'd you want the bamboo chair?"

"*What* bamboo chair?"

"It was in a box on the back porch. All sealed up, but with no shipping label, beyond 'The Goodwin estate' scrawled in marker. I just found it there when I first got here this morning, a little after eight."

"Do you have any idea who sent it?"

"Beats me. Sometimes delivery men leave boxes out there. I brought it in, unpacked it, and left it in the office."

"Maybe it's Mikara's."

"Oh, yeah," Ben said. "That's probably it. I better go ask before I recycle the box, though." He left, heading for the kitchen, and I sorted through the tree decorations. Steve and Henry would be bringing the tree in any minute. Although I couldn't hang the external lights today or trim the tree, my new plan was to get the preliminary steps done—wire the star in place and hang the tree lights.

"She says it's not hers," Ben said, returning to the room. "Meantime, I really gotta get goin' on those front steps."

"I'll look into it on my own, Ben. Thanks."

Curious now, I went into the office to see the chair for myself. It was constructed from cheap wicker and was round with a high back—hardly the quality of anything Sullivan and Gilbert Designs would select. If someone over two hundred pounds were to sit on it, the thing could shatter into daggerlike pieces.

Mikara entered the room. "Is this the chair Ben was talking about?"

"It must be." I started to run my hand over the cane on the seat. There's not a whole lot to—" I stopped and jerked my hand back. "A spider," I said as I watched the arachnid speed across the surface. I spotted two more. Then a fourth.

"Jeez," I muttered. "What's going on? There's a ton of them!"

"What the—" Mikara looked inside the large box, which Ben had left just inside the door. "There's a batch of spiders in the box, too! This is going to be my bedroom! We've got to get this out of here!" She ran out of the room, shouting, "Ben!"

With my skin crawling, I dragged the box over and shoved the chair inside. By then, Ben had rushed to join us.

"I'm telling Henry he has to pay to have this room fumigated," Mikara grumbled. "This was a trap, meant for me! I'm surprised they didn't paint 'Benedict Arnold Woolf' on the chair."

"Nobody could have known this was going to be your room," I replied.

"That's right," Ben said. He hoisted the box off the floor. "I only put it here so it'd be out of the way. Tell Henry I'm taking this thing straight out to the Dumpster."

Mikara watched Ben carry the chair out the door. "This is too much of a coincidence to be an accident," she declared. "I'm deathly allergic to spider bites. And Ben Orlin is one of just a handful of people who know that about me."

Chapter 3

To avoid the rut of hauling out the same holiday decorations year after year, consider completely switching things up every once in a while—employ nontraditional colors and think outside the Christmas box.

—Audrey Munroe

Domestic Bliss

Audrey Munroe arrived at the inn around four o'clock that afternoon. By then we had a magnificent blue spruce in place in the center of the lobby. The tip of the star was nearly level with the third floor, twenty-five feet up. Sullivan and I had strung its lights, holding off on decorating it until Henry'd had the chance to ask Audrey if she wanted to trim the tree herself.

She and I were encamped in a pair of cozy overstuffed chairs in front of a splendid crackling fire in the moss-rock fireplace. We'd decided we deserved a respite from our reasonably productive days, and I was waiting to see if she'd bring up her date with Wendell Barton all on her own. Audrey had completed the last of her December shows to be shot in Denver; her remaining *Dom Bliss* TV segments would be taped here in Snowcap Village. This afternoon, I'd shared a few re-assuringly pleasant hours with Mikara. We'd chosen bedroom furniture and accessories to transform Henry's former office into her own private retreat. She was so pleased, she got over her fear of spiders and unpacked her suitcases, after all.

Audrey eyed the tree, which stood in its regal splen-dor a few yards away and filled the air with a fresh, woodsy aroma. "That's a gorgeous spruce you selected, and the perfect fit. But why didn't you hang its decora-tions? You'd told me you were going to finish off the tree in one day."

Not wanting to steal Henry's thunder, I said, "We thought we'd wait for you. I know how much you love trimming our tree at home every year."

"True. I'd be happy to help. In fact, it feels a little strange this season. Here we are, suddenly spending all our time decorating someone *else*'s home for the holi-days."

I smiled at her. "Decorating other people's homes is pretty much my job description."

"But being away from your own home so much of the time isn't. You're only there on weekends now, and that's right when *I* am likeliest to be up here. It's working out well for Hildi. In fact, the cat-sitter's had nothing to do. Meanwhile, you and I are never back in Crestview together long enough to put our heads together regard-ing the house's holiday decorations."

"True, but then again, I don't recall your ever discussing decorations with me in seasons past. I'd come home from work one day, and the house would be all decked out in red and green."

"Well, yes, but that's just it—I'm not going to go with my standard decorations this year."

"You aren't?"

"No, every five or six years I like to go with something utterly nontraditional, just to keep things fresh and unpredictable. Instead of the standard candy-apple red and kelly green, I'll use only magenta and sage, for example, or hot pink and lime green. This year I thought we'd try royal blue and a deep purple, with just a few splashes of silver here and there."

"That sounds lovely."

"Oh, good! I was hoping you'd approve. Since neither of us will be home all that often till Christmas day, I'm going to do this one on the cheap. I'll rely heavily on blue and purple ribbons, fabric swatches, wrapping paper . . . that sort of thing."

"That's a good idea . . . just so long as the ribbons aren't dangling at Hildi level. I have visions of her knocking everything off the table as she starts swinging from a ribbon."

Audrey nodded. "Point well taken."

"You can put blue and purple bows on the lamp shades, though, and she'll leave those alone."

"Which will look lovely. And we'll use ribbons on the fireplace mantels, and the stair railings, as well." She paused. "I'll just have to be sure to zigzag blue and green boas and ribbons through only the upper branches of the tree so Hildi isn't tempted to play with them. Oh, and I have another idea. You know that deep ceramic bowl I have that looks like a loose-woven basket?"

"The white one?"

"Yes. I'm going to fill it with a string of tiny white Christmas lights, then with blue and purple glass marbles. I'll top it off with a layer of minipinecones . . . with some fake stemmed red berries mixed in, just for an extra splash of color."

"Lovely! Is there anything you'd like me to do, this weekend or the next?"

"No, that isn't necessary, really . . ." Her lingering "really . . ." made it clear that her mind was racing with possible job assignments for me.

"It may not be necessary, but I'd feel better if you'd let me help. Unless you'd like to change policies and allow me to start paying you rent, that is."

"No, don't be silly. I won't accept your money."

"Then what would you like me to do toward creating our blue, purple, and sometimes silver Christmas décor?"

"Oh, well, if you insist . . ." She leaned forward in her seat. "I'd like you to—"

"Hang on. Let me get my notepad." I jumped up to snatch my notepad and pen from my purse, which I'd taken to stashing in Henry's coat closet by the front door. I returned to my seat. "Go ahead."

"We'll need a blue, purple, and silver wreath for the front door. Nothing too ostentatious."

"Any holly or pine boughs on the base, or strictly ornaments . . . spray-painted plastic fruit, glass balls, that sort of thing?"

She shook her head. "No greens. You'll have to wrap fabric or ribbon around the Styrofoam ring."

"Got it," I said with a nod.

"Create table runners for all the tables in complementary patterns. Don't overuse any one fabric. And design the centerpieces as well. Just for the kitchen table, dining room, and coffee tables."

"Not the end tables, though, right?" I asked.

"No. Unless you have extra time."

"I'll see what I can do. We *are* going with a live tree, though, aren't we? Not a blue or purple one? I can have the cat-sitter water the tree periodically."

"You decide. You and Steve can get the tree on Saturday. Oh, and you know what else would be really nice, Erin?"

"What?" I was trying to sound casual, but she was getting the sparkle in her eyes that spelled trouble. I had to figure out a way to curtail this conversation soon, or I'd be working nonstop every weekend from now till Christmas Eve and paying hundreds and hundreds of dollars for materials that wouldn't be used again for another five or six years—if ever.

"Little trees for each of the bathrooms. Just a foot or so tall. They could sit on top of the toilet tanks. As long as they're positioned so that they won't poke into the back of anyone sitting on the john. And we could fasten hooks to all those fancy miniature soaps that people tend to give me . . . you know, those acquaintances who don't realize I'd prefer an inexpensive bottle of wine to a batch of tiny pieces of soap."

"A soap tree would be unusual, but fastening hooks to soap might prove to be harder than it sounds." Although I could always enclose each soap in plastic wrap and attach hooks to the wrap. Truth be told, I wasn't all that keen about the idea of a miniature tree on a toilet tank, so I kept the thought to myself. "Plus, like you were saying, we're not going to be at the house all that much."

"Well, we won't be there until Christmas, but I've got two weeks' vacation built into my taping schedule, and—"

I hopped to my feet. "Speaking of wine, it's closing in on five, and I think I hear a claret calling our names."

Audrey chuckled. "Why, I believe you're right, Erin. And it would be rude of us to keep a fine claret waiting any longer than necessary."

Chapter 4

I love the fresh holly garlands on the stair railings," Audrey said as we passed the staircase and entered the kitchen in search of our beckoning claret.

"Thanks." I felt a pang, knowing I really shouldn't have hung those till she'd officially approved them, but they were fabulous-looking—perfect for this Victorian-style house. "That was a lot of work, actually. I had to take special care to attach them to the bottom of each handrail, so people's fingers won't get jabbed when they grab the rails. The Christmas carol and all those fa-la-las make decking the halls sound so fun, but some of those leaves managed to stab me right through my work gloves." The shipment of holly had arrived around noon. I had grilled the deliveryman on whether or not his company could have also delivered an unmarked box to the back porch, but had learned nothing.

Audrey selected a bottle from the nicely stocked wine rack. Just as I popped the cork, Henry entered from the mudroom, his cheeks still rosy from being outside. "Oh, good, Audrey. You're here. I wanted to talk with you about something." He glanced at me. "You haven't let the cat out of the bag yet, have you?"

"No, the bagged cat is still all yours to release." The mention of cats brought Hildi to mind; now that Audrey would be staying up here more full-time, I dearly hoped the cat-sitter would give Hildi lots of attention.

"What's up?" Audrey asked him.

"Earlier today, Erin, Steve, and I were talking about Wendell Barton. There's a general perception that he's snatching up the best that this region has to offer all for himself."

Audrey cocked an eyebrow. "And do you share in this general perception?"

"Oh, personally, I have no beef with the man. But the scuttlebutt around town was driven home to me this morning, when the building inspector, Angie Woolf, flunked both our front entrance and our tap water. I'd hired her sister, Mikara, to be our new manager. Admittedly, I'd thought that would help us with the inspections. Unfortunately, it only backfired."

"Ah. And you think *I* can help mitigate this situation?"

"I think so, yes." Henry popped a breath mint into his mouth and looked longingly at the lovely, country-style pine table; the three of us were standing by the cabinet that held the stemware, and I got the distinct impression he'd have preferred us all to be seated, for some reason.

I poured two glasses. I held one up to Henry, who shook his head. I gave the glass to Audrey instead.

"Audrey, it's imperative that we actively demonstrate to the people of this community that this is not the Wendell Barton Inn." Henry pounded his palm with his fist, driving home his obviously rehearsed minisermon.

Audrey merely nodded her approval of the wine to me as she sipped from her glass.

"We've got to show everyone that you and Chiffon are equally important owners of the inn," he continued.

She arched an eyebrow at Henry and gave him a wavering gesture that meant: *Not exactly*.

"Granted, he owns a slightly *larger* percentage," Henry continued undaunted, "but the point is that I'm putting you and Chiffon in neon lights, for all the townsfolk to see."

"Neon's not really my color, Henry," Audrey said, taking another sip of red wine.

"Metaphorically speaking, that is. I'm putting you in charge of the Christmas decorations for the inn's interior. And Chiffon will be doing the exterior. She's hard at work on her design, even as we speak."

Audrey eyed him skeptically. "As Erin might have told you, I truly love decorating for the holidays, Henry, but—"

"Wonderful! So you'll work up a design for the inn?"

"If you'd like me to, I will, of course. Although Erin and Steve are as good a pair of designers as you're likely to find, *and* they're paid professionals."

"I realize that. They'll assist both you and Chiffon every step of the way. In fact, I'm hoping you and Chiffon will be able to come up with a unifying theme for the place. But once you've got the theme in mind, you can feel free to leave the details to the professionals." He winked at me. I took a long sip of wine, feeling more than a little patronized. *By all means, don't waste our talents on coming up with ideas; Sullivan & Gilbert Designs is strictly into minutiae!*

Audrey sighed. "As far as being...placed in neon, as you described it, how will the members of the community know that *I* was the one who came up with the holiday theme for the rooms?"

The question gave him momentary pause, but then he said, "We'll be having an open house or two for the neighborhood as we get closer to the grand opening. We'll post announcements then. You can act as tour guide for your design during the parties."

"Well, I love the idea of playing tour guide. And whatever I can do to help make the transition to Snowcap Inn a smooth one, I'm happy to do, Henry."

"Terrific." He glanced at the clock. "I'm late. I've got a quick meeting in advance of our meeting this evening."

"There's a meeting this evening?" Audrey asked.

"At seven," I said. "To discuss the hostile inspector."

"Well. A last-minute business meeting." She topped off her glass and said to me, "In that case, we'd better think about polishing off this entire bottle."

"I believe Chiffon is going to announce her plans for the outside display tonight. Maybe that will spark some ideas for the interior." Henry headed toward the door. "See you soon."

"Thanks, Henry," Audrey tossed after him. She waited till we heard the exterior door of the mudroom shut behind him, then asked, "Why did he suddenly make this decision, Erin?"

"Anxiety over Angie's not immediately being cowed by her older sister's important role here at the inn."

"I see." She took a sip of wine. "I have a hunch that the older sister expressed anxiety about the autonomy of the inn's co-owners, as well. In other words, one of the sisters must have told Henry about my dating Wendell Barton."

Finally! I decided not to rib her about my being the last to know and instead replied, "That was a factor, too, yes." I searched her features. "I must say, I was a little surprised by the news, myself." I waited, but she didn't volunteer any information. "So, when did this dating thing start? And is it going to continue?"

She gave me another of her wavering-hand gestures, which, in this context, meant: *We'll see.* "Friday night was our first date, and Saturday our second. We both enjoyed ourselves, so my guess is, it will probably continue. At least for the immediate future." She grinned. "Besides, as they say—keep your friends close and your enemies closer. Either way, I win."

"So...which do you think he's going to turn out to be?"

"A friend."

"With benefits?"

"Erin, please. He and I are smart businesspeople." She paused. "We're still in the negotiation phase."

"What exactly are you negotiating?"

She winked at me. "All sorts of strictly professional things. You'd be surprised how many decisions need to be made."

Other than his sizable paunch and leathery skin from too much sun, Wendell Barton was a fit-looking, handsome man. To my amusement, he dyed his thinning hair the same shade of ash blond as Audrey's. He arrived a half an hour in advance of the meeting and spent the time flirting with Audrey. Audrey, on the other hand, kept trying to draw me into their conversation. I did *my* part, but Wendell ignored me, not counting a couple of subtle hints that he wanted to be alone with Audrey. Clearly, the man did not understand the dynamics of women's relationships. At this particular moment, all fiduciary aspects were irrelevant; I was first and foremost Audrey's girlfriend. If he wanted to impress her, he needed to show her that he was interested in getting to know her friends.

The third owner, Chiffon Walters, arrived precisely on time. Chiffon, a petite, pretty blue-eyed blonde, struck me as a nice enough person, but she was more than a little spoiled and had a short attention span for anything that didn't affect her directly. Mikara had correctly pegged her as someone who had made her fortune in pop music too young and too easily. We took seats at the enormous sixteen-seat dining room table. With Mikara joining Henry, the three owners, and Sullivan and me, we were now using almost half the chairs. Wendell announced immediately that he was bringing in his personal fix-it man. This key employee, Wendell explained, had recently completed work on Wendell's property back east—a hotel high-rise—and would consider a hostile building inspector to be a breeze in comparison. Mr. Fix-it, Wendell said, was traveling into town that day and should arrive within the hour.

As is so often the case with business meetings, the discussions were repetitive and unproductive. Finally, I suggested that we nip any additional hostilities in the bud and request to bring in impartial inspectors. "Sullivan and I respect all of the building inspectors in Crestview, and we can make a case that the inn needs to use unbiased, out-of-town inspectors."

Mikara cried, "There's no need to call in an out-of-towner! That's the very last thing Snowcap needs! My sister is ethical. And if she says there's something that's out of code, it's wrong and needs to be redone."

"Everybody knows an inspector can nitpick forever, Mikki," Henry retorted. "It's like how, in a football game, the refs can call holding on every play, if they so choose."

"We need to give Angie a chance," Mikara countered, "or we'll be building a wall between us and this town. Whenever we need an inspector's approval from here on out, we'll get the shaft. Whenever we try to hire someone to—"

"It's time to move onto happier topics," Chiffon Walters interrupted.

I stifled my annoyance, truly wanting to get this issue resolved.

"Let's discuss my Christmas décor plan! I want to turn the entire exterior of the inn into a gingerbread house by tacking brightly painted scalloping to the siding. We'd make it from sheets of that, you know, thin, brown wood-like stuff."

"Masonite?" Steve interjected.

"I guess. You guys know those constructiony kinds of words better than me. The design will be complete with fake candy canes, lemon drops, and licorice ropes."

The bile was rising in my throat.

"Yeesh! That sounds hideous!" Mikara exclaimed, putting a voice to my thoughts.

Undaunted, Chiffon continued, "I *also* want Gilbert and Sullivan to find us a life-size sleigh and a team of moving illuminated reindeer for the front yard."

"Ugh," Mikara muttered.

"*And,* I want us to hire a Santa to pose in the sleigh from nine to five, and to toss candy and trinkets to the children."

"Chiffon, I respectfully disagree with your plan," Sullivan said. (I also disagreed, but not "respectfully.")

"You don't like Santa's sleigh?" she asked, drawing her pretty lips into a pout. Santa would disapprove of her facial expression.

"I can take or leave the sleigh idea," he continued. "But this is a large, three-story, historical home. It's not the type of place that can be made to look like a little gingerbread house by slapping up a fake exterior. It's just too grand and too regal. That would be like putting baby clothes on an adult. It won't be cute; it'll just be ridiculous."

"I was planning on a tasteful display of Christmas lights, and a single candlelike lamp in each window," I interjected.

"Lights are useless during the day," Chiffon retorted, "and we can put lights over our gingerbread façade. Besides which, *Henry* is in charge for this year. That means he gets to choose the Snowcap Inn's appearance. Remember? So what he says goes." She gave Henry a Marilyn Monroe–esque smile, complete with batted eyes. "Henry?"

Detesting being asked to "remember" something that I couldn't possibly have forgotten, I was rapidly reassessing my opinion of her as a "nice enough" person. Meanwhile, Henry had looked almost ill at Chiffon's tacky suggestion, but kept looking in turns at each of the three partners of Snowcap Inn as if to gauge their reactions. He must have been truly torn—wanting to massage Chiffon's ego without pimping out his elegant home.

Henry forced a smile. "I'll go with whatever the majority of the board decides."

"I'm voting to dress up the inn in gingerbread," Chiffon declared, raising her arm so high she was rising from her chair.

"Let's go with Erin's tasteful light display," Audrey said, making it a tie vote.

We all looked at Wendell, who, as the tie-breaker, appeared to be cursing under his breath. "Er, I've got to go with my gut here and say that men shouldn't be involved in anything that has to do with gingerbread."

"This from the man with the biggest sweet tooth in town," Chiffon said. She winked at him flirtatiously.

"Give us an answer, one way or another," Mikara said sternly.

Wendell drummed his fingers on the table, then said, "Henry told Chiffon to decorate outside, and he's in charge of such decisions this Christmas. Next Christmas, when the permanent staff is in place, things will be different. This year, if Chiffon has her heart set on gingerbread, we should let her have her fun."

Chiffon bounced in her chair like a cheerleader. "Hooray! This is going to look so great, guys! You won't regret it."

"Oh, we'll see about that." Audrey fired a paint-peeling glare at Wendell. He winced, then averted his gaze. "But so be it." I knew her well; she was simmering, but was far too classy to throw a scene. "I might as well take this opportunity to unveil my design for the house's interior."

"You've designed the *interior*? Isn't that kind of what we're paying Gilbert and Sullivan to do for us?" Chiffon asked with a sneer.

"I meant with regard to the *holiday* decorations."

Chiffon gave Audrey a long look. "Weren't Erin and Steve the ones who put up the tree and the lights and all those garlands in the hall? They're all kind of spectacular, don't you think, Audrey?"

"Of course. Erin and Steve are spectacular designers. Even so, Henry asked me to do this, so I did. There are sixteen rooms in the entire house—counting the four small bedrooms. My idea is that each of the eight rooms on the main floor and the four large bedrooms upstairs should be decorated as one of the twelve days of Christmas."

Sullivan and I looked at each other. I could immediately envision one of those lovely round miniature pear trees centered on top of the desk in the lobby where everyone would see it as they were checking in, a lavish yet still tasteful partridge on its uppermost branch. Ideas for the other rooms were also springing to mind.

"That sounds like a great idea to me," Henry said.

"Me, too," Mikara chimed in.

Chiffon's eyes widened, then her features took on an expression of childlike glee. "Audrey, I take back everything I said, plus everything I was secretly thinking. That's a *great* idea!"

"Thank you," Audrey said in a monotone. "I'm humbled by your enthusiasm."

"Could we do a big promotion with this, over the Net?" Mikara suggested. "Allow customers to stay twelve days for the price of ten, for example?"

"I don't see why not," Wendell said cautiously, turning toward Henry, who truly was supposedly in charge of this type of decision.

"You were already telling me about the housewarming party for the neighborhood," Chiffon said to Henry. "We could make a party game out of identifying the Christmas day in each room...like, we'd list them on our invitations, the twelve days, and we'd put an A, B, C, or so on in each doorway, and make people match the right letters to the right twelve days. Get it?"

"Hey, I like that, Chiffon," Henry said with a big smile. "But getting back to Mikara's suggestion, most of our guests have already booked rooms based on our previous weeklong price breaks. But we'll contact our registered guests and offer them a special rate—pay for ten days and stay for twelve, from December twenty-fourth to January fourth."

"No! That's going to make us sound desperate," Mikara said, shaking her head. "You'll make people think something's up. And what about all our reservations for the week *after* Christmas? We'll be double-booking ourselves."

"But *you* were the one who suggested it in the first place!" Henry cried, throwing up his hands in exasperation.

"Don't yell, Henry," she retorted. "I reconsidered, and recognized a flaw in my idea. It's not like *you* never change your mind and take back things *you* said!" She glared at him till he averted his eyes.

"This is no big deal," I said, "but just so you know, the Twelve Days of Christmas actually begin on Christmas day and end on January fifth."

"Please," Wendell said, with a dismissive wave in my general direction, "nobody but a church nerd would actually know that. We can assign the dates however we want."

"I'm hardly a 'church nerd,' Mr. Barton, but I'll grant that it's your right to time the promotion however you want."

"Which is *not* going to involve a twelve-day rate at this late juncture," Mikara stated emphatically.

The noise level increased exponentially as everyone except Sullivan and me began to bicker. He gave me a loving smile, which I returned. With all parties feuding about something, I reminded myself that, no matter what happened, my relationship with Steve couldn't be stronger. If not invincible, the two of us could at least prove to be unflappable tonight.

Wendell cleared his throat and grinned at someone in the doorway behind me. "Ah. Here's my director of operations. No need to worry about a thing from now on."

I turned. My heart started hammering in my chest as I stared in shock at the tall, handsome man, recognizing him at once.

"Everybody, this is Cameron Baker," Wendell was saying.

Our eyes met, and we both froze with our gazes locked for several seconds. He was my former boyfriend—my first love, and the first man I'd been intimate with—and we hadn't seen each other in ten years. When I was at Parsons School of Design, he'd been a grad student at Columbia.

"Erin?!"

"Cam! You ... came back from London." He was wearing an exquisite black cashmere coat. Other than his upgraded wardrobe, he looked exactly the same.

"Six years ago. I told you I would. You left New York." He grabbed both my hands and helped me to my feet. "My God. Erin Gilbert, as beautiful as ever, standing two feet away from me." He kissed me passionately.

Chapter 5

In our bedroom later that night, Steve was deliberately keeping his distance from me. "I'm sorry about the kiss, Steve. It was just such a shock, suddenly seeing him again."

"So you said. More than once." His voice was cold.

Although I was trying my best to explain, I was failing miserably. Kissing a former boyfriend in front of Steve was something I'd have sworn I would never do in a million years. "His suddenly appearing after all these years just felt so surreal. There we were with our clients and everything, and the—"

"Which *we* are you referring to?" Sullivan glowered at me. "You and Cammy Boy? Because you can't possibly mean you and *me*. I obviously faded into the woodwork for you the instant he walked into the room."

"I only expected it to be a little 'hello' kiss. Didn't you notice that I pushed him away?"

"Eventually you did, yeah."

"Almost immediately!"

He snorted. "You forgot I existed. Your eyes and your head were all full of Mr. Fix-it Man. Then you *eventually* broke off the kiss and introduced me. As your *partner*."

"Cameron got my meaning immediately."

"Yeah, he did. I could tell by the way he glared at me. He seems to be a smart guy. But you could have slipped in that little phrase about our being partners right away. Maybe *then* he'd have settled for a handshake."

"I'm sorry, Steve. Deeply sorry. Letting him kiss me was thoughtless and inappropriate, I know. But, believe me, there's nothing going on, other than my surprise at seeing a long-lost old friend."

"*Friend?*"

"Yes. Cam's and my romance ended nearly ten years ago. I feel nothing for him now except friendship."

"You'd better tell *him* that. That was no friendly peck on the cheek he was giving you."

"I *will* tell him that. And I'll also tell him that I'm in love with you, just in case he's slow on the uptake. He's probably happily married, for all we know."

"Erin. Don't be naïve. No happily married man takes his old girlfriend into his arms like that. At least, not if he expects to *remain* happily married."

"Maybe he's happily divorced, then. In any case, I'm flattered that you're jealous, but you have nothing to worry about."

He looked at me with far more venom than Cameron could possibly have generated when he "glared" at Steve. "Is that supposed to make *me* feel better, or just you?"

"You don't need to be so harsh, Sullivan. I said I was sorry, and I am. I swear to you that I'll never kiss an old boyfriend again, and anyway, there isn't anyone else in my past remotely like him."

"Great. So in other words, you're still holding a torch for him alone."

"No! I just meant that, out of all the guys I ever dated, he was the only one... This isn't coming out right. The point is, I'm not holding a torch for him or for anyone except *you*."

"How lucky for me." Steve stripped down to his boxers and undershirt, then clicked out the light. "I'm tired and I'm going to sleep now."

"Fine. Good night."

"Night."

Although I turned out my own light and laid my head on my pillow, I silently cursed repeatedly while replaying the lowlights of the evening. I *had* honestly believed Cameron was going to give me a quick kiss hello. Sullivan was truly overreacting. Yes, I'd been wrong to let myself get so enthralled by seeing Cam so unexpectedly. But that's the challenge of major surprises—you don't get the chance to prepare for them; it's impossible to react with intelligent forethought. My reaction had been the result of my happiness at seeing the long-lost man who'd once meant the world to me; it had absolutely nothing to do with my relationship to Sullivan—the man who now meant even more to me. Nothing on this earth could make me drop Steve and go back to Cameron. I weighed telling Sullivan that, but he was already either feigning sleep or actually asleep. Besides, considering his current mood and my ineffective babblings tonight, he might take yet more offense. Surely this was all going to turn out fine. If we were going to be in this relationship for the long haul, we needed to know that we could get past bad times. This evening's events definitely qualified as a bad time.

In the morning, Sullivan was fully dressed when I awoke. We traded "good mornings."

"I have to head down to Crestview to meet with some reps at the office, but I'll be back by five," he explained. His voice was as consciously bland as his face.

"Are you still angry with me about Cameron?"

"No. Let's just forget it ever happened."

"Okay. Well . . . bye."

I reached for him, and he gave me a reasonably nice kiss, muttered, "Bye," then left.

A knot formed in my stomach. I'm pretty sure that it's impossible to activate amnesia at will and that, in any case, unresolved small problems have a way of reemerging as bigger problems later. I rehashed my resolve before falling asleep last night. What if we weren't *capable* of making it through bad times?

When I entered the kitchen, Mikara was sitting at the table, cradling a cup of coffee. She offered me a semi-cheerful, "Morning," but followed it up with: "I assume you can serve yourself breakfast. I'm not a morning person."

"Isn't that going to be problematic for running a bed-and-*breakfast*?"

She arched an eyebrow and said, "I'll rise to the occasion once our guests arrive." Then she indeed rose—and marched out of the kitchen. It was not even half past eight, and I was two for two on driving people from the room. I was on a roll!

Even though Crestview residents' fondness for granola was a cliché, that's what I chose to eat. My crunchy meal was augmented by the racket of a jackhammer and a bulldozer outside as Ben and his temporary crew demolished the stoop.

The vibrations in the floorboards were so strong that I had visions of a bulldozer accident weakening the entire foundation. After breakfast, I went out through the back door and rounded the house. Ben Orlin was behind the controls of the small dozer as two Hispanic workmen were loading chunks of concrete into a sturdy truck bed by hand. It looked like horrid, backbreaking labor to me, and I immediately asked Ben if I could bring out a thermos of coffee or anything.

"Nah, we're fine," Ben said affably, shutting off the engine. "We took a coffee break an hour ago."

"You've made a lot of progress, in just a couple of hours."

"Yeah, well, we got started on it last night. On Wendell's henchman's orders."

"*Henchman?* You mean Cameron Baker?"

"Yeah. He made some phone calls and got them to deliver the dozer at eleven-thirty last night. Then he made the deliverymen wait and watch me operate it, 'cuz he was worried this dozer wasn't big enough. I didn't want to wake up everyone in the house by breaking up the concrete steps, but I finally moved enough dirt out here to convince him."

"That was thoughtful of you." That *did* sound like something Cameron would do. He had been a workaholic in college and had scoffed at anyone who chose a less stressful lifestyle.

He shrugged. "The noise still woke Mikara up. She was fit to be tied."

"I'm . . . really sorry that you had to lose *your* sleep last night to do this. Did Henry have anything to say about your having to work that late at night?"

"Nah. He wasn't even here. Out on a date."

Knowing Henry, he probably took out Chiffon Walters, to counterbalance Audrey and Wendell's dating. The Snowcap Inn was turning into a regular Peyton Place. Of course, *I* was no one to talk. I shuddered to think how quickly Cameron's kiss must be spreading through the village's rumor mill.

"Hey, Ben?" one of the workers said. "You better come take a look at this." He was brushing off a bone that he held in one hand.

"Where'd you find that?" Ben asked.

My mind instantly filled with apprehension. I cursed

and approached along with Ben, hoping that this was just a dog's old bone. But there were no telltale teeth marks, and its shape and size looked all too human. Someone's upper arm. R. Garcia's?

"It was in the pile of rubble," the man explained, gesturing with his chin.

Just then I heard someone approach, turned, and saw a grouchy-looking Wendell Barton striding toward us. "What's everyone standing around for?" he demanded. "Ben! Did you fail to understand Mr. Baker's directive last night that this was to be done on double time?! Why do you have a crew of just two men?"

"There's a problem, Wendell," I interjected. "They found a bone in the debris from the steps. It looks like part of a human skeleton."

Ben showed him the bone. "Nah. That's nothing," Wendell said with a dismissive wave. "Probably a dog's treasure trove. That's hardly an excuse to stop working."

"Maybe not, but *this* is," the second worker said, removing his gloves. He pointed at a spot in the top of the pile that the bulldozer had created, and even from where I stood—some ten feet away—I could make out the shape of a human skull. "I'm out of here. I don't need the work this bad." He started walking toward the driveway.

"Wait. You can't leave," I told him. "We have to call the police. They're going to want to know precisely where you found the first bone."

"I gotta go, too," the second man said as he trotted down the walkway. "I'm not waiting for no police...." They both hopped into their respective pickup trucks and drove off.

"Ben!" Wendell scolded. "Are you some kind of an idiot? Those men are obviously illegal immigrants! Didn't you ask to see their drivers' licenses or their papers before you hired them?"

"No, Mr. Barton. I have a hard enough time getting workmen without—"

"This town's chomping at the bit to shut us down!" Wendell growled. "I can't risk getting socked with a fine or work-stoppage due to hiring illegal immigrants!"

While Wendell carped at Ben, I dialed 911 on my cell phone. When the dispatcher answered, I said, "My name is Erin Gilbert and I'm calling from Henry Goodwin's house on Goodwin Road, in Snowcap Village." I paused. "I'm sorry. This isn't an emergency. Force of habit. But a crew that was digging up some cement steps came across some human bones. I'm pretty sure they were from the grave that was robbed earlier in the week."

"How do you know that the bones have been moved from a grave?"

"I don't. It's an educated guess."

"Erin!" Wendell snapped in a half whisper. "Hang up! We can't get the police involved in this!"

"It's too late," I replied calmly. "They're on their way."

Chapter 6

Fifteen minutes later, nicely bundled up in a stylish plum parka and white Lycra ski pants, Chiffon came outside; Audrey was long gone, having left for a film session at the local TV studio. I barely had a moment to consider how interesting it was that Chiffon was emerging from the inn, considering she owned a condo ten minutes away. She appeared to have spent the night here. Ben rushed to fill her in on the workers' grisly discovery.

Some five minutes after Chiffon joined Ben and me, Sheriff Mackey, the superior officer in Snowcap, finally

arrived, driven here by a second officer who had all the as-
sertiveness of a whipped puppy dog. With V-shaped eyebrows that echoed his receding hairline, the sheriff bore
a passing resemblance to Jack Nicholson. Frankly, he
seemed to have no idea what to do. He interviewed Ben;
asked about the men—Pedro and Juan Martinez; asked if
Ben himself had seen "any bones or bonelike fragments"
while he was digging, which he hadn't; and was then
stymied. Ben volunteered the fact that I'd been talking to
him when the bones were discovered, so unasked, I re-
counted what little I'd seen and heard. That took me less
than sixty seconds. Even at that, Mackey acted utterly un-
interested.

"You're one of the designers from Crestview, aren't
you," he stated with obvious disdain.

"Yes, I'm Erin Gilbert of Sullivan and Gilbert Designs.
I'm the one who called nine-one-one."

"Yeah. Why'd you consider it an emergency? 'Fraid the
bones would vanish before I could get here to see 'em?"

"No, I was afraid the workers who uncovered the bones
would vanish. They were already driving away when I
called."

Mackey pivoted and said, "Hey, Ben? Where's Henry
Goodwin? Doesn't he care about these here events?"

"He and Wendell Barton are having a powwow," Ben
replied. "They're someplace inside the house."

Sheriff Mackey snorted. "That figures. Mayor Goodwin's
sellout continues. We'll fix his wagon." Just then, Mikara
rounded the house to join us. Mackey turned to face the
second officer, who was standing sentinel by the patrol car.
"Penderson?" Mackey shouted, "Let's just cordon off the

entire grounds . . . since we don't know what else we might find. Or where."

"That's not really necessary, is it?" I asked. "Several of us are living here, and we know there are no bones inside the house."

"Plus, I don't really have enough tape," the deputy said. "Can't I just . . . circle all the dug-up area?"

"Won't that prevent anyone from building new steps?" Chiffon asked.

"Yeah, so what?" Mackey asked. "You can use the back door."

"Sure. And now that Ben won't be able to work on the porch steps, he can get started on my gingerbread design."

"You've got Ben Orlin *baking*?" the sheriff asked in dismay.

"No, building a big gorgeous Christmas design," she replied with a bright smile. "We're going to make this whole big home look like the candy house from Hansel and Gretel."

"The witch's gingerbread house was where she baked the children in the oven, right?" the sheriff asked.

"I don't remember what happened. Just that the house was edible, and there was a trail of bread crumbs that the birds ate."

Sheriff Mackey grinned. "I sure don't want to stop Mayor Goodwin from turning Wendell's inn into a witch's cottage. Sure, Chiffon. You go right on ahead with your little design project. We'll keep the cordoning of the house confined to the porch steps."

"Awesome! Thanks, Greggy!"

Greggy? "Sheriff Mackey?" I said with a deferential lilt

to my voice, "Do you think those bones could have come from the grave that was robbed a few days ago?"

He gave me the evil eye and seemed disinclined to answer until he followed my gaze and saw that Henry and Wendell were approaching us. Mackey said in a near shout, "That's one possibility, Miss Gilbert. Or maybe these cement steps were built to hide someone's grave... and someone's unsolved murder."

In what struck me as a futile exercise designed purely to annoy Henry and Wendell, the sheriff ordered Ben Orlin to move the two piles of dirt and debris a short distance away. Mackey claimed he needed to see if they contained any more bones. They did not. Two hours later, he told us to leave everything where it was and he'd get back to us about when Ben could complete the demolition. Henry and Wendell tried in vain to get him to commit to a time frame.

Chiffon, meanwhile, showed me her plans for slapping ugly painted gingerbreadish Masonite over the classy gray-and-white-trimmed siding and forest green shutters, and we agreed that none of the existing hooks for lights— along the eaves and window casings—would be affected. Within fifteen minutes of the sheriff's departure, I was ready to devote what remained of my morning and the afternoon to hanging the exterior lights.

Henry had told me that many light strands had been stored in the shed, so I crossed the snow-crusted back lawn, pausing to admire the gazebo. That structure would require additional lighting—all white, miniature lights, I decided. I dearly hoped Chiffon wasn't considering turning the gazebo into a gingerbread doghouse.

I hesitated at the closed door to the shed. The padlock was open and hanging from the hook and, from inside, a woman's voice shouted, "No way! That's a terrible idea!"

"What do you mean?!" a second woman shouted. "It's the perfect solution, and you know it!"

Henry was crossing the lawn from the footbridge over the creek; this was a walk he took early every morning, but today's events had pushed it back to a few minutes after eleven. Just as the first voice retorted, "I know no such thing! It's dangerous!" Henry spotted me and called, "Erin! Did you find the Christmas lights?"

I had no choice but to call back, "Not yet. I'm about to look for them now."

Unsurprisingly, the voices in the shed instantly fell silent. I opened the rustic, barnlike door and stepped inside. Mikara and Angie Woolf were staring at me. "Hello," I said.

"Hi, Erin," Mikara said. "You're ready to hang the lights now?"

"I hope to."

"I'll get them for you. I know right where they are." Mikara turned and headed to a back shelf.

I looked at Angie, who probably felt as awkward as I did. With Mikara leaving us both standing there, I was obliged to say something to Angie, but was at a loss. Saying "Good to see you again" to someone you'd interrupted in an argument seemed inappropriate. Instead I muttered lamely: "Are you just here to visit, or are you giving us another inspection?"

"Just visiting my sister. Family matters." She trudged past me and called over her shoulder, "Bye, Mikara."

"Take care, Angie," Mikara replied. She carried a large box toward me and rolled her eyes when our gazes met. "Family drives you crazy, no matter how small it happens to be." She brushed past me, saying, "I'll take this to the back porch for you. There's more right on that shelf. You'll have to make a couple of trips."

I grabbed a second box and followed, noticing that Angie was heading toward the street, taking a diagonal path across the side yard. Strangely, she'd opted not to pull into the long driveway, or to park anywhere near the inn.

Late that afternoon, Cameron dropped by. I spotted his car—a black Mercedes—from the stepladder. Ben had finished hanging the lights on the eaves of the highest roofs; I was contenting myself with the first- and second-floor windows in the front, skipping the porch roof to avoid violating the police cordoning. I watched Cam approach, noting the same purposeful stride I remembered from a decade ago. I was wrong about him looking exactly the same; he was even more handsome now. His thick, wavy brown hair was neatly styled and nearly as dark as his coat. He could have been a male model, but his aura was one of pure power. Heaven only knows how I'd once fooled myself into thinking I could actually keep up with the man. Life was too short to have to work that hard just to feel comfortable with someone.

He gave me a full-wattage smile, his teeth white as

the snow. "There she is, Erin Gilbert herself, up on a pedestal. The goddess of my dreams . . . and such a sight to behold."

His greeting was so over the top that I had to laugh. "Before you envision a Pantheon around me, notice that I'm standing on an aluminum stepladder, sticking a string of lights onto little hooks. Does that sound like goddess activity to you?"

"Indeed not, Athena. Which is why I've come to sweep you away in my chariot. Can I give you a hand?"

"No, actually, I was just finishing up. But thanks for offering."

"Even better! Come away with me. We'll have an early dinner and get caught up a bit."

"Hang on a sec." I fastened the last strand of lights, my calves and arms aching. As I came down the ladder, I said, "The first thing you need to know if you want to catch up with my life is that Steve Sullivan is not just my business partner."

"I realize that. It's pretty obvious from the way he was looking at you. And glaring at me." (I couldn't help but smile; hard to say which man was really glaring at the other. Maybe it was simultaneous.) "Did my kiss last night cause any friction?"

"A little, actually. But we'll overcome it."

"Invite him to join us." He spread his arms and said with a wink and a big grin, "Steve and I will be fast friends in no time. To know me is to love me."

"Your ego's still intact, I see."

He laughed. "Always. I'm confident by nature. You *have* to be in my line of work."

"Which is *what*, exactly?" I gazed into his eyes. He was only a few inches taller than I. I'd sometimes wondered if he'd picked me out of the crowd strictly because he figured we'd make a tall, striking couple.

"I'm Wendell Barton's right-hand man. I handle the money problems and the employee problems, and hire people to handle the incidentals."

I turned my attention to collecting the boxes. Cameron picked up the ladder for me, and we started toward the shed. "Did you notice the police crime-scene tape in the front?" I asked.

"Some workmen discovered human remains, right? I heard about that from Snowcap's illustrious sheriff. That had to be a dumb prank."

"A bone and a skull. The sheriff has put an indefinite hold on rebuilding the steps."

"I wouldn't worry about that. Even government bureaucracy can be edged along, if you know the right buttons to push."

"You're going to *bribe* the sheriff?" I asked in dismay.

"No way," he said with a chuckle. "I know better than to cross that line. But I *do* know how to motivate individuals."

That was true. Cam had been a natural leader in college. I opened the door to the shed. He followed me inside. "The ladder goes right next to the door." I continued on to the back shelf. He was standing by the door, watching me when I turned around.

"And speaking of motivating individuals, *you*, my lovely Erin, are overdue for a sloe gin fizz."

I laughed. "I haven't had one of those in over ten years!"

"Not since the days of your fake ID. My point exactly. It'd be hard to get more overdue than *that*!"

"I've moved on, Cameron. Which is why I can't agree to join you till I talk to Steve about it." Who, I realized, was still not here. "Excuse me for a moment." I locked up the shed, then dialed Steve's cell phone.

"Erin," he answered immediately. "Sorry I'm late, hon. There was a massive pileup on I-Seventy, according to the radio. I'm waiting till it clears and still haven't left Crestview."

"I'm sorry to hear that. Cameron's here and wanted to know if he could take us both out to an early dinner."

There was a pause. I couldn't tell if the crackling noise was from the faulty connection or Steve grinding his teeth. "Go ahead. No sense in your missing out. Plus I'm sure he's standing right there."

"Yeah." I didn't want to clue Cameron in to the fact that Steve had given me a green light till I was sure that he really meant it. "Okay. No problem. We'll all just do this another night."

"No, you and Cameron will go now, and you'll feel all nostalgic and revel in old times. Then afterward, you'll re-member that you've been there and done that, and that what you have now with me is better."

I smiled, falling in love with Steve all over again. "That's certainly true."

"Yeah, I know. That's why I said it."

"I love you, Steve."

"Love you, too. Have a horrible time tonight."

"Okay. I will."

"See you in a couple of hours." He hung up before I could reply.

"Let me guess," Cameron said when I pocketed my cell phone and looked at him. "He's giving you plenty of rope in the hopes that you'll strangle me with it."

"Something like that."

He took my arm and started leading me to his car. "It's like I told you earlier. I know individuals and how they tick. I'll take you to my favorite place, run by a couple of Aussies who can pull a wonderful pint . . . and can mix up a first-rate sloe gin fizz, as well. Are you still lousy at darts?"

"Unless a ten-year layoff has worked its magic."

"Perfect! The one thing I could always beat you at. I *rule!*"

Despite our handicap system that gave me a point just for hitting the dartboard, Cameron beat me, which, in actuality, had been our general pattern and was in no way confined to just darts. He was exciting and dynamic, and our every minute together reminded me of how it felt a decade ago to be the center of such a force of nature, when he'd had me convinced that absolutely anything was possible. That is, right up until he'd left for London, and my mom slowly died from lung disease, and I found myself alone when I most needed comfort and support. One night, I'd called to tell him so. The woman's voice with the ever-so-cultured accent who'd answered his phone was burned into my memory banks.

Strangely, I learned very little about his personal life tonight; he claimed he'd been "too busy" to date much, and that I was "too tough of an act for any woman to follow." Flattering, but a load of nonsense.

I looked at my watch and realized we'd been gone for more than two hours. Maybe Steve was at the inn by now.

Cameron searched my features. "Has our carriage turned back into a pumpkin?"

I hesitated. "This has been great fun, Cam, but I need to get back."

He rolled his eyes and grumbled, "To Steve, aka the love of your life."

"Yes, actually." It was time for me to step out of the vortex and back into Steve's arms.

"Well, okay, then. Let's go."

We made small talk during the short drive, admiring the lights as we slowly passed the house. Cameron drove me around to the back. Sullivan's van was still nowhere to be seen.

"We'll do this again as a threesome, with your lucky guy. I hope he's good enough to deserve you."

"He is."

"I'll take your word for it." He gave me one of his winning smiles.

"Right. Good night. Thanks, Cam." I got out and, before shutting my door, asked, "Are you coming by the inn tomorrow?"

"Absolutely. Got to keep things hopping. It's my job. See you then." I watched as he drove away, feeling a touch of sadness, though I didn't know why.

I started toward the door, and gasped as I spotted a man

at the corner of the house, his flashlight beam darting along the ground as he walked. I stared until I recognized him. "Henry. You startled me."

"Sorry, Erin. I was just checking the fuses. The lights on the bridge aren't working."

I glanced in that direction. "That's odd. They were working earlier. I remember checking them."

"The fuses are all good, though. Something probably got unplugged. I'll fix it now."

A gust of chilly air hit me, which felt like an omen. My stomach was instantly in knots. The reaction was silly, I knew, but even so, I was worried at the thought of Henry going alone. Henry had taken a couple of steps, his boots crunching through the icy snow.

"Wait. I'll join you."

Henry pulled up his collar against the wind. There was an awkward pause as we headed down the hill. "Cold out tonight," he muttered.

"Yes, it is."

We slipped into silence, our trudging boots the only sound. He had to be curious at how Cameron had dropped me off just now and Steve had been gone all day. Finally, Henry said, "The place is starting to look real nice. You and Steve are doing a great job."

"Thanks. I'm really—"

By the beam of Henry's flashlight, I spotted a dark shape near the foot of the bridge. Henry spotted it, too, and cursed under his breath. "Go back to the house, Erin."

"No."

I hurried my step. There was enough light for me to see

that someone in a dark coat was lying facedown in the snow, and the sight terrified me. Wordlessly, both Henry and I broke into a run. Henry reached the foot of the bridge a step before me and grabbed the person's shoulder.

"Oh, my god. Angie?" Henry cried. He rolled her onto her back. Angie was motionless—and lifeless. She'd been strangled with a string of lights that had been yanked off its hooks.

Chapter 7

This is Erin Gilbert," I said to the 911 dispatcher, my words coming out in a mindless rush. "There's been a murder at the Goodwin estate in Snowcap Village. I'm here with Henry Goodwin, and we found Angie Woolf's body. Outside by the creek."

She said something, but I only caught a couple of syllables.

"Your voice is breaking up. What?"

"Are you two the only ones there on the premises?"

"No. But we're the only ones outside. I think."

She said something that sounded like: "Stay where you are. You'll be hearing the sirens soon."

Henry had already walked a short distance up the hill, partway back toward the house. I followed and told him, "The dispatcher says we're supposed to wait where we are."

He stopped. "I'll watch for the police vehicles from here."

The dispatcher said something else, but our weak connection failed completely. I hung up and stuck my cell phone in my coat pocket. Filled with dread, I kept an eye on the house, watching for familiar silhouettes in the window. Cameron and I had been gone for a couple of hours; maybe Angie wasn't the only victim.

Henry was popping Tic Tacs in his mouth every few seconds, pacing three or four steps and then turning—like an animal in a small cage.

"Henry, how long were you outside before I arrived?"

"I can't—What?"

"How long has it been since you were inside?"

"I don't know. Ten, fifteen minutes."

"Are you sure Audrey's all right?"

"Yeah. She's fine, Erin. We'd just spoken as I headed out the door. She was with Mikara."

"Mikara has no idea that her sister's dead."

"Oh, God." He put his hand to his head. "That's right! I didn't... this was such a shock, I didn't think of that. Damn it! I need to go tell her now, so that..." He let his voice fade as sirens cut through the wintry silence.

A small chartreuse ambulance, with lights flashing,

pulled into the circular portion of the driveway behind the inn. A pair of EMT's emerged. Seconds later Audrey and Mikara burst through the back door, donning their coats as they ran toward us.

"Erin?" Audrey called. "Is that you? What's wrong? What's going on?"

"There was an accident...down by the creek," I called back.

"Are you hurt?" Mikara cried.

"No."

"Is Henry?"

One of the paramedics hustled them back inside as the other approached Henry and me. I couldn't overhear what was being said to Mikara. Was he telling her about her sister? Henry spoke to the second EMT and started to lead him to Angie's body, but the EMT flicked on his powerful flashlight and told us both to wait for the police where we were. I watched from a distance as he checked Angie's vitals, which I knew was pointless.

A patrol car arrived. Two sheriff deputies emerged and quickly separated us; one led Henry into the patrol car and one stayed with me on the high point of the path that led down to Angie's body. The deputy took my name, birth date, address, and phone before asking me what had happened. Shivering uncontrollably despite my warm parka, I told him that I'd gone to the pub for about two and a half hours with Cameron, and had returned and spotted Henry. Then I described our grim discovery.

A crunch of car tires on gravel distracted me, and I

recognized the headlights of Steve's van. He abandoned his car in the middle of the parking area. Another vehicle pulled into the driveway behind him—a second patrol car.

"Erin, are you okay?" Steve started to trot toward me.

"Yeah, I'm—"

"Halt!" an amplified voice boomed at us. Sheriff Mackey got out of the passenger side of the patrol car and was using a police bullhorn. "Stay right there!"

This was probably the first murder case Sergeant Mackey had ever been charged with investigating. There was no chance that he'd prove to be up to the task.

"It's all right, Greg," one of the EMT's called back to Mackey. "That's just her boyfriend."

Jeez! This town really *was* gossip central!

"That may be so," Mackey retorted into the bullhorn, "but he's not allowed onto the crime scene."

"What's going on?!" Steve demanded.

I watched the back door; Mikara was still inside and couldn't possibly overhear me. "Angie Woolf was murdered," I called back. "Down by the bridge. Someone strangled her with a string of Christmas lights."

Steve was still standing on the edge of the parking area. I could tell how perturbed he was by his stance and balled fists, though it was too dark to see his features.

"Look, Sheriff," Steve said. "I haven't been here all day, so I've got no idea of what happened. All I want to do is go talk to my partner. Can I please go do that?"

"No, sir, you cannot," Mackey retorted. "You can wait in your vehicle, or you can wait in the house."

"Steve, I'll talk to you soon," I shouted, waving at him.

"I'll wait in my car," he called back to me.

"Silence!" Mackey said, again using his horn. Steve returned to his van and closed the door.

"There's really no need for the bullhorn, Greg," Henry said, emerging from the passenger side of the patrol car. He slammed his door shut. "We can all hear you just fine."

"That so, Goodwin?" Mackey said, his amplified voice, if anything, a notch louder.

"Yeah, that's so! I'm still the mayor, and I appropriate the police budget, including the equipment that you're now misusing! I'd rethink your attitude, if I were you."

Raising his bullhorn once again, the sheriff announced, "I am in charge of this murder investigation, Mr. Mayor, and *you* are one of my suspects!" He chucked his bullhorn into his car.

"Suspects?!" Mikara shrieked, suddenly standing in the doorway. "The paramedic won't tell us who's been hurt! Who's the victim? What the hell is going on?!"

"I'm so sorry, Mikara," Mackey said, his voice kind. "Just go back inside, and I'll explain everything in a minute or two."

"What's that supposed to mean...you're 'so sorry'? Last time you said that to me was when my dad had his—his heart attack."

"Just...go back inside," Mackey repeated sadly. "Please. I'll be in as soon as I look at the crime scene."

"Oh, my god!" Mikara cried. "Something must have happened to Angie, didn't it?" She started trotting down the path.

"Wait!" Mackey started to follow her.

"No! I need to see my sister!"

"You can't!" Mackey slowed his pace. "Stop! We have to keep everyone away. There are footprints in the snow. You could destroy the evidence without even realizing it."

Mikara hesitated, but only for a moment. She tried to rush past us down the shoveled path to the creek. The deputy closest to me grabbed her arm.

"Come on, Mikara," he said. "Let's go back to the house. I know how hard this is, but you—"

"Don't tell me that!" She yanked free of his grasp. "Don't you dare tell me you know the first thing about how hard this is! Have you ever had your only sister get murdered?!"

Henry headed toward us down the path, past Mackey and one of the deputies. "Henry!" Mackey shouted. "You need to stay right where you are, or—"

"Shut up, Greg," Henry growled. "You folks can go do whatever you need to do. *I* need to show some kindness. Nobody *else* is. You got a problem with that, you can come handcuff me and haul me away."

Henry kept walking, and nobody made a move to stop him. He gently pulled Mikara into his arms, where she promptly broke into wracking sobs. It was excruciatingly difficult to hear someone in such agony, and it brought back painful memories of the losses in my own life.

"Why?" she cried into his shoulder. "Why would anybody kill my little sister?"

"I don't know, Mikki. It doesn't make any sense."

"You were outside for so long," Mikara cried to him. "Didn't you see anything? Hear Angie cry for help?"

"No. Obviously, I'd have come to her rescue."

Steve, meanwhile, got out of his car and walked beside Mikara as Henry led her back toward the house. Thank God that Henry, at least, was showing some basic human decency.

And yet, I couldn't help but wonder if Henry had lied to me earlier about how long he'd been outside before I'd returned.

After a miserable two hours of braving the cold in sepa-rate patrol cars, Henry and I were finally allowed to go inside; Steve had long since gone into the house, unable to convince the officers to let us do so, as well. We were directed to sit on the bench in the mudroom and remove our boots, which the deputies then collected as evidence, along with a beat-up pair of men's boots from the cubby underneath the bench. Drops from melted snow had been left underneath those well-used boots. Henry told the sheriff and his men that he'd noticed those boots a week or two ago and had assumed Ben Orlin had left them there for use on a snowy day.

"Are you absolutely certain they're not yours?" Mackey asked Henry. "They're your size."

"Yes, I'm sure. I know my own boots, for chrissake."

"It's important, Henry." Mackey held the boots out for him to examine. "These are the same tread patterns that we found near Angie's body."

"Do you remember seeing those boots on the shelf earlier today?" I promptly asked Henry.

My question was rewarded with a dirty look from Mackey. "Hey! You're in Snowcap now! No one gets to play Nancy Drew on my turf!"

Because Nancy would solve the murder so much faster than you could, I thought bitterly.

Henry ignored him and turned toward me. "I have no idea if they were here or not today. I remember seeing them yesterday afternoon. I considered asking Ben about them this morning, but the whole hullabaloo with the bones was going on, and I just let it drop."

Mackey whisked me off to a separate room to take my report again, although most of my time was spent in silence; he obviously just wanted to keep me sequestered from the others. It was almost two A.M. before he and his underlings finally left the house. Audrey and Steve were waiting for me by the fireplace. Steve embraced me and told me that Mikara had been given a sedative and was asleep in her room. Henry, too, had recently gone upstairs to bed. Steve and I sat down on the love seat across from Audrey.

"Were both Henry and Mikara in the house with you this evening?" I asked Audrey.

She shook her head. "Unfortunately, I had an early dinner with my producer tonight. I think I must have left the house right around the same time as you. When I got back, Mikara and I chatted for a couple of minutes, and then Henry came in from outside, saying it was 'sure nippy out there,' but that this was his kind of weather. Then he said he was going to take a look at all the lights you'd hung, and he left. I wasn't paying attention to time. It must have been half an hour or so later when Mikara and I heard the ambulance." She sighed, her features looking a little drawn. "I nearly had a heart attack. Mikara started cursing, wondering if Henry had hurt himself and had called for an ambulance. I immediately started worrying about *you*."

Steve gave my hand a squeeze at Audrey's last remark, and I laced my fingers between his. "Had both of them eaten dinner here, do you know?" I asked.

Audrey shook her head. "Mikara was putting away dishes when I arrived. She asked Henry if he'd eaten, and he said something like: 'I'm fine.' " She sighed again. "Wendell called my cell a couple of hours ago. He'd heard about Angie through the grapevine and told me he'd been home alone all evening. I haven't seen or heard a thing about anyone else connected with the inn—Ben Orlin or Chiffon Walters."

The next morning when Steve and I came downstairs, Henry was setting his cereal bowl in the sink and not in the dishwasher—the typical male morning ritual. I still felt run ragged by last night's events, and my head was pounding from lack of sleep. We greeted him, and Steve poured us both coffee.

"Mikara still hasn't emerged from her bedroom," Henry told us. "Last night she said she was taking a sleeping pill and knocking herself out for the next twenty-four hours. Or for as long as she could manage." He stared straight into my eyes as he spoke. "I've never seen her so upset. Both her parents have passed away. I'm not sure she can take losing her sister. It's been nearly twelve hours. I'm worried."

"Do you want me to check on her?" I asked.

"Could you?" Henry replied. "I'd do it myself, but... the thing is, we have a history. She might resent my knocking on her bedroom door, let alone entering, if she's unable to answer. Something like eight or nine years ago, we got engaged. And I broke it off. Word around town was she took it pretty hard. Obviously, she got over it a long time ago, but still, it's best if I keep my distance now. I don't want to dredge up old feelings in either of us. I'm just... not the marrying type. You know?"

Now he looked solely at Steve, which, frankly, I resented. Steve didn't move a muscle, except to shift his vision to me. I think he felt trapped by Henry's question. I deserted my steaming cup on the counter and left to check on Mikara. The swinging doors into the kitchen weren't soundproof, and I heard Steve mutter something to Henry, who responded, "No kidding." That froze me in my tracks for a moment, as my mind raced to figure out what Steve might have said. Unfortunately, Henry's voice had been so flat that it was impossible to tell if he'd meant: *No kidding?! You're proposing to Erin tomorrow?!* Or: *No kidding; we truly are better off as bachelors for all eternity.*

I hesitated at Mikara's door, listening for snores or footfalls. Even so, my thoughts wandered. My Christmas present to Steve would be vastly different if only I knew for sure what he'd said just now; if he felt as strongly about me as I did about him, I'd like to upgrade his skis, or maybe get him the 'his' half of his-and-her mountain bikes. But if he'd denigrated marriage the very moment I wasn't there to overhear him, a half dozen cereal bowls and a Scrubby would suffice.

Mikara's room was completely silent, and things snapped into perspective for me. Here I was at the door of a woman whose sibling had been brutally murdered, and all I could think about was whether or not my boyfriend intended to propose. How self-centered could I get?! From now on, I was putting all such thoughts out of my head.

I knocked softly.

No answer.

"Mikara?"

I rapped loudly on the door. Still no answer.

Uneasy now, I opened the door and entered slowly. Her bed was neatly made and empty. "Mikara?" I turned. She was standing in front of the window, staring outside.

"I can see some of the path to the bridge from here," she said. "If I'd been here last night, watching out this window, I might have seen him. Or her. Angie's killer might be behind bars right now. Or I would have realized Angie was out there and gone to check on her. Maybe I could have prevented it."

"I'm so sorry for your loss, Mikara. It's all so terrible."

She started crying. "I had to leave her there. In the snow. A batch of strangers poking and prodding for evidence. My only sister!"

I rubbed her back a little. She should be with a friend now, not me.

"Why did she have to come here last night?" she asked me.

"She must have been coming to visit you again, right?"

"I guess so." Mikara dried her tears. "Sheriff Mackey told me they found her car on a street, at the other side of the open space. Which makes no sense. Why would she walk all that way in the dark? Why not park near the house?"

"Could she have been out on a late-afternoon hike, maybe?"

"That's possible, I guess. There's a space between fence posts wide enough to walk between. And the path's only a couple of miles long, round-trip. Henry walks that way every day and has it all tamped down. She might've been inspecting a construction site in the cul-de-sac at the end of the day, decided to drop by to see me, and that's when she was ambushed."

"Was she familiar with the path?"

"Yeah. We call it—" She broke off and her face fell. "We used to call it 'Henry's hike.' Since it starts on his private property. When Henry and I were...friends, years ago, we used to walk there. Angie and her ex-husband were here with us a lot back then."

"Angie was married?"

"Yeah, but she'd been divorced for several years now. Alex, her ex, left Colorado after they divorced. That was my first thought when I heard she was dead—that maybe he did it. I even told Greg...Sheriff Mackey I thought so. But, when I thought about it some more, it's really unlikely. Somebody would have seen him and told me if he'd come to town. Our local government sucks, we get blackouts all the time, can't always count on running water. But something like Angie Woolf's ex-husband sneaking back into town? *That* would spread to every corner of the town within ninety minutes, tops."

She rubbed at her forehead and slumped onto her bed. "How can this be happening? Angie. Murdered. She's the only family I had left in the entire world."

"Mikara, I'm so sorry. That's all I can think to say, and I know you'll hear it dozens of times in the next few days."

She sighed and nodded. She wiped a tear from her cheek.

"Can I fix you some breakfast?" I asked. "I could make you a tray if you're not up to having company in the kitchen."

"That's really thoughtful of you, Erin. That'd be great, actually. I'd just like a cup of coffee, black, and a cereal bar. I brought a couple of boxes over yesterday. They're in the pantry, by the door."

"Be right back."

I closed the door behind me and returned to the kitchen. Henry was pacing by the stove and promptly asked, "How's she doing?"

"She's awake. Depressed, of course. Maybe still in shock. I'm bringing her some coffee and a cereal bar. She's not really up to facing people yet."

"Of course. I'm going to tell her to just come and go here as she pleases, for as long as she likes. I figure she might feel better here than at the apartment she shared with her sister."

I poured the coffee as he got out one of Mikara's cereal bars and handed it to me. "Tell her I asked about her. I just . . . feel so guilty. Maybe none of this would have happened if I hadn't hired her."

"You can't know that. Angie's death might have had nothing whatsoever to do with Mikara, or with the inn."

"Yeah. Or it might have had *everything* to do with it. "

Chapter 8

Sheriff Mackey returned to the inn that afternoon, holding court in the dining room and interviewing everyone separately. He spoke first with Chiffon, who'd been sitting at the kitchen table when I returned from bringing Mikara her coffee and breakfast bar. Mackey then interviewed Audrey, Henry, Mikara, and Ben.

Annoyingly, Mackey had asked all of us to stay close as we awaited our turns. I settled into the wonderful wing-back chair in the minilibrary on the second-floor landing. I was searching for leaping-lord figurines on my laptop when Ben came up the stairs. Because there was no door, he rapped on the wall. His beard, I noticed, was starting to get heavy; he was still a couple of days from shaving. Tomorrow, I remembered incongruously, was Friday, when the filter was supposed to arrive.

"Sheriff Mackey wants to talk to you now," Ben said wearily.

"Okay. Thanks. He sure kept you in there for quite a while, considering you'd already left for the day before anything happened."

Ben hung his head. "Not according to the time of death. Or the footprints in the snow. Although I'm not supposed to repeat anything Mackey said."

"So those boots he took from the mudroom were yours?"

He hesitated. "I have a feeling I'd better talk to a lawyer." He looked at me with vacant eyes. "I'm going to head home for the day. I'm not good for much right now anyway."

He turned and trudged down the stairs without meeting my eyes. I followed him downstairs, but he clearly didn't want to talk.

Mackey was standing at the head of the table when I slid open the pocket door to the dining room. "Close the door behind you," he said.

I did so, and then took a perversely childish pleasure in seating myself at the opposite end of the long table. Mackey hesitated, annoyed, but then picked up his notepad and headed closer. He dropped his pad in front of a chair near mine but continued to stand. "I've done some checking around." He hitched up his pants and rocked on his feet. It looked like a move I'd seen the law-men make in B-grade Westerns on TV. "I can't help but wonder why death seems to follow you around."

"I don't know the answer to that question."

"You seem to have created a nice little alibi for yourself and your old beau . . . Wendell's hatchet man."

"Cameron Baker and I had dinner together, like I told your deputy. We were getting caught up on old times, not deliberately establishing an alibi."

"Good thing for you," Mackey said with a snort, still choosing to loom over me. "'Cuz the alibi thing's coming up short. See, the coroner can only put the death within a three-hour time span ahead of when Angie's body was dis-covered. You'd've had plenty of time to kill her before you went out on the town with Mr. Baker."

"Oh, my god! You can't possibly suspect me! I had no motive whatsoever to kill Angie Woolf! I barely knew her! Besides, I was hanging the lights on the house! Passersby would have seen me up there. All you have to do is check with the neighbors, and they'll confirm my whereabouts!"

He pulled out the seat beside mine, angling it to face me, and then sat down, eyeing me the whole time as if this proximity might cause me to crumble. "'Fraid that's not what I'm hearing through the local grapevine, Miss Gilbert."

"Then you're getting garbled information from some-body!" I took a couple of calming breaths. It was terrifying to have an officer of the law suggest that I was a murderer. "I only met Angie twice. Once when she came out here to inspect the gazebo, and a—"

"That's when she told you the place wasn't up to snuff, setting your design schedule back considerably."

"Which is something that happens all the time in my line of work, and which, frankly, often leads to an increase in my earnings. The second time we met was when I interrupted her and Mikara arguing in the shed. Yesterday morning. We were all a little embarrassed, and she left quickly."

"Yeah. Mikara already told me about that."

"So you *also* already know that Angie and I are all but strangers!"

"Nobody's disputing how well *you* knew the victim."

I was baffled by the remark and looked at him, waiting for the other shoe to drop. He started jotting notes in his pad, and when he finished, he sneered at me.

Even though I was certain he was trying to intimidate me, it worked. I was scared. Could the townies here hate us so much that one of them was now framing me?

"I'm not following you, Sheriff Mackey. What exactly is somebody 'disputing'? Every word I just said is the complete truth!"

Mackey rose. "You and your partner might want to get your story straight." He collected his cap from the far side of the table and centered it on his head. "Be seein' you, Miss Gilbert. You'd better not plan on leaving Snowcap Village without checking with me first."

He let himself out through the kitchen door, walking with a studied saunter. The moment I was sure Mackey had left the house, I snatched up my cell phone and called Steve. Barely giving him time to answer, I said,

"Sheriff Mackey just left. He implied that I had a motive to kill Angie Woolf. And that *you* would know what it is."

There was a pause. "Pardon?"

"Had you been talking with Angie Woolf, or something, the day she was killed?"

"Yeah. Didn't I tell you? I forgot to get myself coffee for the trip to Crestview, so I went into town to grab a cup. I ran into Angie in the coffee shop. I figured it was in our best interest to chat her up, so I paid for her latte, and we shared a table for a few minutes."

"What did you talk about?"

"Nothing much. Just small talk ... ski conditions and what the mountain was like before the resort opened. Our plans for the holidays. That kind of thing. How could something that trivial possibly be of interest to Sheriff Mackey?"

"Apparently he thinks I could have killed Angie in a jealous rage." I felt queasy at the thought of being a murder suspect—in a town that hated outsiders.

"That's ridiculous! It was a five-minute conversation over coffee, for God's sake!"

"Well, that was apparently all that it took to get that damned Sheriff Mackey to focus on me, instead of on whatever clues there might be that point to the actual killer."

"Jeez. I'm sorry, Erin. I had no idea ..."

"It's not your fault." Suddenly exhausted, I dropped into the nearest chair. "Obviously the sheriff's an idiot. It's just that *he's* heading up the murder investigation, *and* he's got a big chip on his shoulder regarding outsiders. As does half the population of Snowcap Village. So who knows if he'll be able to convince a judge to issue an arrest warrant?" Audrey came into the dining room, no doubt to check on me. "Are you heading back soon?" I said into the phone. He'd gone to an antique store in Denver to select some miscellaneous items for the bedrooms.

"I'm on my way."

"Good. See you soon."

Audrey immediately asked me what was wrong, and I filled her in on the gist of my conversations with Mackey and now Steve.

"Oh, sweetie, don't let it get to you. Apparently the sheriff's doing that with everyone. He insinuated that I'd go to great lengths on Wendell's behalf."

"Including murdering the building inspector? He thinks that would keep your relationship going smoothly?"

"Apparently. He advised me not to leave town."

"He told me the same thing. This is beyond infuriating."

"I agree," she said. "Meantime, Chiffon Walters seems to have all the men in town wrapped around her little finger. Including Sheriff Mackey."

It would be in keeping with the way things had been going lately if Chiffon, the one person Sheriff Mackey did not seem to suspect, turned out to be the killer.

Chapter 9

It's fun sometimes to experiment with recipes. Especially when the taste-testing involves my favorite ingredient...booze!

—Audrey Munroe

Domestic Bliss

"It's time to get serious about Christmas preparations," Audrey announced after dinner. The two of us were just putting away the last of the dishes. Steve and Henry had made our dinner of grilled chicken, green beans, and baked potatoes tonight.

"I can't think about Christmas preparations right now, Audrey," I replied. "It's been 'firmly suggested' to me that I don't leave town. I can't go back home to Crestview without raising the sheriff's suspicions. I can't even go home to Hildi this weekend, let alone make blue-and-purple runners and wreaths."

"I realize that. That's why we're working on something fun and low-key this evening."

"I'm with you so far."

"We're coming up with a new eggnog recipe. Based on an old reliable one I've used for years. You can be my co-taster."

I grinned. "Wonderful idea, Audrey! That's the kind of project I can fully throw myself into."

She lifted a bottle of rum from the liquor cabinet. "There's the spirit."

"Rum? Not bourbon?"

"Good point." She grabbed a bottle of bourbon, too. "We'll try both and choose the best flavor." She turned on the radio, which was already set to a classical station playing a seasonal piece.

"So what should I do first? Separate the eggs? Beat the yolks?"

"Done. I've already got the basic eggnog recipe made up and properly chilled. All that's left for you and me to do now is select a new, special ingredient to jazz it up, and choose between the bourbon and the rum." She gestured at the stools behind the island.

I sighed happily and slid into the closest seat at the kitchen table. "I love cooking."

She removed a bowl with a spout built into its rim from the refrigerator.

"I wanted to try to add something that might turn the eggnog a Christmas color."

"Eww. We're talking red or green, here, aren't we? Not blue or purple?"

"Yes. So originally I was thinking maybe lime juice . . ."

"You actually *want* to get us halfway to Dr. Seuss's *Green Eggs and Ham*?"

She clicked her tongue. "That book has a happy ending, if you'll recall. In any case, lime juice wouldn't really get us to green, so I thought we'd try a nice green crème de menthe in the eggnog. For the second and third experiments, we'll add cranberry juice and sugar to cut down on the tartness of the juice. One with rum, the other bourbon. For the last one, I thought we'd go with chocolate sauce and kahlua, just because it's hard to go wrong with chocolate. With just a dash of rum. And a dollop of whipped cream. Possibly leaving out the eggnog altogether."

She whisked and stirred and slid me a cup of the slightly green eggnog, which she'd sprinkled with nutmeg. Gamely, I took a sip, which almost made me gag. "No to the crème de menthe."

"Would adding rum or bourbon help?" She took a sip herself, made a face, and promptly chucked the drink down the drain. "I'm going to say no."

We both loved the cranberry eggnog with rum, which tasted better than the bourbon version, and then moved on to her version of a white Russian—eggnog in the place of milk and rum replacing the vodka. She kept fiddling with the combinations, but after my fifth or sixth sip, I said, "You know, Audrey, I much prefer the cranberry nog. It's pretty and pink, and if I want a chocolate-flavored drink, I really prefer a shot of schnapps in my cup of cocoa."

She nodded, poured herself a cup of the cranberry nog, and we clinked glasses. "Good teamwork, Erin."

"Glad I could help."

Cranberry Nog

6 egg yolks
6 tablespoons sugar
1 teaspoon vanilla
1½ cups chilled medium cream
4 cups cranberry juice
6 egg whites
6 tablespoons sugar
1½ cups rum
½ teaspoon nutmeg

Beat egg yolks, sugar, and vanilla until very thick and lemon-colored. Gradually add cream and continue to beat until blended. Stir in cranberry juice and rum.

Beat egg whites until frothy. Gradually add sugar, beating well after each addition. Continue to beat until soft peaks form.

Gently fold egg whites into cranberry mixture. Chill in refrigerator 20 minutes before serving. Sprinkle with nutmeg for garnish.

Chapter 10

Monday morning, I watched Ben tack up the last sheet of Masonite board. The rough backing of the panels truly *was* the color of gingerbread, and so that was the side that Chiffon had told Ben to expose. Although, she'd thankfully resisted having him retile the roof in pseudo Thin Mints, Ben had dutifully added rows of scalloping just under the eaves, extending halfway down the third-story windows. Chiffon had painted the scallops pink, purple, and lavender. She'd also cut out a hundred corrugated cardboard circles, which she then spray-painted red or green — M&M's, presumably. These she'd had Ben staple in a zigzag pattern to the ghastly façade between the second-floor windows.

The only good thing about her design was that she'd done nothing to mar the shutters; she'd instructed Ben to cut the Masonite to fit around them. (I'd warned Chiffon that I love the aesthetics of shutters so much that if she messed with even one, I'd quit on the spot. That might have factored into her singular nod to good taste.) Even so, the overall emotional impact that her design had on me was tantamount to having a toddler run amok in my living room with a set of permanent markers. Shamefully, I endured the outrage by imagining myself shaving Chiffon's head and gluing zigzagging red and green dots to her scalp, followed by painting pink and purple scallops on her face.

Acting very much like the teenager that she'd been just a couple of years ago, Chiffon came bounding out of the inn to stand beside me on the sidewalk and observe the finished product. Behind us, the sparse traffic was slowing down as drivers and passengers paused to gawk. "You see that, Erin?" she cheerfully announced. "We're attracting all kinds of attention to the inn!" She waved at the driver of an SUV who was gaping at the inn in apoplectic dismay. He drove off without acknowledging her.

"Yes, we sure are." In less than a week's time, the Goodwin estate had gone from the highlight to the lowlight of my career. I was now going to have to park my Sullivan & Gilbert Designs van in the back parking area, out of eyeshot from the road.

Chiffon sighed happily. "It's going to look really pretty

at sunset, when your Christmas lights first turn on. The place will look like a gigantic lit-up candy cottage."

"And it will look even prettier when the sun's gone down completely."

She missed my sarcasm and called out compliments to Ben for his "outstanding job." He climbed down the ladder and then approached, his shoulders slumped and his gait heavy. He looked physically pained by the monstrosity he'd been forced to create. I said to him, "Do you think you can install a mooring, for lack of a better word, in the front yard? We'll have to figure out a way to secure the large sled that Steve's renting. Snowcap Inn is liable if the thing gets stolen."

"No problem," Ben said. "I could just sink a metal fastener into a cement pylon in the rock garden at the head of the driveway. And get a long, sturdy chain."

"That should work."

"It's too bad Steve Sullivan said he wouldn't be able to rent a team of reindeer," Chiffon said. "That would have really made an impression on everyone in town. We could have put jingle bells on their collars and harnesses, and pulled the sleigh through downtown Snowcap Village. And we could have gotten Wendell Barton to dress up like Santa. I was going to make up flyers attached to little bags of candy for Wendell to distribute to all the downtown shoppers and children. I even wrote an advertising slogan: 'You always win when you stay at Snowcap Inn!' "

"Catchy," I replied.

"Oh, that's nothing, really. I've written several songs myself, you know. I'm chilling for now...taking a break from the stress and grind of the life of a pop star, but I have a natural talent for words."

"That must be really fun for you."

"Thanks." She gestured at the house. "And I have a passion for design, as well."

I managed a nod, and more important, to hold my tongue; at the moment I'd been thinking that it was too bad her "passion" wasn't for being the first woman to walk on the moon.

Five days had now passed since Angie's murder, and I was growing uneasy. All indications were that no progress whatsoever had been made in the investigation. With Sheriff Mackey's instructions not to leave town, I'd had to extend my cat-sitter's duties to include weekends, even though I desperately longed for the comfort of home, hearth, and Hildi. Making matters worse, Steve had seemed to take my melancholy personally, as if his presence should fill my each and every want. Yesterday afternoon, Audrey had been unable to attend Angie's service, but Steve and I had suffered through the discomfort of whispered voices and stares from the countless attendees. In a town that had recently been tiny and close-knit, it would have been human nature to assume that the killer was an outsider, as opposed to one of their own.

We were also getting into a time crunch. Christmas Eve was two weeks from today. The steps were still barricaded behind crime-scene tape. The water filter had been lost in transit—the shipment seemed to have gotten bogged down somewhere in Milwaukee, probably while the deliverymen made a pit stop at a brewery.

"Ben? Erin?" Chiffon said, jarring me from my reverie. "Look! Some of our neighbors are coming over to say hi."

I followed Chiffon's gaze. A dozen neighbors were gathering on the sidewalk at the base of the hill. They all stood together chatting for a minute, then they headed toward us. "At least they don't seem to be carrying any tar or feathers."

"What do you mean?" She looked at me, blinking in the bright sun. A sincerely baffled expression put small worry lines on her otherwise flawless skin. "Why would anyone want to add tar or feathers to our Christmas decorations?"

"Erin means that this group is unhappy about our turning the inn into an oversized candy cottage," Ben explained. "I tried telling you 'bout that the other day. They have town ordinances that limit the size of the holiday display."

"That just seems very un-Christmassy of everyone to me," she muttered. "They need to get into the true spirit of the holidays." But she quickly turned on a full-wattage smile as the minimob reached the property line. "Good afternoon, friends! Merry Christmas! I'm Chiffon Walters, part owner of the inn. And you are . . . ?"

"Irate at your tacky Christmas display!" the middle-aged woman who appeared to be leading the pack retorted. "If you want to call this monstrosity a 'Christmas display,' that is. Seems like blasphemy to me. Why would you want to hide the lovely siding behind ugly brown boards and all those red and green dots?"

"Because gingerbread is brown, and the dots are M-and-M's. And I'm putting up candy cane light poles, all along the front walk, which will help tie everything to-gether. Plus, we're in the process of getting a Santa's sleigh, silver-painted chocolate kisses, and big gumdrops. This house is every kid's dream!"

"Every *dentist's* maybe," the woman scoffed. "It goes against the neighborhood covenant. Nothing is supposed to be hung from our homes except lights."

"You know what, Ms. Spokesperson?" Chiffon replied cheerfully. "I checked into that, and because we have re-classified our property as a *business*, your covenant no longer applies. But to be totally honest, I was hoping everyone in Snowcap Village would share in my enthusi-asm for Christmastime, and join in that childlike, Christmas morning joy for things like"—she gestured at the house—"candy and gingerbread."

Ms. Spokesperson, as she'd been dubbed, was non-plussed at Chiffon's response and glanced back at her minions for a rebuttal.

An elderly woman stared at the house and said, "The display *is* unusual, at least."

"Yeah," a white-haired man grumbled, "but so is find-ing *human remains* underneath your porch steps. And having the building inspector get strangled by your Christmas lights. The Goodwin estate has been through all that, too, this past week. You ask me, enough is enough."

Did he mean to say that it was okay to endure a murder or two, but that he drew the line at ostentatious Christmas decorations? In any case, his proclamation stuck in my craw. "We'll take everything down by the second Saturday in January," I said. "There are no flashing lights aimed at anyone's windows, no blaring music or honking horns."

"But you *are* stopping traffic," Ms. Spokesperson pointed out.

"It's all in good fun," Ben added. "It's not like we're out to hurt anyone."

"Absolutely we're not," Chiffon said. "So I'll tell you what. If it would be over the top according to your general opinion, I'll scale back on the lawn ornaments."

"*Lawn ornaments?*" Ben and I asked in unison.

"Something in addition to the sleigh?" I added.

"Yeah. Just a couple things." She shrugged. "I was hoping to get inflatable elves, Santa, and maybe a miniature Santa's workshop. Along with a big nutcracker."

There wasn't a nutcracker in the world that was big enough to work on Chiffon's head, I mused uncharitably.

"No!" at least four of the group of neighbors cried at once.

"Does everyone feel that way?" Chiffon asked the assembly on the sidewalk.

They all swiftly voted down the idea of any inflatable decorations. "This cheesy-looking junk you've slapped on the outside of the house is a big enough eyesore as it is," the grouchy man added.

"Well. You've certainly made *your* opinion clear enough." Chiffon sniffed. "Tell you what. We're throwing an open house tomorrow night. The entire neighborhood is invited."

I couldn't maintain my poker face at this news. "We *are*?" I asked, incredulous.

"Yes, indeedy. We'll put up flyers downtown. We'll have

hors d'oeuvres, wine, cocoa, and tons of candy." Her face lit up. "*And*, in the place of the inflatable elves and so on, I'm herewith giving all you nice people a challenge: Come make snowmen and snow animals in the front yard of the inn's grounds."

"I don't know if there's enough snow," a fifty-something man said thoughtfully. "Is it all right if I cart in some extra snow from my front yard?"

"All the better!" Chiffon replied. "Everyone here, plus all of your kids, can get started anytime, and we'll officially view your creations tomorrow night, at the party. Which will start at . . . let's say seven P.M. and end no later than ten, seeing as tomorrow's a school night."

Ben and I exchanged surprised glances; how bizarre that Chiffon's crazy but creative brain could concoct the all-time tacky Christmas display on the one hand, yet also pop out the idea of a combination block party/snow-sculpture contest. The mob-in-the-making soon quickly and happily headed back to their homes, and my own spirits lifted, as well.

The following day, to everyone's delight—especially Henry's—Chiffon's idea was working magnificently. Inviting everyone to create snowmen and snow critters in the front lawn had been a huge hit. Henry, Audrey, Chiffon, Wendell, and Mikara periodically took turns bringing out cups of cocoa and chatting up the neighbors who dropped by the property to build snow figures. For such a serious, nonmaternal type, Mikara proved to be surprisingly terrific with children and was looking happy for the first time since her sister's murder. She supplied the kids with various vegetables to augment the snowmen, and branches to serve as antlers for the "snow reindeer" that a trio of middle-schoolers built. The creations used up every bit of untamped-down snow in front, but the nearby neighbors got into the spirit and periodically supplied us with cartfuls or sledfuls of additional snow.

That night, Henry got those same neighbors' permission to run floodlights across the sweeping expanse of the front yard; the dozens of snowmen and snow animals built by the townspeople were utterly delightful. Mikara and Chiffon had managed to employ an excellent catering crew, and Audrey did her usual magnificent job of organizing a big party. Wendell, Audrey, and Chiffon acted as the primary party hosts—not unlike a three-person family, with Wendell glued to Audrey's side. Henry was taking a slight backseat in hosting duties, even though he was technically in charge. The guests were quite clearly merely tolerating Wendell, who had amassed a huge debt of acrimony over many years, but at least no blatant hostility was evident.

A woman from yesterday's neighborhood brigade excused herself from a friendly conversation with Ben Orlin and another couple to join me at the snack table. Audrey and I had decided to put our new eggnog recipe to good use, and we'd rented an enormous punch bowl to fill with the creamy concoction.

"This was such a great idea," the woman said to me.

"Yes, it really was."

"How odd that the same person who dreamt up such a god-awful outdoor display could have come up with it."

I couldn't help but laugh. "The human mind is quite a mystery, isn't it?"

She laughed, too, and added, "As they say, there's no accounting for taste." She lifted her chin to return Henry's smile of greeting, as he crossed the room and joined Ben in conversation. "It's nice to see that Ben Orlin and Henry Goodwin have become friendly, after all these years."

"They once weren't, you mean?"

"Oh, well, they grew up together, but were kept at a distance. Everyone says that's because of Ben's father. He worked as a master carpenter on this house over the years and was always very conscious of not being in the same social class as the Goodwins. So, from what I gather, Ben was told he couldn't be friends with Henry. Which just seems so sad, don't you think? I'm roughly their age, and back when we were all kids, Snowcap Village was so tiny! You *had* to find a way to be friends with your neighbors, because there just plain weren't enough people around to be choosy."

Times must indeed have changed; Snowcap had been plenty "choosy" when it came to welcoming Steve and me. That thought darkened my mood, and I soon had to shake off an image of Angie's body by the bridge. Forcing a smile, I said, "When you think about it, that's always the case. None of us has the kind of time to foster animosity."

She held my gaze for a moment. "You're absolutely right." She paused. "In fact, I have to admit that you and Chiffon and this gathering tonight have altered my opinion. I hope the Snowcap Inn is a great success. I really do."

The sound system was now playing a recording of dogs

barking the notes to "Jingle Bells," and I told the woman honestly that her words were "music to my ears." I decided to make it my goal to try to get to know each of the seventy or so guests at the party. I started purposefully mingling and joined two couples sitting in the den, but was distracted when Cameron—overdressed but killer handsome in his tuxedo—took a seat beside me. "Evening, Erin. I'm starting to get the impression that you're avoiding me."

"Not at all. I'm simply trying to meet and greet all our guests."

"Ah, of course. You're working the room. Good for you." He grinned at me. "Now that you mention it, I think *I'm* going to make an effort to get to know your illustrious Mr. Sullivan."

I glanced at Steve, who was visible through the doorway, chatting with some people in the next room. Catching my eye, he started to smile, until he spotted Cameron sitting beside me. Sullivan promptly turned his back on us.

Chapter 11

Before I could give another thought to Steve's reaction, a thirtyish woman spilled red wine on the Oriental rug a few feet away from me. I excused myself to grab the closest bottle of seltzer water, one of several that we'd strategically placed throughout the house for this very purpose. We chatted a little as I doused the would-be stain, and working together, we soaked up the wine with napkins. I assured her that she should get another glass for herself and let me finish dabbing up the last signs of the spill.

Chiffon, meanwhile, flounced over to claim my vacated seat and said to Cameron, "Hi. You work for Wendell, don't you?"

"Yes, and you're one of the co-owners of the Snowcap Inn."

"That's right. I'm Chiffon Walters. You've probably seen some of my videos, or heard my recordings."

"I'm not up on pop music. Sorry. I'm sure you're very good at what you do, though."

Much as I was enjoying eavesdropping on Cameron and Chiffon's conversation, Wendell, looking a little soused, walked over to me and bent down a little. "My, my. You're a designer *and* a cleaning woman. Do you do windows?"

With difficulty, I mustered a smile. He held out his hand and helped me to my feet. "Great party, Erin. You should try the eggnog."

"Thanks. I will," I replied.

"You're almost as tall as the Woolf sisters, aren't you?" he asked, looking up at me. Although he'd taken a wide stance, he was weaving on his feet. "It feels like either you're getting taller, or I'm getting shorter."

"I haven't grown lately. But I *am* wearing heels."

"That's a relief. I was starting to worry I was turning into one of Santa's elves." He laughed heartily, and I managed a small chuckle, to be polite.

He wandered off, and I returned my attention to Chiffon and Cameron. "You don't have a napkin," Chiffon was telling him, practically sitting in his lap now. "Let me give you this one. It's got my private cell phone number on it. You can call me anytime you want."

He looked at the napkin, but didn't take it from her. "That's not going to happen, Ms. Walters, but thank you." He rose and said, "Excuse me."

She glared at him as he walked away. Although I tried to disguise the fact that I'd overheard their exchange, Chiffon immediately approached me. "Your ex is really hot. But I guess he thinks he's too old for me. Can't blame a girl for trying, as they say."

"Better luck next time, *as they say*."

"Oh, it's hardly like I need any luck, Erin." Suddenly, there wasn't an ounce of the harmless bimbo in her voice or countenance; perhaps alcohol had dislodged her ditsy routine. "I simply enjoy flirting. My dance card's pretty full, actually. Henry Goodwin and I are dating."

"He's at least a dozen years older than Cameron is, you realize."

"I like *mature* men."

The implication was that my ex was immature. The remark rankled. In the corner of my vision, I could see Mikara and Henry chatting like the best of friends. "I wonder if your dating Henry bothers Mikara at all. The two of them used to be engaged."

Chiffon shrugged. "Everyone knows that." Chiffon turned and gazed at Mikara and Henry. "She's fine with it. We all know it's nothing serious. And Mikara and I are hardly in the same league."

"Meaning what?"

She hesitated. "Much as I hate to say this, she's, you know, kind of old and tired." She giggled, as if the airhead in her had returned. Her small mood swing made me wonder if she was cagier—and more formidable—than I'd considered her to be.

"Were you friends with Angie at all?"

She gave me a slight shrug. "We were acquaintances, really, but we were friendly enough. I can't believe someone killed her."

"I know. It's horrifying."

"I can't believe anybody I know would be capable of murder. It had to be some pervert looking for a random victim. Some itinerant who wandered into town. And who's probably long gone."

"I wish I believed that. But who would come up here, the outskirts of town, hide out till someone happened to walk by the property's little bridge, and *then* kill the person? It doesn't make any sense."

Again, Chiffon shrugged, now looking around the room as if blatantly searching for better company than my own. "But it's better than the alternative . . . than thinking one of us could have killed Angie Woolf." She grinned at Henry. "Speaking of dearest Henry, I think I'll go see how he's doing." She trotted toward him.

Cameron, I noted, had made good on his word and was now talking one-on-one with Steve. Things didn't appear to be going well, however, judging by body English; Steve's arms were crossed and he was frowning at the floor. Regardless, my worrying about their conversation was keeping me from being a festive cohost. It was time for me to mingle with more neighbors. I saw a pair of couples I hadn't met and started to head toward them. Audrey, however, intercepted me. She grabbed my elbow and pulled me into a conversation with some obviously wealthy friends of Wendell's. Several minutes later, I began to realize that I was going to have to scale down my meet-everyone goal. When I finally excused myself and turned around, Steve was standing there, waiting to talk to me.

"I have to tell you honestly, Erin," he said into my ear, "Cameron's a player... the type of guy who'll step on anyone to get ahead. He's like a young Wendell Barton, only worse. And he's definitely more dangerous."

"Dangerous? Cameron?"

Steve merely nodded.

"Cameron's driven, highly ambitious, and enjoys amassing power. But he's not what I'd call a *player*, and he's certainly not *dangerous*. He's basically a nice guy."

He shook his head. "Your opinion of him is colored by your history." He glanced around as if to ensure he couldn't be overheard. "I don't trust him in the least, Erin. If I didn't know that you were his alibi the night of the murder, he'd be my number-one suspect."

"You dislike him *that* much, from a ten-minute conversation? What on earth did he say to you?"

"That he wants to make his fortune in the next five years, then return to New York City where he can 'live large.' The man doesn't care about anything but making money and gaining power. Frankly, I can't imagine the two of you ever having been a couple in the first place. He probably hit on you just because of your looks."

"And all this time I thought it was my personality and charm that captured his interest."

Steve shrugged. "No offense, Erin. I'm just saying... the guy's really shallow."

"Your attitude is getting on my nerves, Sullivan. Why are you telling me this?"

He seemed taken aback and ushered me to a deserted corner. "Isn't that obvious?" he asked, lowering his voice. "Because I'm worried about you, and you have a blind spot where Cameron Baker is concerned! We have to be on the lookout. Angie Woolf was killed on this property a few days ago."

"But we *know* the killer wasn't Cameron," I replied in a harsh whisper. "I saw him drive up, and he was with me from that point on."

"Even if he's innocent of the physical murder, he might have played a part in it."

"Oh, come on, Sullivan! You don't honestly believe he hired a hit man! I just don't get why you think you should be judging someone I knew ten years ago. And who, after a couple of weeks from now, I'll most likely never see again!"

"Because he's here *now*, and I think Cameron's bad news and should be avoided!"

"You've made your point more than enough times, Sullivan," I fired back at him. "There's nothing like having your boyfriend lead you to a quiet, dimly lit nook of the room just to chastise you! You'll have to excuse me. I'm going to go mingle with our other guests now."

I marched into the dining room, refreshed my eggnog, then continued past Sullivan and into the living room, where a couple of dozen people were milling around. I walked up to a small circle of women and introduced myself. They were more than pleasant, but very soon, I was distracted by a pair of unsupervised young boys—five or six years old—who were fidgeting with the drapes. I had visions of them trying to scale the walls with the curtains as climbing ropes and asked, "Do any of you know those boys?"

" 'Fraid so," one woman replied. "We call them Dennis the Menace One and Two."

"Their parents probably snuck out the back door a long time ago," another added. "They have a terrible habit of doing that."

"Don't they, though?" the first woman agreed. "Remember when they did that at my Halloween party?"

I set down my glass on the coffee table and headed toward the boys. In remarkable unison, both youngsters jumped up and grabbed hold of separate drape panels. I raced over and caught the drapery rod as it fell, barely preventing the heavy rod from clonking both boys on the head.

"Hey, you two! These curtains are not climbing ropes! The curtain rods cannot support your weight! Where are your parents?"

"I dunno," they said in unison.

"We're going to go locate them right—"

"What are you doing to my sons!" I whirled around to see Ms. Spokesperson shoving her way past a group of onlookers and marching toward the boys and me.

"Your sons just pulled down the draperies and nearly injured themselves in the process."

"Mathew, Peter, apologize this instant." Although the words themselves sounded stern, it was a rote delivery, and she was scanning the room for someone to chat with next.

"Sorry," one said, while the other said, "Star pee." A truly heartfelt apology, if ever I'd heard one. Their mom, I was certain, heard the insincerity in their apology, but seemed to feel we were now even.

"That's all right," I replied somewhat testily. "We can replaster the holes in the wall and rehang the supports for the curtain rod."

"It was just an accident!" Ms. Spokesperson proclaimed.

"Which is why it's fortunate that nothing happened that can't be easily fixed."

She pursed her lips and shot me a hateful glare. "Come on, boys. Get your coats. It's time to leave."

While that trio marched away, I returned to my eggnog, still on the coffee table where I'd abandoned it. A couple of the women I'd been talking with earlier were now grinning at me. Planning to rejoin them, I started to take a sip of my drink, then froze. The contents of my cup suddenly didn't smell right; it now bore an acrid odor. I turned my back on the women and discreetly sniffed again. I got a distinct whiff this time.

My eggnog smelled like bitter almonds! Cyanide!

Chapter 12

My heart started hammering in my chest. I'd helped make the first batch of this eggnog myself, and it hadn't smelled even *remotely* like bitter almonds. Maybe Audrey had added almond flavoring to the second batch, though. I scanned the room, but she was not in the immediate vicinity.

On second thought, could I have been drinking poison all along? My stomach felt queasy. I set my cup down on an end table. I felt dizzy. This must just be my imagination running wild. I couldn't possibly have missed the aroma earlier.

Maybe my sense of smell was playing tricks on me. I strode into the dining room. The bowl of cranberry nog was half full. I lifted the ladle and took a whiff. No almond scent.

Cameron appeared through the kitchen door and headed toward me. "You look upset. Is something wrong?"

"Maybe." He was holding a cup of eggnog. "Let me try some of that." I snatched the plastic cup from his hand and took a quick sip. "I knew it! This tastes fine. And the eggnog in the bowl smells normal, too." Although part of me knew there was no cause for panic, my stomach was doing flip-flops.

He stared at me as if my face had been turning colors. Maybe it was. "Why are you so—"

I brushed past him. "I have to throw up."

"Erin?" Cameron called after me as I rushed toward the bathroom. "Are you okay?"

That was what's known as a stupid question. Suddenly it felt like the temperature had shot up twenty degrees and I was burning up.

Two women were standing next to the door to the downstairs bathroom, waiting their turn. My distress must have been readily apparent because they both backed up. One said, "Go ahead. We can wait."

I pounded on the door, which was quickly pulled open. I brushed past the startled-looking man as he exited, and raced over to the toilet in the nick of time.

After a minute or so, I pulled myself together and both my breathing and my stomach returned to normal. Linda, my police officer friend, had once told me that cyanide turned a person's tongue cherry red. I examined my tongue. It was a dark pink and in no way bore a cherry red hue. After splashing water on my face and using toothpaste on my finger to brush my teeth (and tongue, just on principle), I emerged from the bathroom. Steve was waiting for me by the door, with nobody else around. His eyes were wide and his lips were set in a grim line.

"Good Lord, Erin," he said quietly. He reached out and caressed my cheek. I got the impression that the caress was meant, in part, to gauge if I had a fever. "What's going on? I just now overheard some woman I've never seen before in my life telling someone *else* I've never met that you were in here throwing up. They were speculating that . . ." He held me at arm's length and searched my eyes. He whispered, "Are you pregnant?"

"No," I answered in a harsh whisper, "although those women are undoubtedly still happily spreading rumors to that effect, even as we speak. I was nearly poisoned!"

"What do you—"

"Somebody slipped cyanide into my eggnog. I caught a strange whiff of bitter almonds before I took a sip. I didn't drink any of it."

"Thank God," Steve said, looking pale. "But you got sick to your stomach anyway?"

"Finding out I came so close to getting poisoned did quite a number on me. But there was nothing toxic in my glass when I was drinking from it earlier. For one thing, Linda Delgardio once told me that cyanide turns your tongue bright red."

He furrowed his brow. "Let me see your tongue."

A couple was passing by, and the woman gave me a

long look. I gave her a friendly nod. "My tongue is fine," I told Sullivan under my breath. "I checked."

"Then just let me verify."

I sighed, but then dutifully stuck my tongue out at him. He nodded. "It's your normal magenta color."

"More of a dusty rose, really. Not that I've held color swatches against it. I've got to get my glass back before anyone else takes a sip." Thank heavens those rambunctious boys already left; they were just the sort who'd view a deserted cup as a chance to have their first taste of alcohol.

"We'll take your drink to the sheriff's station and insist that it be analyzed."

With Steve just a step behind me, I rushed back over to the table where I'd left my glass. I stamped my foot and looked back at Sullivan. "My glass is gone."

Chiffon was standing not far away. I dashed over to her. "Chiffon. I had a glass of eggnog on the table. Did you take it?"

"No, Erin. Of course not! I'm a celebrity. I can't risk being seen drinking at parties. Next thing you know, my image is splashed all over the front page of the society sections. And the paparazzi always intentionally take shots where I'm blinking or when—"

"Did you see who *did* take it, then?" Sullivan interrupted.

"It had to be one of the waiters or caterers. That's their job, after all . . . to pick up deserted cups and things."

"It was nearly full," I told Steve. "Maybe I can recognize the glass in the kitchen."

"There's plenty of eggnog in the punch bowl, Erin,"

Chiffon said, clicking her tongue. "It's really okay to pour yourself some more, you know."

"I'll keep that in mind. Thanks." We rushed into the kitchen. I raced toward a woman wearing a caterer's uniform—black slacks and a white Oxford shirt—standing at the double sink. She was rinsing out a pair of glasses and slipping them into hot, soapy water. "Damn it all," I grumbled.

"Is there a problem?" the woman asked.

"Did you pour out a full glass of eggnog just now?"

"I...think so. Why?"

"Let me see if the sink smells funny."

"Excuse me?" she asked, although she stepped aside.

The water was on full force and there were no traces of the creamy dregs of my drink in the rinsing half of the double sink. I shut off the water. No odor.

I reached into the scalding-hot sink, grabbed a glass, and lifted it to my nose. "Damn! It just smells like dishwashing liquid!"

"Are you with the department of health or something?" the woman asked.

Ignoring the question, I asked: "When you were handling leftover glasses of eggnog, did you smell almonds?"

"No. Why?"

"It's too late, then. It doesn't matter. Thanks anyway."

Steve was speaking in low tones to Audrey, who must have followed us into the kitchen. She shook her head sadly at me.

I walked over to them. "I don't know what to do." I looked at Steve. "Should we stop the party? Tell everyone they need to get tested, in case anyone else's glass was poisoned?"

"Maybe we should," he replied.

"Are you absolutely certain your drink was poisoned, Erin?" Audrey asked.

"It smelled wrong... like bitter almonds. But I suppose I'm only ninety-nine percent sure."

Audrey drummed her fingers against her upper arm. "There's nothing wrong with the batch that's in the punch bowl. I was drinking some just now. Let's end the party now, without spreading panic. If we let everyone know they might have been poisoned, that's going to put a swift end to our hopes of opening a bed-and-breakfast here anytime within this decade."

"More importantly," I said, "I think there's zero chance that anyone was spiking more than my glass alone with poison. Let's face it—for whatever reason, I always seem to be a prime target for murder attempts." I mentally ran through a list of suspects who could have killed Angie and perhaps believed that I'd unknowingly seen something from my rooftop perch that evening—Mikara, Ben, Wendell, Chiffon, or Henry.

Audrey glanced at the clock on the stove, and I followed suit. It was eight twenty-two. Originally we weren't going to wind things down till ten. "I'm going to have the waitstaff put away all the unserved munchies and beverages," she said, "starting with the eggnog. Then I'll get everyone to leave the house. Nicely, of course."

"How are you going to manage that feat?" Steve asked.

"Easy." She grabbed the phone and started dialing. "I'll announce that my TV show is about to arrive to film a segment on snow sculptures. And I'll get a crew out here immediately by chipping in a hundred-dollar bonus for each of them. Then we'll have the partyers wave at the cameras from behind their creations. And once everyone's outside and the filming's complete, we'll thank all our guests for coming."

Over the phone, Audrey told her producer that this was "a personal emergency," and she needed a cameraman and van within fifteen minutes. She explained that "someone may or may not have slipped poison into a friend's drink," so she needed to get the police out here—without causing our guests to panic.

Once she hung up, Steve said, "That's an ingenious plan, Audrey."

"Thanks." She patted his arm. "Having a camera crew at the ready is one of the fringe benefits of my job. I just wish I'd had my own show when my sons were teenagers. You can get all sorts of speedy results by promising to produce a television camera."

"Let's go do our civic duty," Steve said to me, "and make sure Mackey doesn't manage to ruin everything and get himself on TV."

While Audrey made her announcement, Steve and I grabbed our coats, slipped out the back door, and drove to the sheriff's station at the jail. The tiny boxlike structure had been built according to recent stringent town ordinances, which required wooden siding painted from a range of light hues and using two complementary colors for the trim. The effect was more like an ice-cream shop than town jail, inside and out. A long counter delineated the front room. Behind the counter, Sheriff Mackey and the sad-sack deputy who seemed to serve as his driver sat behind fake-wood Formica desks, separated by a partition that was arranged so that Mackey had twice the area as the deputy did.

"Aw, jeez," Mackey said in the deputy's direction as we entered. "It's the decorators." He sneered at us. "You got some more info for us? 'Cuz otherwise we're closed. We already got the state investigators riding our asses and have enough on our hands." The deputy, meanwhile, stared at us blankly.

"Can you give us that number?" I asked Mackey. "We'd be happy to talk directly to them."

"That depends," he replied, smoothing his greasy hair back against his scalp, looking and sounding more than ever like Jack Nicholson. "Are you here to confess?"

"Someone tried to poison Erin tonight," Steve said.

The deputy maintained his blank stare, but Mackey regarded me with an increasingly haughty expression. "Come on in and tell me all about it."

Sullivan opened the half-door in the counter and held it for me. Mackey gestured at one of the two molded plastic chairs in front of his desk. I took a seat, and Sullivan sat down beside me.

Mackey stared at me for a long moment. "You look all right to me. How close did this poisoner come to succeeding, Miss Gilbert?"

"I don't know how to answer that. We were hosting an open house at the inn for the neighborhood. I had to desert my glass of eggnog for several minutes, and when I returned to it, there was a strange odor . . . bitter almonds."

"This was eggnog, you say?" Mackey asked.

"It was cranberry eggnog, to be precise," I replied.

"Cranberries? Mixed with yellow eggs? Eww. Doesn't that make it orange?"

"No, slightly pink, but that's really beside the point."

"So do you still use the, uh . . ." He glanced toward the top of the partition. "Hey, Penderson? What's that brown seasoning stuff they put on top of eggnog?"

"Nutmeg," the three of us answered in unison.

"Yeah, that's it. Maybe they ran out of nutmeg in your kitchen, and someone threw in some ground-up almonds instead. Hey, Penderson? Do you know if nutmeg is made from powdered nuts?"

"Doubt it. I don't think 'meg' means powdered, or else they'd call it *gun-meg* and *dusting-meg*. I bet nutmeg is a weed of some kind."

I concentrated on tapping my toe in an attempt to keep from losing my patience. "I'd been drinking from that same glass of eggnog till I was pulled away. It smelled fine until I picked up my glass a second time."

"Someone slipped poison into Erin's cup when no-body was looking," Steve said firmly. "There were fifty or sixty adults at the party, and it could have been any one of them."

"Did your eggnog *taste* like almonds, too?"

"I don't know. I didn't actually drink any, because I know that cyanide smells like bitter almonds."

"So, where's the glass? You did bring it, didn't you?"

I shook my head. "One of the caterers at the party must have picked it up."

"Or," Sullivan added, "whoever tried to poison her grabbed it when she ran to the bathroom, and he or she realized the murder attempt had failed."

"I got an upset stomach," I explained, "when I realized I almost drank poison."

"You puked, eh?" Mackey said with a grin. "You must've been the life of the party."

"All I cared about at the time was not to *die* at the party," I retorted.

Mackey rocked back in his chair, looking contemptuously at us both. "This story strikes me as far-fetched. Poisoning somebody at a party? Running off with the glass? Sounds to me like you just got yourself an overripe cranberry or a rotten egg."

"No, Sheriff, my drink smelled specifically like bitter almonds! Not rotten eggs. Or stale cranberries."

"Did any of your guests who were also drinking eggnog start puking their guts out? Or suddenly start to get spooked about being poisoned?"

The phone rang.

"Penderson? You got that?"

"We're not suggesting that the entire punch bowl was laced," Sullivan replied, his voice far more patient than mine. "Erin's *glass* was poisoned."

"And why's that? Have the two of you been trying to spread that gingerbread décor from—"

"Sheriff?" Penderson interrupted. "It's Wendell Barton on the line for you again."

The sheriff winced. "Tell him I'm busy," he said with false bravado.

"He says it can't wait."

Mackey snorted, his cheeks turning red. "Speaking of the devil, was Wendell Fat Cat Barton at the party tonight?"

My warning flags rose. Mackey was at Wendell's beck and call. The sheriff was now trying to cover for himself by acting like a big shot and bad-mouthing Wendell.

"Barton left the party early," Sullivan replied.

Sullivan's remark jogged my memory. "He walked through the room right when I was arguing with the mom of the kids who'd broken the curtain rod." Steve and Mackey both looked puzzled, and I explained. "Wendell was nearby just when I'd deserted my glass, and immediately before it smelled like poison."

"Huh. So *Barton* might have done it." Mackey gave a rueful shake of his head, then picked up the phone and said, "Yeah?" by way of a greeting. My thoughts raced. His gruffness felt like an act; I suspected that he and Wendell Barton had much more cordial a relationship than the sheriff wanted to let on. Sheriff Mackey wasn't inept; he was corrupt!

Steve and I exchanged glances, and I knew he'd picked up on the same thing. Mackey followed up his greeting with a series of "yeahs" and "nos." He then looked at me and said into the phone, "I'm going to nab Angie Woolf's killer. No matter what it takes. I'm taking this personally." He continued to hold my gaze, his own eyes blazing with intensity. "Nobody comes into my town and acts above the law." He slammed the phone down in a childish fit of pique and shifted his eyes toward Steve. "Barton thinks he's an important man. His money may give him special privileges at the spa, but not here. Not as long as I'm town sheriff."

Was it just a coincidence that Wendell was calling the sheriff, right after I'd nearly been poisoned? Could he be planting the idea that I, having killed Angie, had made up the story about poison in order to divert suspicion from himself?

My mouth felt dry as my imagination started to run away with me. If the sheriff was in Wendell Barton's pocket, and Wendell was, in fact, guilty, not only would Angie's killer never be brought to justice, but an innocent person would very likely be framed for Angie Woolf's murder: me.

Chapter 13

Sheriff Mackey leaned his elbows on his desk and shifted his gaze from me to Steve and back. "Now. Where were we? We got no eggnog to test for toxins, no glass for fingerprints, and fifty or so suspects. Right?"

And a chief investigator who's on the take. I nodded, my feelings of helplessness only deepening.

"Any witnesses? Did your fellow partyers see anyone handling your glass?"

"I don't know. Maybe."

"Penderson?" Mackey called over the partition. "Looks

like we're in for even more overtime. We gotta go to a party at the mayor's mansion and ask if anyone saw anyone carrying around little bottles with a skull and crossbones on 'em."

"Everybody will have left by now," I said. "The party ended a few minutes ago."

Mackey rolled his eyes. "That's gonna make this even harder to investigate. You got a list of the invites?"

"There weren't any invitations," Steve explained. "It was a come one, come all type of thing for the neighbors."

"This gets better and better, Penderson," Mackey called out again. "We'll be doing a door-to-door."

Door-to-door questioning by the police would be a disaster for the inn's reputation, and, if anything, would amp up the killer's sense of urgency. I had to put a stop to this right now. "Never mind," I said, rising. "I'm withdrawing my complaint. Or my claim. Whatever." In the corner of my vision, I saw Sullivan's eyes widen in surprise. "You can't possibly catch whoever did it at this point, and it's just not worth the effort."

"You sure?" Mackey said. "I don't want you claiming this office ignored an attempted murder."

"I'm sure."

Steve muttered, "Thanks," and followed me out the door. We got into his van. He started the engine and pulled out of the space, neither of us saying a word. After a lengthy silence, he asked, "Why did you make such a hasty exit?"

"Because I needed to think. If Mackey is Wendell's lackey, and Wendell killed Angie and tried to poison me, I'm a sitting duck."

"But why would Wendell poison you?"

"Maybe he thinks I know more than I do. We had a strange conversation earlier. He was pretty drunk. He made a remark about the Woolf sisters . . . my being approximately their height. Maybe he panicked afterward and thought he incriminated himself somehow. Or maybe somebody made a comment at the party that led him to believe I'd seen something when I was hanging Christmas lights on the roof."

Sullivan said nothing for a minute or two. "You should head back to Crestview, Erin. Let me finish up at the inn by myself."

"No. If I *am* being set up, that's only going to make me look guilty. And it's not as if Sheriff Mackey is ever going to find the real killer."

"Isn't it more important that the killer doesn't succeed in making you the *second* victim, Erin?"

"Of course. But if Wendell Barton's the killer, I'm no longer in his crosshairs. Because I've just inadvertently turned myself into his perfect patsy. It now seems I made up a story about a poisoning so that I can look like I escaped the killer's clutches myself . . . when, all the while, *I* killed Angie."

Although we were within a mile of the inn, Steve pulled over. He shut off the engine and turned toward me. "Erin. I know you're not going to want to hear this, but you have to listen to me anyway."

With an introduction like that, I was steeling myself. I hoped if I waited long enough to answer, Steve would just say: On second thought, never mind. "What?"

"Wendell calls Cameron his fix-it man. That's a euphemism for the guy who does all the boss's dirty work. That's what I was trying to get at earlier at the party."

"You seriously believe that Wendell Barton is a Mafia-style kingpin, and that Cameron Baker is his hired hit man? Because if so—"

"No! I'm not implying that they're underworld criminals! But they aren't scrupulous businessmen, either. Those two are perfectly willing to cut corners, regardless of the law. You already said as much yourself...the sheriff is in Wendell's pocket. I'm certain that Wendell bribes other officials, probably with Cameron as his go-between. And who's to say where those two draw the line? Maybe they figure that Angie Woolf's life was insignificant, compared with their financial goals for expanding the resort."

"You're telling me you think it's possible that my ex-boyfriend strangled Angie Woolf and slipped cyanide into my eggnog?" The charge was outrageous and insulting to me, and I couldn't keep the anger from my voice.

Steve sighed and raked his fingers through his light brown hair. He returned his hands to the steering wheel and sat and stared through the window for what felt like a full minute or two. "Yeah, Erin. That's precisely what I think. I think Cameron handles the sleazy parts of Barton's jobs and could have killed Angie over her stonewalling the inn's remodel. And if you can't at least acknowledge the possibility, you really *are* a sitting duck."

"But again, Sullivan, I was *with* Cameron the night of Angie's murder!"

"You were with him for a couple of hours. Before that, you were hanging lights on the roof! Your back would have been turned at least half the time, and the evergreens block the view to the footbridge where she was killed. I checked when I was helping Ben install Chiffon's painted scallops."

"So you're saying that Cameron strangled Angie, drove up to the inn immediately afterward, invited us to dinner, then chatted with me over our meal as if he hadn't a care in the world. And that I never sensed anything was wrong. That simply is not possible! I *know* the man!"

"If you knew him so well, why were you so shocked that he was here in Colorado?"

"We'd lost touch years ago!"

"Yet you're certain he hasn't turned monstrous in the meantime?"

"Fine! I acknowledge that there's a one-in-a-million chance that Cameron's guilty. I appreciate the fact that you're trying to protect me, and I'll keep your suspicions about him in mind. Now let's please drop the subject!"

Sullivan and I might as well have slept in separate bed-rooms that night, we took such care not to acknowledge each other, and I still hadn't cooled off much the following morning. I couldn't seem to get past the thought that Sullivan had so little faith in my ability to judge people's character that he believed my ex not only was a murderer, but would actually make an attempt on *my* life. It was almost as absurd as suggesting that Audrey was guilty.

Granted, I'd read statistics, and ex-lovers were prime suspects in homicides for very good reason. But we'd been separated for ten years and then had a coincidental reunion! Besides which, the entire notion of Cameron

Baker as a murderer was insane! A ruthless businessman, yes. He was all about personal accumulation—wealth and all its trappings. We hadn't been able to sustain our feelings for each other when he put an ocean between us by accepting a position in London after graduating from Columbia. But the more I thought about it, the more certain I was that an ocean had already been forming between us. Even if he'd stayed in New York and remained faithful to me, our relationship would never have lasted much longer than it did.

Ironically, Steve and I had planned to sit down today to finalize our Twelve Days design. What fun to discuss what "my true love gave to me" with the true love who thinks you're a fool. Sullivan would be presenting his ideas to me for the odd-numbered days in the song, and I was showing him the even numbers.

Not eager to enter into an all-day design discussion that was bound to devolve into a quarrel, I took an exceptionally long time to shower and get dressed before coming downstairs, my folder of themed Christmas decorations in hand. Sullivan was waiting for me at the kitchen table, seated behind his notebook computer. Our floor plans were spread out to one side of him, and pictures of figurines, birds, and whatnot were spread on the other. I tried to shore myself up. We'd worked together for a long time before we'd become a couple, and we could be detached professionals today. We would make no mention of previous disagreements and definitely steer clear of discussing Cameron Baker. I breezed past the table and headed straight toward the coffeemaker.

"Good morning, Erin."

"Morning."

"Did you sleep okay last night?"

"No." I poured myself a cup and added a splash of milk, then turned to give him the briefest of glances. "Is this decaf?"

He shook his head. "Industrial-strength."

"Good." Although tempted to sit across from him, I instead grabbed the adjacent seat. Wounded feelings aside, we needed to look at plans and pictures at the same time.

"Are you ready to pay homage to the all-time worst gift giver in the history of the world? Most people get it wrong once or twice, but *this* guy gave lousy gifts twelve times in a row."

I couldn't help but smile. "Well, he did get *one* of the days right."

"The five golden rings, you mean?"

"Yes, and it's surprisingly out of character. He could have given his love 'five cawing crows,' yet for some reason, he gave her jewelry on day five. Maybe his sister was visiting him on that day and intervened."

Steve chuckled. "If so, it was a short visit. The very next day, he goes back to the birds, and two days later he resorts to gifting the poor woman with whole sets of people behaving bizarrely."

"I like to think that he took her to the ballet for his dancing ladies and his leaping lords. And maybe the drummers and pipers were trips to listen to a pair of symphony orchestras."

"In addition to taking his true love on an outing at a dairy farm?" Sullivan asked with a grin, his dreamy hazel eyes sparkling as he gazed into my eyes.

"Your guess is as good as mine. I've always found the milkmaids baffling. And you're dead wrong about Cameron, by the way." *It was weird how that slipped out. Maybe Sullivan was less at fault for our spat than I wanted to believe.*

"I hope so. Except for the *dead* part."

I adjusted his floor plans for the three main levels of the house so that we could both see them. "Let's start by figuring out which room goes best with which day of Christmas."

"We should base our selection for each room on our original vision for that space. The Christmas decoration should enhance what we've already created."

"Right. And our original vision for the lobby was that it's going to be the first room guests will see."

"Which means it should have the partridge in the pear tree."

"Yes. Which also means our pear tree is going to be competing with the Christmas tree."

"I had a thought about the Christmas tree," Steve said. "We should feature miniature versions of our twelve designs on the tree. Although we'll need to procure an additional seventy-something ornaments."

"That's an excellent idea, even so. It'll help unify everything. Besides, this is the kind of thing that Audrey would be happy to do. She can make milkmaids and lords out of old-fashioned clothespins. I'll ask her if she's willing to help."

Sullivan was fishing through his stack of decorative items and didn't appear to be listening. "So we've got that huge, sturdy coffee table in front of the fireplace in the lobby. That can support the pear tree, and it's in the sitting area—a visually separate space, as delineated by the area rug."

He passed me the photograph he'd found of a gilded pear tree. It was the same one that had caught my eye when I surfed the Web, the day after Audrey first suggested the design concept. "Perfect. All lush gold hues, four feet tall, quite spectacular."

"Unless you'd rather go with an actual miniature pear tree and a live partridge," Sullivan said. "But then we'd have to deal with shedding leaves and such. Plus it'll take forever to train the partridge to stay put in the tree."

I chuckled. "Actually, I was planning on wiring his little feet to one of the branches."

"Gilded pear tree it is."

"I located two cross-stitched pillows featuring turtle-doves that will pop against the brocade fabric of the Sheridan chair and the lace comforter in Mikara's bedroom." I showed him the photograph.

"You don't think that's too subtle?"

"Maybe, but I think a mixture of subtle in some rooms, primary focal point in other rooms is what we're aiming for here."

"Agreed. I found some rather pricey porcelain French hens. Which can go in the den." He handed me the photograph, and we tentatively agreed to put them in the den. "Not to jump the gun, but what exactly is a calling bird?"

I shrugged. "One bird that's calling to his birds of a

feather. It would be fun to place them in a Christmassy centerpiece for the dining room table. Maybe four bird figurines, with built-in recordings of their songs. And push-button controls."

I was pulling Steve's leg about the sound recordings. The "calling birds" that I'd chosen were four lovely and colorful porcelain figurines of birds with open beaks. I saw him grimace a little. When he held his tongue, I said, "Or, better yet, we could set up a motion detector, so the birds will sing the moment anyone enters the room."

He furrowed his brow. "Have you been getting advice from Chiffon, by any chance?"

I gave him my best injured look. "Are you saying you want the birds to remain silent? No minirecordings of them calling out: 'Yoo hoo! I'm over here!'?"

He fought back a smile and returned his attention to his file. "The five golden rings will be gold wreaths. That's a natural for the parlor."

Cameron stepped into the kitchen from the mudroom, bringing our chat to an abrupt halt. He greeted us cheerfully, then said, "Great news. The building inspector is here. And the front steps are perfect. Furthermore, I had the lab retest the water, and the inn is within legal limits after all. So everything's good to go."

"I'm ... amazed," I said, painfully reminded of Steve's assertions that part of Cameron's job description for Wendell was to bribe officials.

"Yeah. Seems a bit too good to be true." Sullivan's voice was rife with skepticism.

Cameron spread his arms. "That's how I get my name. I arrive in town, and I fix the problems."

"Great," I said with false cheer. "Henry's going to be thrilled."

"As will my boss."

"Thanks, Cameron." Knowing Steve had to be galled to no end, I glanced at him, but he held his tongue.

"I'd like us all to go to lunch to celebrate," Cameron said. "The three of us, plus Audrey. What do you say? Got any other lunch plans? Not to be mundane, but I was thinking we could go at high noon."

Steve and I looked at each other. I assumed that he wanted me to say no. "Actually, Cameron—"

"We can't speak for Audrey, but Erin and I are free."

I glanced at Steve in surprise.

Still wearing his coat, gloves, and boots, Ben entered the room, carrying a pink sheet of paper. He bore his typical hangdog expression. "Bad news. The inspector found a problem after all."

"But... he was leaving!" Cameron exclaimed. "I walked him to his car! And everything was fine!"

"Yeah, but right after you came inside, he shut off his engine and said he'd forgotten Angie hadn't logged the measurements for the handicapped-access ramp on the back door. He measured it himself, and turns out it's too steep and needs to be replaced. I told him how the ramp had already *passed*, but he insisted Angie must have used the old standards by mistake. I argued for all I was worth, but he said, 'Rotten luck for you,' got back into his truck, and took off."

Cameron grabbed his head. "The ramp is made of concrete! We can't just add on to make it longer! I left you and the inspector all of sixty seconds ago! How the hell could you have put up this big, huge argument inside of a minute?"

That struck me as a very good question.

"It was more than a minute," Ben grumbled.

"Ben," Cameron said, his eyes smoldering, "this is a huge screwup! The only question is, was it *your* incompetence, or the inspector's?"

"I followed the specifications precisely!" Ben retorted.

Cameron balled his fists. "And did you get them from Angie, or from a Cracker Jack box?"

"Cameron, Ben, we'll figure out how to fix this quickly," I said. "There's no reason to get upset."

"I'm not *upset*, Erin," Cameron snapped. "I'm just articulating my discontent." Cameron gestured toward the door. "Ben, let's talk outside. Show me precisely what the problem is with the ramp."

Ben pivoted and stormed out the door. Cameron followed.

Sullivan cursed under his breath and rose.

"The inspector had to have done this intentionally, the moment Cameron's back was turned," I said, looking up at him. "He wanted to keep Cameron in the dark about his plans to flunk the inn."

"Probably so, but that's Cameron's problem, not Ben's. Ben looked ready to sock Cam in the face. If Ben quits, we really *won't* be able to open on Christmas Eve. All our work will have been for nothing. I'm putting a stop to it, right now. No way am I going to let Cameron louse everything up for us."

Chapter 14

W ait!" I grabbed Steve's arm before he could open
the back door. "Let me handle this. We'll get better results
if I go and play the part of the clueless female. By the time
they're done explaining to me what the problem is, they'll
both have cooled off."

"Seriously? That's an actual tactic women use?"

"I don't understand your question. Maybe you can explain it to me later, darling." I dashed into the mudroom,
donned my coat, and headed outside.

Cameron was shouting: "I'm paying you to fix—" He

stopped when he spotted me. He had been wagging his finger in Ben's face, but now he lowered his voice and said, "—this ramp." He forced a smile in my direction. "Everything's under control, Erin. We're just trying to decide on a strategy to get the okay to open for business on time."

"Yeah. A strategy," Ben repeated, his features and voice justifiably full of venom.

"Sorry to interrupt. But, Ben, I've seen you work magic more than once. We're not going to miss our grand opening on Christmas Eve, are we?"

"Not if I'm allowed to do my job," he grumbled.

"That's all I've been asking you to do," Cameron fired back.

"What exactly is wrong with the wheelchair ramp?" I asked gently. "How far off is it from the regulations?"

"Three inches," Ben replied.

"Which might as well be three feet," Cameron said. "Those three little inches are going to cost us a ton of time and money. Ben needed to begin the ramp three inches farther back from the door in order to give it the proper slope. Now all the concrete has to be broken apart and hauled away, then new cement's got to get poured, smoothed, new railings put up, et cetera, all because Ben, here, blew it."

"I didn't blow it! I got the code from Angie Woolf, and I followed it to the letter! She set me up!"

"That's real nice, Orlin," Cameron said. "So *now* you're blaming the whole thing on a dead woman!"

"Cam, it isn't Ben's fault if the two inspectors used different sets of codes for their inspections," I said firmly.

"Isn't there a city official who should be notified about this? Somebody in the local government? I don't really know who we could talk to about maybe granting us some sort of temporary permit. Do you have any ideas?"

Cam released a sigh of frustration, but conceded, "I've got a couple of connections. Not counting the town *mayor,* who's obviously got no clout here whatsoever."

"That'd be great. Thanks, Cameron." I shamelessly gave him a grateful smile. *Desperate times, desperate measures and all that rot.* "Come to think of it, maybe I should be the one taking *you* out to lunch. Have you asked Audrey yet if she can join us? She's around here someplace."

He glanced at his watch. "I'll go track her down." He patted Ben on the shoulder. "Sorry for taking my anger at the inspector out on you. Thanks for getting right on this."

"Sure thing," Ben said in a near growl.

Cameron brushed past us and went inside. Steve was right. Cameron claimed he knew how to motivate individuals, and yet he was allowing his temper to disrupt our relationship with a highly competent builder—in a town where we couldn't even manage to hire a plumber for a one-day job. Cameron should have realized that for himself and handled the situation like a grown-up.

After giving Ben a few moments to cool down, I asked, "Is there any way to get the ramp up to code *without* having to tear it out and start over from scratch?"

Ben shrugged, but I could see by his expression that he knew it was a possibility. "We can affix a wood ramp on top of the concrete one. It won't look too pretty, and it'll only last a couple of years, but it'll be inexpensive, and I can get it ready for inspection in two days. Three, tops."

"Brilliant! That's perfect, Ben!" Although my gratitude was sincere, I was laying it on a little thick to compensate for Cameron's behavior. "Thanks so much for bailing us out, yet again."

He gave me a small smile and nodded. "That water filter you ordered arrived today. Do you want me to go ahead and install it? Even though the retest measurements say the water's fine?"

"No. But, just to be cautious, let's be sure to hang onto the filter till after the inn actually opens."

"Will do." Ben stared at the ramp, probably envisioning how he was going to rebuild it to avoid making the top of the ramp higher than the back porch itself, even though he'd essentially be enclosing the existing concrete ramp in wood. He'd managed to pull off comparable feats in the past, however. "Cameron Baker is a horse's ass."

"You do seem to be getting exposed to Cameron at his very worst—first when he called you here at midnight to work on the front steps, and now over this trouble. Maybe he fell off a porch as a boy and was scarred for life," I joked.

"Yeah. I wanted to punch his lights out just now. Probably would have, if you hadn't happened to come out right when you did."

"I'm glad I interrupted things, in that case. The concept of breaking into fisticuffs over a handicapped-access ramp just seems wrong to me on a cosmic level."

"I know. But that guy has a knack for getting under

my skin. Him and his boss. They're both total jerks, you ask me."

He still struck me as very close to throwing up his hands and quitting. "Honestly, Ben. You're a bigger man than both of them for putting all that aside and doing such excellent work here."

He shrugged, but the hints of a proud smile tugged at his lips. "I owe my father that much. And I owe this house. Guys like Cameron and Wendell can't begin to understand what it means to build something with your own two hands. They're too busy building big bank accounts." He gazed up at the house. "I look at this place, and I see my grandfather's craftsmanship, and my father's, and now mine."

I followed his gaze. "I'm sure the fact that Chiffon's ghastly gingerbread façade doesn't cover every square inch of the house must make you feel better. We can still see its elegant siding from this angle."

He chuckled. "True."

"At least nobody can accuse Chiffon's design of being too understated."

"You can say that again. But I gotta admit, I like the Santa's sleigh. It's just like the one folks are always drawing in picture books and everything."

"I like the sleigh, too. It looks so perfect with its cherry red paint. I just wish they hadn't knocked over half a dozen snowmen when they delivered it yesterday. All of which reminds me, thank you for getting it so nicely secured." His equanimity seemed to have been restored, but for extra measure, I told him, "Like I keep saying, Ben, I don't know what we'd do without you."

"Tell that to Henry," Ben muttered.

"Henry?" I repeated.

Ben winced a little. "Cameron, I meant."

Steve and I rode in the backseat of Cam's Mercedes,
Audrey gaily keeping up a steady patter of pleasant conversation with Cameron and, occasionally, me. Clearly,
Steve was not doing a very good job of masking his resentment of Cameron's interference; otherwise, Audrey
wouldn't have been ignoring him like this.

Immediately after I'd filled Steve in on what was said
while he'd been waiting in the kitchen, he had launched
into yet another lecture about Cameron. My saying "Let
it go, Sullivan! The problem's fixed, so let it *stay* fixed!"
had only darkened his funk. It was strange how I seemed
to have endless patience for my clients but next to none
for my boyfriend.

"You two are sure quiet back there," Cameron said,
eyeing us in the rearview mirror. "Everything all right?"

"Yep," Steve replied, while I simultaneously answered,
"Just peachy."

"Awesome," Cam said. He pulled into the valet parking for the one four-star restaurant—but with *five*-star
prices—in Snowcap Village. "You'll like this place."

We stepped into the enclosed front porch of this regal,
converted Victorian-style house. The space featured gray
slate floors and paned windows above the pale green wainscot. Tasteful pine boughs and ribbons were on subtle display throughout the room. Cameron strode ahead of us
and held open the inner door. The bar was overflowing,

and at least a dozen people were awaiting tables in front of the maître d's oak stand. "Are reservations required for lunch?" Audrey asked Cameron.

"It won't be a problem," he replied. "Wait here a moment."

He spoke quietly to the maître d', and moments later, a hostess in a black dress said, "This way, please." We were whisked ahead of the long line, past the main room of diners, and toward a set of paneled pocket doors. Audrey, leading the way, hesitated as we stepped inside a private room. An instant later, we learned that our party was actually five members, not four; Wendell Barton was seated at a round, elegantly set table.

"Wendell," Audrey said. "This is a surprise." He smiled broadly at her and rose. They bussed each other's cheeks, and he pulled out a chair for her next to his. I detected a hint of stiffness in her demeanor; she had to be wondering why he'd been so scarce since the party. I allowed the hostess to seat me on Wendell's other side. Steve greeted Wendell and sat beside me. Cam wound up seated between Steve and Audrey.

"What's this all about?" Audrey asked Wendell as soon as we were situated.

"It's my way of apologizing to you for voting to let Chiffon go all hog-wild on the holiday display."

"Heavens, Wendell," she exclaimed. "An apology lunch for Sullivan and Gilbert Designs and myself was hardly necessary! All that you owe us is a simple acknowledgment that we were right and *you* were wrong." She paused, but he held his tongue. "In fact, I've been wondering what was taking you so long to admit to your mistake. After all, you saw the results of Chiffon's design at our housewarming party. I would think that the tawdry appearance of the inn when you look at it from the street speaks for itself."

"It's pretty bad," Wendell said with a nod. "That's why I felt a primo meal was appropriate."

"Ah. So you admit you were wrong and we were right," Audrey prompted.

"Yes, dear." He rolled his eyes, but took Audrey's chiding in good fun. "I was wrong. You were right."

"Thank you." Audrey patted his hand. "Now, was that so hard?"

Wendell had already ordered a couple of bottles of a truly delicious white wine; I was too distracted to catch the vintage. Truth be told, I'd entertained hopes that with Audrey's social skills, Steve would get past his unfounded suspicions about Cameron, and the four of us could form an alliance. That was unlikely to happen now that the endlessly pompous Wendell had thrown himself into the mix. Cameron managed to draw Steve into conversation, however, and by the time we'd ordered our meals, Steve began to relax.

Wendell was being quite personable and treated Audrey like a queen. Yet, even after half a glass of wine (by my best estimation; the waiter was dangerously skillful at filling my glass unobtrusively), there was something about Wendell that grated on me.

Just when I was on the verge of admitting to myself that I was being unduly harsh to the man, he turned to Cameron and said, "Congratulations again for getting things all cleared up with the new building inspector."

Cameron grimaced. "I didn't have time to fill you in on the latest. The handicapped-access ramp has to be rebuilt. No big deal, but technically, the inn still hasn't got the green light till the ramp passes its third inspection."

"At *this* late date! What the hell am I paying you for if you can't get a simple ramp inspected?!" Wendell erupted. "In all the assignments I've given you over the years, you've never been this sloppy before."

Cameron spread his arms. "We've never had a building inspector get murdered on our property. I'm working with a whole new set of rules this time."

"That was a coincidence. Bad luck. It has nothing to do with me or with Barton Enterprises. It *certainly* shouldn't affect what the new building inspector says."

"Human nature being what it is," Audrey interjected, "knowing that someone's been murdered *has* to impact the poor person assigned to complete the victim's job."

"Sure, but the 'impact' should have helped us," Wendell retorted. "Not to be callous, but after the original inspector was killed, you'd think that the new guy would just give everything an automatic thumbs-up."

Audrey arched an eyebrow. "It's rather impossible not to sound callous when you make a remark like that."

"All I'm saying is, that's what *I'd* have done in his shoes. Wouldn't you? Inspecting buildings is just a job. It's not worth risking your life over."

"You think the new inspector should have been in fear for his life when he told us the ramp wasn't up to code?" Steve asked pointedly.

"Not literally, no. We're all speaking in hypotheticals here, right? I'm sure Amy...Angie...whatever...was killed by an ex-lover or something. I'm just saying, purely hypothetically, like Audrey said before, human nature being what it is, wouldn't you think a murder victim's replacement *wouldn't* want to follow exactly in his predecessor's footprints?"

Audrey set down her wineglass with a thump, sloshing a small amount onto the immaculate white tablecloth. "Let's talk about something less depressing, such as global warming."

Cameron chuckled sarcastically and guzzled his glass of wine. Wendell glared at him, but then said, "Fine," to Audrey. He shifted his attention to Steve. "So, Mr. Sullivan. Tell us how a macho guy like yourself wound up choosing to become an interior decorator."

There's no accounting for taste ran through my mind as I looked at Audrey complacently sitting beside her boor of a boyfriend. Steve, however, was well used to this line of questioning and immediately replied, "I knew it'd be a great way to meet women." He gave my hand a squeeze and added, "And I was right."

I wanted to kiss him, but settled for giving him a loving smile.

Wendell chuckled. "How'd you wind up in this profession, though? Seriously."

"I started out wanting to be an artist, but interior design was something I naturally gravitated toward."

"Why not architecture, then?" Wendell asked. "Something more masculine?" He suddenly flinched, and I was certain that Audrey had kicked him.

I felt like clocking the guy myself and searched desperately for the perfect witticism on Steve's behalf, but my mind was unable to get past the thought that Wendell Barton was a total ass.

"Hard to say," Steve replied evenly. "Maybe it had something to do with being the only boy in a family with five kids."

Three waiters arrived, providing a natural—and much-needed—break in the conversation. I gave Steve's hand a quick squeeze, and we all turned our attention to our scrumptious meals.

A minute later, however, Cameron's cell phone rang. He glanced at the phone's screen, announced, "I've got to take this," and left the room.

"I'll bet that's one of his inside connections," Wendell said as he watched Cameron slip out the door, "letting us know to watch out for Ben Orlin."

"What do you mean?" Steve asked.

"Just thinking out loud, is all," Wendell replied.

"Wendell," I snapped, "Ben is a highly capable craftsman and can be trusted implicitly."

"I wish I could agree with you, Erin. But I think he's pulled the wool over your eyes."

"In what way?"

"Before Cameron arrived at the inn, he did some poking around. According to his sources in City Planning, Ben Orlin was behind their taking a closer look at the front steps."

"What?!" I cried.

"Evidently, he called Angie Woolf and suggested she take a look at the code for business property and check the measurements of the steps."

"That can't be true," I retorted.

Wendell swirled his wine as though it were port brandy in a snifter. "In other words, you don't think your builder has plenty of reason to drag his feet right before Christmas? Maybe contrive to get a hefty check for lots of overtime...?"

My mind raced. *Was* that something Ben would do? He certainly detested Wendell and probably felt no guilt over taking the man's money. Heck, neither did I, even though, with Audrey a part owner, thirty percent of my salary was basically coming from her. Still, Ben was a hard worker, and he was such a nice guy! The Goodwin estate was such a source of honor and pride for him. And had been for his ancestors.

I eyed Wendell, disliking him more than ever, try as I might to give him a fair chance for Audrey's sake. "You're saying that Ben deliberately built the ramp wrong? After which he blew the whistle on himself?"

Wendell made a slight gesture with one hand. A tacit: *What do you think?*

A wave of frustration washed over me. I really didn't know *what* to think, or who to trust.

Chapter 15

With a purposeful stride, Cameron returned to the room. He glanced at me, then at Barton. "Erin, Wendell, everybody, I'm afraid there's trouble at the ski resort. I have to run."

"What *kind* of trouble?" Wendell asked.

"Apparently, a twelve-year-old girl panicked when she got on the chairlift, jumped off, and broke her leg. The parents are screaming their heads off that the operator should have shut down the lift sooner. They're threatening to sue Barton Enterprises for every penny you've got."

"That's the first thing everyone threatens me with after an injury," Wendell scoffed. "It's a *ski* resort. Stuff like this happens every couple of months. And it's what I pay my ski lodge managers and my lawyers to handle." He gestured at Cameron's empty chair. "Sit down. There's no need for you to interrupt your lunch."

Cam shook his head. "This one sounds like something that could explode in our faces. I'm nipping it in the bud."

Wendell gave him a long stare. "You're micromanaging. Let my team at the resort handle it."

"I'm just doing my job, Wendell."

"But I'm your boss, and I want you to stay and enjoy your meal." He forced a smile. "That's an order."

"I can't do that. You pay me to decide when a work problem is more important than lunch. If you can't trust me to do that, my salary is way too high."

Wendell appeared to be grinding his teeth. He gave Audrey a little glance before returning his gaze to Cameron. "Fine. Suit yourself, then."

I couldn't tell if this power struggle between the two men was for Audrey's benefit—and maybe, to a small extent on Cam's part, for mine—or if Wendell was embarrassed to be arguing with his employee in front of us.

Cameron scanned our faces. "I apologize for having to leave. Don't let my rushing off like this put a damper on things." His gaze settled on me. "Take care, Erin." He gave me a peck on the cheek, and I could feel Steve cringe as Cameron walked away.

Audrey cleared her throat and asked Wendell, "You'll be able to give us all a ride back to the inn after lunch, won't you?"

Wendell winced slightly at the question, and it dawned on me why he'd tried so hard to prevent Cameron from deserting us—Wendell must have had romantic plans for Audrey this afternoon. He'd probably prearranged for Cameron to give Steve and me a ride back without her.

"Certainly," he said. "I'll make sure that you all get back...no thanks to my overly eager employee. That boy's becoming a workaholic. You'd think he could take one little lunch off."

"Cameron's working hard on your behalf, Wendell," Audrey said. "You should cut him some slack."

"Yeah, maybe you're right," Wendell said. "He's run off to put out some fire so that I don't have to. Instead, I can enjoy this wonderful food with this wonderful company." Wendell emptied Cameron's wine into his own glass, which he then lifted. "Here's a toast to many more enjoyable meals like this one, and to our great success at Snowcap Inn."

We clinked glasses. Heaven knows I was all for achieving some success at the inn. Yet it seemed obvious to me that we still had a number of fiery hoops to leap through.

As we got out of Wendell's BMW, Wendell told Audrey he had something he wanted to ask her, so Steve and I went in alone, using the front door, with its government-approved steps.

"That was fun," Steve said sarcastically as he shut the door behind us. "We'll have to hang out with Cam and Wendell more often."

"Enough with the put-downs of Cameron, already!" I

chucked my purse into the coat closet, removed my coat, and stuck it on a hanger. "He is who he is, and he'll be out of our lives for good in another couple of weeks."

"*If* we finish on time. Otherwise, God only knows how much longer we'll be stuck here."

"Sorry you're having such a terrible time."

"I didn't mean that as a personal affront." He removed his coat and hung it up, shutting the closet door with unnecessary force. "A woman's been murdered. You've been named as a suspect, all because I talked to her for five minutes at a coffee shop. Your ex still has a thing for you. Everyone's snapping at everyone else. Building codes are being changed by the hour. So, yeah, I'm getting anxious to finish up and get back home."

"He doesn't still have 'a thing' for me. And even if he does, it doesn't matter because the feeling isn't mutual."

We glared at each other. I was getting really tired of this tension. "This isn't a contest for my affections or my esteem, you realize. You won both a long time ago."

"That's not it, at all. I just think the guy is—"

Audrey entered. We both turned and looked at her. "I obviously interrupted something. My apologies."

"No, we were just—"

"Having another stressful discussion," she interrupted. "How are things going with the Twelve Days of Christmas design? Is there anything I can do to help with that?"

"No, but thanks," Steve said.

"Actually, there is one thing. We were thinking about hanging ornaments that duplicate the Twelve Days in miniature on the Christmas tree. If you could maybe shop for things like pipers, ladies dancing, and so forth, on the Net, that'd be a big help."

She smiled as she unbuttoned her coat. "That's going to be great fun. I could buy a whole set of 'Twelve Days of Christmas' tree decorations, I'm sure, but that would be too easy. I'll make most of them myself, and any that I don't feel like making, I'll buy."

"Wonderful! Thanks, Audrey."

"Oh, don't mention it." She folded her coat over her arm. "Also, I'm sorry Wendell was acting so arrogant during lunch. He sometimes gets like that, especially when he drinks. When he and I are alone, he's really very sweet."

Yet why was she willing to continue to date a guy who turned into a pompous ass when he was in the company of anyone besides *her*? Not to mention that he was also a murder suspect! "It was good of him to pick up the tab."

She held my gaze for a moment and said, "I'll leave you two to have at it, and I'll start shopping for materials for my ornaments." She left.

Sullivan waited a few seconds, then asked, "What number of Christmas days did we get up to this morning?"

"Six."

"Oh, good. An even number, so it's yours." We started to amble toward the kitchen, where we'd left the folders containing our decorating ideas. "Six what?" he asked. "I forgot the carol again. I can never remember the stupid thing, except days one to five."

"It's really simple from seven swans on down. Seven swans a-swimming has excellent alliteration."

"So does *six* swans a-swimming."

"But it's six geese a-laying. Think about the fact that eggs are sold in a dozen, and that a goose egg is twice the size of a chicken egg, and so laying half a dozen eggs is comparable to a chicken's dozen."

"I can do that. Although, technically, I only have to remember the odd numbers, since you're designing the even ones."

Although it was a little silly, he held open one of the barroom-style doors for me. As I walked past him I admitted, "I have a hard time remembering how many lords are leaping, pipers piping, drummers drumming, ladies dancing, or my personal design horror—maids a-milking."

"Oh, hey. No problem, Erin. *I'll* do the milkmaids. I always mentally picture them in short black dresses with white collars, their feather dusters in hand."

"You're thinking of French maids, Sullivan," I replied, although I knew full well he was pulling my leg. "That's hardly the same thing."

"Oh, right. Too bad. French maids would have been great for one of the more masculine bedrooms."

"Apparently so. But, remember, this song is about a woman's gifts from her true love. Not to mention that I shudder to think what a French maid's action verb would have been."

"That's obvious. 'French maids a-cleaning.'"

I laughed in spite of myself. "Okay, fine. I take it all back. *Now* you're talking about a *woman's* ultimate fantasy Christmas gift."

"Yes!" He pumped his fist. "It worked!"

"*What* did?"

"My devious plot to discover what you wanted me to get you for Christmas."

"A cleaning service would have been nice, except it's Audrey's house, and she already has one."

"Damn! I'll have to stick with my Plan B, then."

"Plan B?"

"Yeah." He narrowed his eyes. "Apropos of nothing, Audrey's house only has the one bathtub, right?"

"Right. *Why?*"

"No reason, really." He hesitated, but there was a twinkle in his eye. "Just . . . off the top of your head, would you say that your tub is big enough for seven swans to swim in?"

I started to laugh, but my attention was suddenly drawn to my manila folder, which had been lying on top of the neat stack we'd made of our work before we'd left for lunch. The folder now had a stain that looked like a drop of blood.

Chapter 16

Every time I vacation in a new place, regardless of the season, I purchase a Christmas tree ornament. They never fail to conjure up wonderful memories as I trim the tree.

—Audrey Munroe

Late morning the next day, Audrey was hard at work in the kitchen when I cheerfully approached, expecting to find her creating an ornament related to our theme. Instead she was fastening ribbons to meticulously halved, scooped-out orange rinds that formed perfect little round bowls. "Are you in the middle of a crafts project involving orange rinds, Audrey?"

"Yes," she said with a smile. "I wanted fresh-squeezed orange juice this morning, and there was no sense in wasting the rinds. So I saved them for the birds."

"Birds like to eat orange peel?"

"I'm going to fill them with birdseed and little pieces of suet." She dangled one off her index finger to show me. She had knotted loops of plaid ribbon underneath the halved rind. "See? I'm making a half dozen of them."

"Nice."

"I'm also decorating the pine tree in the front yard, just to add a special touch to the lights that you hung."

Henry and Ben had actually hung the lights on the tree, but I smiled and said, "So the seventy-eight decorations I asked you to make for the indoor tree wasn't enough work for you?"

"Oh, that's been keeping my hot-glue gun and me plenty busy, thanks. I'm multitasking. Although it *was* my cookie cutters that got me started on decorating the pine out front, as well."

"Cookie cutters?"

"Yes. Fortunately, I was planning on baking for the holidays, so I brought up my full set of cookie cutters. I made a lot of the decorations for the indoor tree out of a basic Play-Doh recipe." She slid a shirt box across the granite counter toward me. "I painted them on both sides so they wouldn't be strictly two-dimensional."

"Three French hens," I cried, delighted. She'd cut miniature berets from green felt and glued dainty pieces of lace to the hardened hen-shaped dough. "These are so cute!" I looked closer at a dove-shaped cookie. "Is that a green turtle on the two doves' bodies?"

"For the two turtledoves, yes. And fortunately, I had a swan-shaped cookie cutter, so those were a breeze, and a cow-shaped one for the maids to milk. I'm making the people out of clothespins. With felt jackets and pipe cleaners, and drinking straws for the pipers, small spools of thread for the drummers. I painted their faces and the details. I did take the easy route and ordered tiny ballet dancers for the ladies dancing and the lords a-leaping. And I've got five linking rings from gold pipe cleaners to make into one larger wreath. Plus this little guy here." She showed me a plump bird sitting on a yellow pear, which she'd sculpted from artist's clay and baked.

"Ohh! That's adorable, Audrey!"

"It's sitting on a pear, if not a pear *tree*. Still, it gets the general idea across. I'm going to need another couple of days to complete the decorations for inside, but I want to finish with the pine tree outside tonight."

"Can I help?"

"Thanks, but actually Mikara already volunteered. She cut stars and circles out of the heels from three or four loaves of bread. She's out there hanging them now, along with the old standby pinecones." My blank expression spurred her on. "You mix equal amounts of Crisco with peanut butter so that the birds can swallow it, spread it onto a pinecone, then roll the pinecone in birdseed. They're messy as all get-out to make, but the birds love them. Provided the squirrels don't immediately run off with them."

She frowned a little as she tied a ribbon around the last orange-find seed bowl. "I wish I could have found biodegradable ribbon. I was actually considering licorice strings, but I'm worried about the animals' teeth. The last thing I want to do is give them cavities."

"Birds don't have teeth."

"But we have so many squirrels around here. It's not like they can go to the dentist."

"I've never thought about squirrel dental hygiene before."

"Neither have I, but then, I never considered using candy on an outdoor tree before. At any rate, lastly, I'm shaping suet into ornaments and just kind of squeezing them onto thread. Like little meatballs."

"That sounds a bit gross, frankly."

"Yes, but think of it this way: The tree itself will have dozens of lovely birds perched on its branches. What could possibly be a nicer decoration than that?"

Chapter 17

That afternoon, I returned from picking up some supplies that Audrey needed at the nearest hobby shop and found Chiffon and Henry sitting on the bench in the mudroom, removing their outerwear. I watched as Chiffon hung her pink skates by their laces on a wall hook. I quickly shed my own coat and gloves and said, "Chiffon, suspending something with razor-sharp blades directly above a bench isn't a good idea." Having a skate fall onto even just the *empty* seat below would aggravate me no end. That bench was divine—an elaborate nineteenth-century Russian piece, its green paint faded to a lovely copper patina.

"But my skates are so pretty, Erin. You should really hang them over the fireplace."

I'd just as soon hang my ski boots on the mantel. Knowing I'd be wasting my breath by suggesting she use one of the numerous cubbies for boots and skates, I said, "They'd look better hanging in the corner. Where there's less visual competition."

She mulled this over for a moment, but then moved the skates to this safer location.

"How was the skating?" I asked Henry.

"It was sort of fun," he replied, "in a falling-down-a-lot way. Chiffon's many times better at it than I am."

"When I was little, I had to choose between my music and ice skating," Chiffon interjected. "I very nearly opted to enter the Junior Olympics."

"Oh, really?" I said.

Henry continued, "The ice on the small pond out back is nice and smooth. Which is more than can be said for my skating technique."

"At least you got out there and gave it your all," Chiffon said, squeezing his arm.

"That wasn't really 'my all.' That was just me staying upright for as long as possible, while balancing on steel blades."

Chiffon laughed as though he'd said something hilarious. She glanced back at me, and I forced a smile before heading into the kitchen. Audrey was removing a cookie sheet from the oven.

"I got everything on your list," I told her, indicating the shopping bag as I set it down in the corner.

"Perfect. Thank you, Erin. I'm just finishing the last of my baked-clay tree ornaments for the tree in the central hall," Audrey said.

Henry and Chiffon entered the kitchen. "Did you see my candy canes yet?" Chiffon asked us. "Aren't they darling?"

"I saw them," I said. They were rather impossible to miss. Poor Ben had been installing a dozen five-foot-tall illuminated candy canes on either side of the front walk for at least two hours now.

"They're certainly in keeping with the rest of the display," Audrey said tactfully. I decided to let her reply suffice for us both.

"Ben's biggest problem has been getting each one anchored down properly," I said. "With the Chinook winds that we get up here, that's quite a challenge."

"Yeah," Chiffon said. "You know, I'd thought that those illuminated reindeer we put out in front of the sleigh last week were getting blown about, but let's face it—the wind couldn't possibly have blown them into obscene positions four nights in a row."

Henry laughed heartily. "It's the teens in the neighborhood, my dear."

"That's what I finally gathered," she replied. "How juvenile can you get? In any case, Ben sunk six-inch tent stakes into the ground this morning. Now the vandals will have to get the hooks out with a crowbar, before the reindeer can be repositioned."

"I wouldn't want to place bets on the teenagers' perseverance," Henry said. "Snowcap Village still doesn't have a whole lot of nighttime entertainment. Especially for minors."

"So is this the sort of entertainment you engaged in when you were a teenager here, Henry?" she asked. "Did *you* mess with your neighbors' Christmas displays?" She was grinning at him, her tone of voice more than a little flirtatious.

Henry chuckled. "I sure did." He leaned back against the kitchen counter. "As the Goodwins' only son, I had to be careful not to get recognized. Back in those days, nativity scenes were a whole lot more popular than they are now. My friends and I used to steal all the baby Jesuses out of their crèches, and we'd put one of the animals in the cradle. This one neighbor kept his lawn gnome outside, year round. So we'd line up all the babies and the gnome at a street corner downtown and make up a sign like they were hitching... 'Bethlehem or Bust,' for example."

Ben entered the kitchen, looking a bit worse for wear. Beneath his scruffy beard, his cheeks were red with windburn. Henry was still engrossed in his memory.

"Hey, Ben. I was just telling them about the time we'd go do the Hitchhiking Baby Jesus during winter break. Remember?"

"Yeah. I remember, all right." Ben scowled. "I wasn't ever actually a part of your group, though. Even so, I got three weeks of clean-up duty at church because one of your cronies lied and gave the pastor *my* name."

Henry grimaced. "Oh, man, yeah, that's right. You must've hated my guts back then."

Ben shrugged. "If I say yes, would you give me a raise now out of guilt?"

"Probably."

"In that case, yeah. I hated you. You ruined my life. In fact, my dad beat the daylights out of me when the pastor called."

"He *did*?" Henry asked in horror.

Ben smiled a little. "If it gets me a decent *raise*, he sure did."

Henry chuckled and raised his palm. "That's that, then. I'm giving you another buck an hour, starting today."

Chiffon had begun to grow impatient. "Hey, Henry? We were going to go over those documents you said you had upstairs, weren't we?" She stepped closer and pushed her chest against him in case he failed to get the point of what she was really talking about.

"Oh, right. We should see to that right away."

Chiffon and Henry headed upstairs to his bedroom, no doubt. Ben brought his hand out of his jacket pocket. His hand was crimson with blood.

"Ben!" I exclaimed. "What happened?"

"I'm fine. It's just a minor scratch. I need an antiseptic and a Band-Aid."

"Let me get the first-aid kit." Audrey rushed over and pulled open the kitchen drawer right under the phone. "Go stick your hand in running water. How did this happen?"

"Just poked a couple fingers through a seam in one of those plastic candy canes. I cut my pinky, and it started bleeding like a son of a . . . gun."

He was obviously going to be fine, so I said, "That reminds me. Yesterday there was a drop of blood on my folder. You didn't cut yourself then, too, did you?"

"Nope. Had to be somebody else who had a—"

Mikara burst into the kitchen from the main hall. She was animated and happy for the first time since we'd met. "You are not going to believe—" She cut her announcement short as she caught sight of Ben and Audrey, hunched over the kitchen sink. "What are you doing?" she asked Audrey.

"Applying some minor first aid. Ben cut his finger."

She turned away. "Don't let me see it. I faint at the sight of blood." She did look a little wan. "I wanted to announce that I'm interviewing a chef this afternoon. This kitchen needs to be sparkling clean and appealing by then. In other words, no blood and no baking-clay odors."

"No problem," Audrey said. She shut off the water and started drying Ben's hand. "The sink's already clean, and I'll make cinnamon toast. That's the quickest way to make a kitchen smell inviting."

Still not looking at them, Mikara nodded. "Excellent. Thank you. I'd better get out of here. Sorry to be such a wimp." She strode out through the double doors.

Several minutes later, Steve and I claimed a cozy reading nook in the living room to finalize our discussion about the Twelve Days. Yesterday we'd only gotten as far as deciding on six geese for the game room, seven swans for one of the bedrooms, and the kitchen for the milkmaids.

The former would take the masculine form of wooden decoylike sculptures and goose-hunting paintings. (We'd chosen to ignore that the geese were supposed to be a-laying.) And swans had such soft, flowing lines that they were a natural for a bedroom. Sullivan, in fact, had ordered the swan artwork; I couldn't object all that vehemently about being kept out of the loop, because the geese I'd chosen were already being shipped.

I had also managed to find seven tasteful images of young women milking cows: an old-fashioned pitcher with blue ink artwork, a toile fabric suitable for framing, a Currier & Ives–style mirror frame, a bowl, a butter dish, and a couple of paintings. I planned to do a decoupage on a tray for the final one. We were debating the idea of using a similar hodgepodge approach to the dancing ladies and the leaping lords—which we agreed would be female and male ballet dancers—in two of the bedrooms when we heard heavy footsteps approaching.

Cameron leaned in the doorway. I could feel Steve's tension—and my own blood pressure—rise. I didn't want to deal with Cameron right now. Even though I knew he was innocent of poor Angie's murder, it felt like he'd been the harbinger, and he was certainly becoming Sullivan's and my bad-luck omen.

"There you are," he said with a smile. "Did you two enjoy your lunch yesterday?"

"Very much," I replied. "It's an excellent restaurant."

"The meal was first-rate," Steve replied. "Thanks. Since you're here, I've been meaning to tell you something. Don't interfere with Ben Orlin. Let us handle him from here on out. All right?"

I cursed inwardly. Cameron gave Steve a crooked, haughty grin. "Hey, dude. I'll talk to Ben whenever I need to. Wendell put me in charge of making sure this joint's up and running and filled with happy clients on Christmas Eve. That's precisely what I'm going to do. Whether or not we've got some conflicts of interest to deal with."

"What conflicts of interest?" I asked. "We all want the inn to open on time."

"The three of *us* do," Cameron replied. "*Ben*, not so much."

"Yeah. Wendell told us about how you think Ben supposedly blew the whistle on the front steps being too steep," Sullivan said. "You need to let it go."

"*Let it go?*"

"That's right. It doesn't concern you. Sullivan and Gilbert Designs is in charge of the remodel, and that puts us in charge of Ben Orlin. Everything that he does goes through us first."

Cameron held Sullivan's gaze for a long moment. "You know, I'm familiar with the terms of your contract. It doesn't stipulate that you get a bonus for the inn opening on time."

"So what?" Sullivan fired back, rising.

"So the inn's time line isn't as big a deal to you as it is to me!" Cameron balled his fists.

"Knock it off!" I cried. "Both of you! This is ridiculous! It goes without saying that it's in our best interest to make our clients happy and get everything done on time, Cameron. A payment bonus isn't necessary to motivate us."

"I'm just trying to ascertain where everyone's coming from," Cameron said, spreading his arms.

"And you're implying that we had something to do with the inn's failed inspection," Steve said.

"No, he isn't, Steve."

"Jeez, Erin!" he shouted. "He's accusing us of sabotaging the job!"

"Untrue," Cameron countered. "I'm just pointing out that I have a bigger stake in the inn's launch than Gilbert and Sullivan Designs does. Maybe that's why I want to take it more seriously."

"The correct name is Sullivan and Gilbert," Steve declared. "And if by 'taking it more seriously' you mean causing conflicts and undermining our work here, maybe so."

Someone coughed, and the three of us looked toward the sound. Mikara, her cheeks slightly pink, was standing in the doorway next to a blond, ultratanned man in his fifties. He looked vaguely familiar. I realized I'd seen him on television but couldn't yet place him.

"This is Alfonso," Mikara said. "He is interviewing for a position as pastry chef and head cook." She gestured at the three of us. "These passionate folks are what we call 'short-timers' and won't be here by the time the doors open for business. Erin and Steve are decorators, and—"

"Hi, Alfonso. I'm Cameron Baker, chief of operations for Wendell Barton."

"The owner of the Snowcap Ski Resort?"

"That's right," Cameron said proudly. "As well as the majority owner of the Snowcap Inn."

"Wendell's real estate company owns and operates the

ski resort and properties all across the country," Mikara added.

"Ah. Good."

"Everyone associated with the inn normally gets along great," Mikara said to Alfonso, unconvincingly. "We must happen to be in a weird biorhythm today."

"It's no problem," he said, with a smug attitude that was already grating on me. "Overall, your inn's quite nice. Your kitchen needs work but is adequate for the short term."

"How short-term were you thinking?" I couldn't help but ask. We'd installed a large, dual Wolf convection oven and range and a huge Sub-Zero refrigerator; every inch of the kitchen was professional caliber from top to bottom.

Alfonso gave a one-shoulder shrug. "Maybe for a year, provided the inn never expands into a full-operation restaurant. And by that I mean, of course, never opens for dinner. If you ever hope to serve dinners, you would need to double the size of the workspace and build a dining area out back, roughly the size of this room."

"That's never going to happen," Mikara said. "Not on *my* watch, anyway. We're not looking to expand the profile of the Goodwin estate. We just want it to be the premiere bed-and-breakfast inn in the state of Colorado. If not the country."

"Good to see that you're keeping your goals modest," Alfonso said with a nod. "I've seen all I need to see. You know how to reach me. We'll talk again, maybe."

We exchanged a brief round of good-byes, and he left. Mikara sank into a chair. "Oh, damn it all," she said on a sigh. "I came so close to pulling a rabbit out of my hat, just now. Only to watch him hop out the front door."

"I'm sorry, Mikara," Cameron said. "I didn't know he was here."

"He might want the job yet," I said.

Mikara looked at me. "You think so? Really?" Her voice was rife with sarcasm.

"Why wouldn't he?" Cameron asked. "For all he knows, we were dickering about the cost of the drapes."

"Every kitchen in Snowcap Village is trying to get Alfonso to sign on the dotted line! The man has won Top Chef awards. He just happens to be trying to scale down under orders from his doctor, who said he needs to avoid stress. Stress! Like, oh, I don't know, people shouting at one another!"

"Well, in that case," Cameron retorted, "God only knows what he's doing, looking to settle in Snowcap Village. Half the town will want to lynch him for bringing yet more of the Vail/Aspen scene to Snowcap, and the other half will worship at his feet and want to elect him mayor. Come to think of it, he couldn't help but do a better job than Henry."

Chapter 18

I heard footsteps descending the stairs and rolled my eyes, knowing that Henry had just overheard Cameron's last remark. Cameron turned around and said, "No offense, Henry." After a beat, he added, "Hello, Chiffon."

Henry stepped through the doorway, Chiffon hanging onto his arm. "I'm mayor till next November, no matter what happens, and I'm not seeking reelection. Who's the poor slob you think 'half the town' might want to elect to replace me?"

"I was just talking about the cook that Mikara was interviewing. His name's Alfonso, but he—"

"Is that his first or his last name?" Henry asked.

"*The* Alfonso?!" Chiffon cried. "Omigod! He's like only one of the hottest chefs on the planet! We have *got* to try to convince him to come here." She scanned our faces, stopping at Mikara, who was still flopped in the easy chair across from Sullivan and me. "Does he know I'm a co-owner? Did anyone tell him I was here?"

"It slipped my mind somehow," Mikara said in a droll voice.

"Did Alfonso say where he was going next?" Chiffon asked. "I don't mean to brag, but he needs to be made aware that there is already a celebrity associated with the inn. He'll be more inclined to accept a position here once he knows that."

"I told him about Audrey Munroe," Mikara replied. "In fact, the two of them had a lovely chat about her show just before she had to leave for a taping at the studio."

"Ha-ha," Chiffon said venomously. "You know full well that I was talking about my own celebrity status. This is an opportunity we can't afford to waste. As co-owner, I need to track him down and talk up the inn." She strode up to Mikara's chair and leaned down to whisper, "Would you guess that Alfonso is gay or straight?"

"I'm afraid I can never trust my own judgment on that," Mikara replied. "And maybe that's because I just plain don't care either way. People are just people to me."

Chiffon straightened and trotted back over to Henry. She grabbed his arm and nuzzled against him. "No offense, sweetie. I'm just trying to get the skinny on how I can best present myself to Alfonso."

"How about *not at all*?!" Mikara retorted.

Chiffon ignored her. All of the men had mildly pained expressions on their faces, and, like me, were probably mentally concocting excuses to leave the room. "Steve? You're a designer. You've got to have good gay-dar, right?"

"*Gay-dar?*" he repeated.

"What's with all the fake birds?" Cameron asked, in an obvious diversionary tactic. He indicated the ornaments on the coffee table, where Audrey had stashed many of them until we had the chance to hang them.

"They're miniature versions of our holiday theme decorations. Audrey made them for the tree."

"*Holiday theme?*" He curled his lip. "You're not doing 'Hansel and Gretel' indoors, too, are you?"

"Of course not. It's the Twelve Days of Christmas. One day for each of the twelve largest rooms in this house."

"Good. That will look much nicer than a house full of edible gingerbread furniture." He glanced at his watch. "I have an appointment nearby, so I'd better shove off." He smirked at Sullivan. "Don't worry, Steve. My appointment isn't with Ben."

"Super," Steve snapped.

Cameron glared at him, then shifted his gaze to me and opened his mouth as though he was about to tell me something, but thought better of it. He turned and left without a word.

———

Wendell joined us for dinner that night at Audrey's insistence. She made such a fabulous meal—roasted leg of lamb with new potatoes, green beans, and spinach salad—that none of us was about to complain. Afterward, Wendell, Henry, and Steve went to the den to watch some minor football bowl game. Mikara insisted that it was her turn to do the dishes. Audrey and I hung her new Christmas ornaments; she had nine of the twelve days' worth of decorations ready to go.

With Audrey supervising, I gamely hung the partridge-on-the-pear on the highest bough and worked my way down. I was able to get off the ladder by the time I reached day eight; we were going to have to leave a gap for uncompleted days nine through eleven, but we could hang the twelve drummers down low.

"Should we each hang six of these?" I asked Audrey.

She was staring at me with a stern look on her face. My first thought was that I'd somehow loused things up, but I gave the tree a quick backward glance, and it looked stunning to me.

"Erin, I think it's important that you don't lose sight of your priorities."

"Meaning what? Am I putting too much emphasis on the tree? The holly? The Twelve Days decorations we ordered online will start arriving tomorrow, so we're going to get into that full-tilt then, and the whole house really won't take us all that long."

"I mean with regard to you and Steve."

She'd thoroughly surprised me, and I asked in complete sincerity, "What are you talking about?" I glanced toward the den to make sure he wasn't in earshot. The television set was still blaring. "My priorities are completely straight where Steve is concerned."

"You're making him jealous over Cameron."

"No, I'm not! I told Steve flat out that I don't love Cameron; that I love *him*."

"And yet the message doesn't seem to be getting through to either one of them. Earlier today, Steve told me that he's afraid to leave you and Cameron alone, even."

I clicked my tongue. Lowering my voice to ensure that Mikara couldn't hear me from the kitchen, I said, "That's because Steve has this ridiculous notion that Cameron killed Angie Woolf. Even though that's next to impossible. Cameron would never kill anyone. Plus, I saw him arrive that day. He whisked me off to dinner minutes later...all the while acting perfectly normal."

Audrey hesitated for a moment, then put a hand to her chest. "Oh, thank goodness!" She grabbed my arm and gave it a squeeze. "I assumed Steve believed that you and Cameron were having an affair...but he's just afraid you'll be killed!"

I sighed. "It's symptomatic of how my life's been going, that your statement made perfect sense to me."

She gave me a sly grin. "So this is really it for you, isn't it, Erin? You're going to settle down with the love of your life...produce a bundle of joy or two...future kick-ass designers, maybe?"

"We haven't talked about settling down yet." Annoyed, I turned my back on her and started to circle the tree, paying little attention as I randomly stuck drummers on the bottom branches. "And quite frankly, I've vowed not to think about it till I'm absolutely certain that Sheriff Mackey isn't going to throw one of us in jail for a murder that we didn't commit. In other words, I'm *keeping my priorities straight*."

"Oh, pish posh! Women are natural multitaskers. Your romantic life has absolutely nothing to do with the murder investigation."

"Unless you consider the fact that my lover thinks my ex-lover is guilty of the crime."

"Fine. The investigation and your romance *are* loosely related. In any case, you don't mind if I do some checking into Steve's intentions, do you?"

"Yes, Audrey! I do mind! Vehemently, even! I don't know if Steve's ready to propose to me. If anything, he's probably feeling less like doing so now, the way things are falling apart here at the inn. But one thing we *all* know is that a woman was strangled a few yards from where we're standing! Now is not the time for you to be snooping into things like if or when Steve is thinking about proposing to me."

It suddenly hit me that we were standing in the infamous lobby/central hallway, where sound carried as if we were on an acoustic stage. I turned a full three-sixty and saw no one. The television still blared. For once, a truly inappropriate statement had apparently been uttered in this hall without being overheard.

Audrey, meanwhile, arched an eyebrow. "Fine, Erin." She set down her handful of drummers on a step of the ladder. "Never let it be said that I butt into people's lives where I'm not welcome."

She walked off in a huff, and I refrained from retorting

that she rarely *failed* to butt into my and Steve's lives, regardless of our pleas otherwise.

Something awoke me from a sound sleep. I sat upright, my heart racing. I must have had a bad dream, but, if so, it had already erased itself from my memory banks.

The other side of the bed was empty. The ray of light surrounding the edges of the drapes was muted. I glanced at our alarm clock. It wasn't even seven A.M. Steve had risen early.

I arose and parted the curtains, peering toward the street. There was a group of a half dozen people gathering out on the sidewalk. How bizarre! Sullivan was trotting toward them from the house, gesturing for everybody to move away from the Santa's sleigh.

I stared in horror. Below me, I could see Steve slowing his pace as he approached the sled.

Someone must have played a prank on the inn again. Surely that was the only possible explanation. And yet, for all the world, it looked like a man was upside down in the sleigh.

Chapter 19

I ran downstairs, stepped into my boots, threw a coat over my nightgown, and dashed out the front door. The snow was dappled in red near the runners of the sleigh. Blood. This was not a prank. A man had been murdered. It hadn't snowed since before the open house and all of our snowmen, so the entire front yard was a mass of foot-prints.

I neared the now gruesome sleigh but, for several seconds, was unable to fully comprehend what I was seeing. The black cashmere coat, tailored slacks, and Italian leather shoes were indisputable. Cameron Baker had been murdered.

"Cameron! Oh, my god!" I cried. I had an image of his poor parents and his little sister. They would be devastated beyond repair.

The half dozen people who'd gathered were watching me, nobody speaking, their expressions blank.

"Erin," Steve said, grabbing me. "You don't—"

"Who would do something like this?!"

Steve pulled me into his arms and forced me to look away from the hideous sight. "Erin. I'm so sorry."

"How long have you been out here? Why didn't you call me? Why are all these people here?"

"A jogger spotted Cameron's body. Just a couple of minutes ago. He didn't have a phone with him. They'd already called the police by the time I awoke and looked out the window. I was going to go back inside and tell you the moment the police arrived. It didn't feel right just . . . deserting him."

Rage welled inside me. Was this my lot in life? My permanent curse? To have people I cared about get murdered? "Deserting him? You hated him!"

"Stop," he said gently.

Police sirens were growing louder. Damn it all! We were going to have Sheriff Mackey arrive any second now! Cam was dead, and now I was going to have to face an interrogation by an arrogant idiot. He who would probably assume *I* had killed the first man I'd ever loved! Or else that Steve had killed him out of jealousy.

"It's going to be all right, darling," Steve said. "We'll get through this."

"How?" I asked as the first patrol car pulled up. This time Sheriff Mackey drove himself, his hapless deputy riding shotgun.

Mackey emerged from his vehicle as the second car arrived, parking behind his at the foot of the driveway. He gestured at the six bystanders across the street, half of whom, like me, were wearing coats and boots over their pajamas. "I need a ten-yard periphery around the body!"

They looked at one another, nobody moving. "You mean you want us to form a circle, Sheriff?" a man in a jogging suit asked.

"No! Just back up a step or two!"

Steve and I were the only people anywhere near the sleigh, so we both took a small step back. Steve took my hand and gave it a reassuring squeeze. A slaying in the sleigh, I thought as Mackey approached the grisly sight. Apparently, I was losing my mind in the face of my ever-deepening troubles.

"Ah, Christ," Mackey said, looking into the sleigh. "Here's the murder weapon. Looks like he got stabbed right in the carotid artery with the end of a skate. Either of you know whose skates these are?"

"Chiffon Walters's," I replied. "She left them in the mudroom yesterday afternoon."

Mackey looked at the two of us. "Did you notice if the skates were still in the mudroom last night?"

"I noticed a pair of pink skates hanging on a hook the last time I used the back door, which was around five or five-thirty yesterday evening," Sullivan said.

"I don't think I've been in the mudroom since four-thirty yesterday," I said.

"The killer had access to Goodwin's back room last night," Mackey said to himself. "That's a start."

Frankly, I was surprised; that was the most intelligent thing I'd heard the man say to date.

The front door flew open, and Mikara raced across the snow-covered lawn toward us, her eyes wide and her face flushed. "*Now* what's happened?" she asked.

"Stay back!" Mackey yelled.

Mikara stopped running and stood staring at us from several feet away.

"Penderson," Mackey called over his shoulder. "Tape off the area. And stop anyone else in Goodwin's house from coming—"

One after the other, Chiffon, Audrey, and Henry charged out the door toward us. "Hold it right there, everyone," Mackey called. The deputy strode purposefully toward them as they stopped next to Mikara.

"Oh, my god," Chiffon exclaimed. "That looks like Cameron Baker's coat! He was wearing it last night!"

"You saw him last night?" Audrey promptly asked.

"Yeah. We had dinner at The Nines." She grabbed Henry's arm and said to him, "I just needed to talk to him about the inn, is all. It was important. I knew he could help us figure out how to land Alfonso as our pastry chef, to raise the inn's profile."

"You don't owe me any explanations," Henry replied in clipped tones.

"Did you and Mr. Baker go ice skating after dinner?" Mackey asked her.

"Ice skating?" she asked. "No. Why?"

"A pink ice skate is, uh, in the sleigh," the deputy replied.

"Oh, jeez!" Chiffon exclaimed. "That must be mine."

"Cameron's car is still parked behind the house," Mikara said. "Didn't anyone else notice that this morning?"

"He must have never made it home," Chiffon said. "I . . . went upstairs to see Henry just as Cammy was leaving."

"Do you know if your skates were still in the back room at that time?" Mackey asked.

"No. I gave them to Cameron to hang in the ski lodge."

"You gave Cameron Baker your ice skates," Mackey repeated, more a statement than a question.

"Yes. The lights were still on downstairs, so I asked him to come in and discuss his ideas for hiring Alfonso with Henry and Audrey, but Mikara was the only one around. We got to talking about my skating. I was a competitive skater when I was younger, and we all know how museums and restaurants always like to have souvenirs from celebrities to put on display. So I gave Cameron my skates to put on public display at the ski lodge."

"I don't remember any of this," Mikara said.

"You'd already left the room," Chiffon countered.

"In other words," Mackey said, "Baker was carrying your skates out the back door when you last saw him?"

"Right. At about ten-thirty last night."

"And you spent the entire rest of the night with Henry Goodwin?"

Chiffon paled visibly and hesitated. "That's right." She released Henry's arm and stuffed her hands in the pockets of her plum-colored parka.

I met Steve's gaze. It was true that Audrey had said she was tired and had gone to bed early, but Steve and I both knew that the rest of Chiffon's story was a lie. Henry had left the house at a few minutes after ten P.M., joking to Steve and me that he was heading out on the town, and we were not to wait up for him. Not wanting to deal with Chiffon, we had tiptoed up the stairs half an hour later when we heard the back door open and her calling out, "Oh, good, Mikara. You're still awake." Although it was quite possible Cameron had been with her at the time, *Henry* had definitely not yet returned.

Mackey announced that he wanted to take everyone's statements at the station house. He and his deputy brought Steve and me separately to start the process. Mackey realized once we arrived that he'd made a tactical error; there wasn't a solid wall between the two desks, which meant that we'd hear what the other was saying. Mackey and his underling conferred, then the deputy led Sullivan through a door in the back, which, judging by the building's dimensions, housed the jail cells. My heart was not only racing but seemed to be beating irregularly—palpitating every few minutes. I'd rather have been thrown into a tiny cell than forced to endure Mackey's questions, but my choices were limited; en route I'd told him about the inconsistencies in Chiffon's story, and I wanted to back that up by being as cooperative as possible.

Mackey offered me coffee and displayed a veneer of basic humanity as he asked about my relationship with Cameron. His veneer cracked after the three or four minutes it took for me to give him the gist of our personal history. "From what I hear tell," Mackey said snidely, "you and Cam had quite the reunion kiss at the inn last week."

"We were both happily surprised to suddenly see each other again, a decade later."

"You're sure he was surprised, too? That the whole thing hadn't been secretly prearranged?"

"*Prearranged?* No. That doesn't make any sense. Cameron was as surprised as I was."

Mackey bobbed his head as though he hadn't been listening and was instead framing his next question. "One thing that's not a secret is how jealous Steve Sullivan was of Mr. Baker. Care to comment about that?"

I clenched my fists below his eye level, trying hard not to let him goad me into snapping at him. "Yes. Steve was angry about the kiss. We both got over it. Cameron accepted that I was now in a serious relationship with someone else. Steve was with me all last night. Neither of us killed Cameron Baker."

"You sound pretty upset, Miss Gilbert."

"I am! Of course! A man I once loved was brutally murdered right below my bedroom window! It's highly upsetting to me!"

Mackey peered at me and rocked back and forth in his desk chair, a spring making an annoying high-pitched squeak all the while. I wasn't doing well on my vow not to snap at the ignoramus. "And you have no idea who killed him?"

"No, I don't. I can't begin to understand how he could have brought Chiffon to the inn, come inside, and then been killed on the front lawn. All without my having heard a sound."

"Yeah. That's pretty hard for me to believe, too."

"And yet, that's what happened. And, like I told you earlier, Henry left the inn at ten. So I don't know why Chiffon apparently lied about being with Henry from ten-thirty on."

Mackey started taking notes now. "And you didn't hear Henry come in last night?"

"Right. Nor did I hear Cameron's voice. It's an old house, very solidly built. When your doors are open, you hear everything in the central hall where the Christmas tree is. Once you've got them closed, though, you can't hear a thing that's going on in the lower levels."

Mackey's jiggling in his chair increased, as if he was trying to shake an idea loose in his thick skull. "Henry could have killed him. I wouldn't put it past him to kill a man out of jealousy over Chiffon."

"*I* would! They only recently started casually dating. Those two truly are not a committed couple, Sheriff Mackey."

"Yeah, the 'committed couple' is you and Sullivan."

"But we were together all last night! We're both innocent!"

"Barring either of you being a real solid sleeper." He leaned his elbows on the desk and gave me a sly grin. He tapped his notepad. "Could have been either one of you, once you take deep sleep in this soundproof house into consideration."

I stared at him, dumbstruck. The man had seemed to be stupid, yet he'd managed to elicit self-incriminating statements from me.

By the time the sheriff's deputy gave us a ride back to the inn, I felt miserable. The police tape had marked off a substantial area, but the driveway itself was still unblocked. Cameron's car was not there, so the police must have towed it away while we were at the station.

Steve put his arm around me as we made our way toward the back door. "Maybe it'd be best if you stayed in bed all day today and just ... zoned out," he suggested.

I shook my head. "I know Sheriff Mackey won't approve, but I'm going back to Crestview tonight. I want to talk to Linda about all of this."

"It's not in her jurisdiction and—"

"I know that! I want to talk to her as a friend. And get her advice. I'm not going to let Sheriff Mackey railroad one of us and make false accusations against us."

"Okay. I'll come with you."

"No, please don't. I need some time alone. And at home. I'll drive back up tomorrow morning."

Steve hesitated, then replied, "Okay. Well, then, I'll just ... hold down the fort here."

Chapter 20

I packed my overnight bag and drove directly to the Crestview police station. The woman at the desk in the lobby told me that Linda—Sergeant Delgardio—was out, and so I asked to see Detective O'Reilly. When his tall but unathletic frame leaned in the doorway, I'd never been happier to see him; in truth, this was my first time being glad to see the man. He tended to act highly skeptical at my every statement, a habit that had driven me up these eggshell-white walls on numerous occasions. After dealing with Sheriff Mackey, though, I felt like kissing O'Reilly's feet.

Even as he was holding the lobby door for me, he told me, "We don't have any jurisdiction up in Snowcap, you realize."

"I know. I'm just hoping for some good advice on what to do."

Our eyes met and I could sense from his somber expression that he'd heard the latest reports. "Was the second victim a friend of yours?"

"My college boyfriend. Cameron Baker."

"I'm sorry."

"Thanks."

He escorted me to his desk, and I dropped into the cheap chrome-and-gray-fabric chair facing him. As he took his own seat, I told him honestly, "I never realized how good the Crestview Police Department was until I ran into Sheriff Mackey."

He seemed to mull my statement in silence for a long time. Finally, he glanced to either side and leaned forward. "Erin, my advice, as a . . ." he paused, then continued, "off the record, is to get a lawyer. And to stay here in Crestview. Walk away from this place in Snowcap you're designing."

"That's what I want to do. But, the thing is, a man who once meant the world to me was murdered today. There's a buffoon in charge of the investigation. And I think he might be taking payoffs from Wendell Barton."

"Wendell Barton is the business mogul who pretty much owns the town of Snowcap, right?"

"Right. Cameron's boss. I think it's very possible that Wendell either killed these people himself, or that he hired a henchman."

O'Reilly rubbed at his temples. "Would he have any reason to kill his right-hand man?"

"Maybe. Cam seemed to be getting into something of a power struggle with Wendell. A whole lot of rancor could have developed over time. Or maybe Cam had recently uncovered information that Wendell was bilking businesses in town...something along those lines." I was speaking off the top of my head, but during the long drive down from the mountains, I'd been formulating a theory. "One possibility that occurred to me is that Wendell's ski resort could be a link between both victims. Angie Woolf—the first victim—and Cameron could have discovered that Wendell's resort had been cutting corners. Just the other day, there was a ski lift accident, and a girl's parents were threatening to sue. Angie was a building inspector, but she also did other types of inspections. She could have done a safety inspection of some kind on the lifts and discovered serious problems."

O'Reilly pondered this for a moment. He pinched the bridge of his nose, and I suspected he was either battling a headache or was surprisingly worried about me. "Is this all just conjecture, or do you have evidence?"

"Conjecture."

"Then let's look at this realistically for a moment. With all of Barton's money and power in the town of Snowcap, even if you're right, Erin, a crack investigative team is going to have to amass foolproof evidence."

"What exactly would you term 'foolproof evidence'?"

He sighed. "A half dozen witnesses plus a visual recording of Barton committing one or both murders, along with a taped confession. At which point you'll still only have a fifty-fifty chance of conviction."

"Barton will go scot-free."

"*If* he's guilty." O'Reilly held my gaze for a long moment. "After fifteen years as a cop, it pains me to suggest this...Then again, I've already told you to get a lawyer, which is like an atheist chanting to Allah, so... Hire a good P.I., Erin. Also, stay the hell out of Snowcap. And, whatever else you do, steer clear of the investigation yourself."

Feeling more discouraged than ever, I drove to Audrey's house, eager to cuddle with Hildi and a cup of mint tea, and to spend a couple of uninterrupted hours alone with my thoughts and my cat. Hildi trotted partway toward me as I entered the front room through the French doors. As if suddenly remembering my unforgivable absenteeism, she stopped, raised her hackles, *rr*-red at me, then pranced out of sight.

Half an hour or so later, after I'd ensconced myself in my favorite sage-colored sofa in the den, she gradually warmed up to strutting past me with her cute little pink nose in the air, flicking the white tip of her tail at me. (I've always considered that gesture feline for a raised middle finger.) An hour after my return, she deigned to join me at the far end of the sofa. Several minutes later, after much suitably reverent coaxing on my part, she climbed into my lap and purred as I stroked her black, satin-smooth fur and thought about Cam. We'd been the center of each other's universe at one time. He'd had an uncanny ability to sense my moods, and always knew the perfect thing to say or do. We couldn't wait to be together, and whenever we were apart, nothing felt real or significant till we'd had the chance to discuss it in detail. For an entire year after we'd first met, I'd half suspected he could read my mind and barely cared either way; he was so kind and loving that I never had any negative thoughts about him. He made me feel wonderful about myself.

When the doorbell rang within a minute or two of Hildi's and my reconciliation, I jumped a little. Hildi let out an indignant growl, hopped off my lap, and rushed from the room, leaving a trail of silent recriminations in her wake. I marched toward the door, silently composing the tirade I would deliver if this was a door-to-door sales-person. I threw the door open without looking through the sidelight.

Steve stood on my front porch, a sheepish smile on his face.

"What are you doing here?" I asked.

"I came to find you. I was worried about you."

"I'm fine, Steve. I'm just extremely upset. Cameron is dead. And I can't talk to you about that." My words, how-ever unfair or unprovoked, were coming out in a torrent now. "I don't want to have to think about your feelings every time I say something or remember something about him. I want to be selfish and sad for my loss just for this one putrid day in my life. Without having to always guard myself, to always consider how my grief affects you." Even as I was speaking, I was horrified at myself; just because my statements were true didn't mean I should voice them.

"You can be as unguarded as you want, Erin." Steve's voice was steady, although I could see the pain in his eyes.

"You don't have to worry about my feelings. They aren't going to change, no matter what. I'm in love with you."

"That's wonderful to hear, Steve. It is. And I'm sorry, I truly am. But . . . I can't be with you right now. I need to be alone. I need to think about the past."

"Okay. You know how to find me. Take care." He kissed me on the forehead and walked away.

I went back inside the house, reclaimed my seat, and started to cry. Hildi, the sweet little kitty that she was, promptly dropped her finicky behavior and hopped onto my lap once more. An hour or so later, we were both in the kitchen and in better spirits when the doorbell rang a second time. I assumed it was Steve and weighed deserting my quest for private time, but it was Linda Delgardio.

"You've been crying," she said the instant I opened the door. "You're grieving over the second murder in Snowcap Village?"

I nodded.

She pulled me into a hug, and I realized then that I'd really come to Crestview and spurned Steve because I needed not *alone* time, but rather *girlfriend* time. Although not without considerable guilt, I asked Linda if she could stay for a while. She wound up staying for hours, discussing the murders and the fool in charge of the investigation, but also my grief for poor Cameron. It was wonderfully cathartic, and afterwards, I was able to call Steve and talk freely about my feelings.

———

The next morning, my cell phone rang at six-thirty. My heart started pounding when I saw that it was Audrey. She immediately asked: "Erin, are you all right?"

"I'm fine. Why?"

"No reason. It's not an emergency. But Wendell's calling a meeting of everyone associated with the inn at nine this morning."

"That's a relief. I'm glad that's all it is. I've gotten so I panic when the phone rings at an odd hour."

"Is Steve with you?"

"No, he spent the night at his house."

"Oh, dear. I'm so sorry. I *told* him not to drive down after you, but he wouldn't listen. I knew things would get strained between you two. Cameron's death is so . . . horrible and heartbreaking."

"We're okay, Audrey. I called Steve last night and spoke to him at length. He said all the right things."

"In that case, could you see if he can possibly get up here by nine? I'm assuming you'll want to stay put, and it's not a problem if neither of you makes it back up today, but Wendell wants to speak with each of us. He's concerned about everyone giving up on the inn."

"So we're supposed to vow our allegiance to the inn? The day after finding Cameron's body in the front yard?"

Audrey clicked her tongue. "He's also worried about morale. He means well, Erin."

"But, Audrey . . . what if he *doesn't*? What if he's behind the killings?"

"I'm sure he isn't, Erin. Call Steve for me, would you?"

She hung up without waiting for a reply.

Steve wanted me to stay in Crestview (as did Linda and Detective O'Reilly), but Sheriff Mackey was probably already on the verge of issuing an APB for my arrest. Besides, finishing our job at the inn was growing into an obsession with me.

Steve and I caravanned back to the inn and arrived at about ten minutes after nine. By then, everyone — Ben, Mikara, Audrey, Chiffon, Henry, and Wendell — was gathered around the kitchen table, making small talk. As soon as we grabbed the last two chairs at the table, Wendell said, "Let's get this thing under way. Folks, we've had big shocks in the last couple of weeks. It's inconceivable that two such fine young people have been murdered here on the grounds."

"You can say that again," Mikara muttered.

"Even so, we can't allow ourselves to fall apart," Wendell continued. "Personally, I suspect that there's someone in town who's responsible for these murders and who is trying to frame us. I'm cooperating fully with Sheriff Mackey, and I've hired my own investigative team to get to the bottom of these murders."

"You have?" I blurted out. "Who?"

Wendell ignored me. "In the meantime, we all deserve and *need* a break from the routine. I've hired a van to take us and our equipment to the resort, and the driver has your all-day passes for each of you. I want everyone to breathe in some fresh air, get some exercise, and take a holiday from the tragedies that we've been forced to endure."

This was utterly tasteless and shallow! Taking a group

ski day to recuperate from a murder? Everyone else was looking around, gauging reactions. Chiffon broke the silence. "I think Cam and Angie would want us to quit moping around the house. Excellent suggestion, Wendell. Thank you for being so generous."

"I don't actually own skis," Ben said quietly.

"I made out a few passes for free rentals, for just that very reason," Wendell countered.

Feeling a bit like a little child shoved out the door to "go have fun" despite terrible weather, I rose, as did Steve, and we went with the flow.

"Oh, look, Erin!" Chiffon said as she and I schussed our way toward the first ski lift at the base of the lodge. "You and I have identical skis! How funny!"

I glanced at her feet. She was right. "They might be the same skis and bindings, but I have no doubt that they look better on you," I said.

"Oh, I don't know about that. Actually, you look right at home."

"That's only because we're on level ground."

Steve grinned at me. The four of us—Chiffon, Henry, Steve, and I—had been able to head straight for the lifts. Mikara and Ben were renting equipment, and Wendell was taking Audrey on a tour of the lodge itself.

She smiled. "Maybe so, but you're looking pretty comfortable. The real rookies can't even manage that much."

Henry and Chiffon were ahead of us in line and shared a chairlift; Steve and I got onto the next one. The view from the lift was magnificent. As I quietly said to Steve, much as I hated to admit it, Wendell was right. This fresh, nippy air and the glorious scenery were lifting my spirits in spite of myself.

We skied off the chairlifts. Feeling hesitant to reveal my lack of skills on skis to the others, I hung back at the top of the slope. Sullivan waited with me while Henry and Chiffon took off, zigzagging expertly down the trail. The sky was crystal clear, and I could see the inn from where I was standing, visible below the still-natural portion of the mountain. Till now, I hadn't realized how close the inn was to the unused half of the mountain, where no trails were located. Many large sections of land in Colorado were owned by the state parks and national forests and could not be built upon, so maybe Wendell didn't own that property.

Sullivan and I pushed off. Gentleman that he was, he allowed me to go first. Remarkably, I felt completely in balance as my skis flew along the snow. Chiffon was right! Apparently my body had decided it was sick and tired of falling down. I could ski! I was able to turn, and roughly a third of the way down the course, I even managed to come to a nice crisp stop.

Sullivan beamed at me as he came to an effortless stop right beside me. "Damn! You've been holding out on me! Were *both* you and Chiffon in the Junior Olympics?"

"As it turns out, skiing must be a little like getting the feel for riding a bike."

"Awesome, dude," Steve joked, parodying the typical ski bum. "So let's take advantage of it and get on down the slope. Follow me!"

I pushed off with both poles and stayed right behind

Steve. After a minute or two, it felt as if I was going a tad too fast. To slow myself, I made a sharp turn and dug in with my edges. To my horror, the heel on my right boot seemed to jerk free from my ski.

My binding had failed! Urging myself not to panic, I tried to shift my weight to my left—good—ski. My tips crossed. A split second later, I was crashing into the slope, falling head over heels, utterly out of control. My right binding released immediately, and I couldn't have hung onto my poles if I'd tried. Yet my second ski wasn't releasing, causing all the more stress on that knee. My helmeted head cracked against the ground.

It felt as though I was helplessly careening down a roller coaster—without the car. My teeth were hitting together so hard, they were sure to shatter.

I regained just enough control to dig the edge of my lone ski into the side of a mogul, and my bone-jarring tumble finally came to a stop. I lay still, sprawled out for several seconds, just breathing and collecting my wits. I heard Steve yelling my name from below me, and I lifted a hand to let him know that I was still conscious.

I sat up and saw Steve running up the incline toward me as fast as he could in his clunky boots. I'd struggled to my feet by the time he arrived at my side.

"Erin." He was panting. "Are you okay?"

"I think so. Amazingly."

"Thank God! That was one of the worst wipeouts I've ever seen!"

"It looked even worse from my vantage point."

I turned. My poles were above me. Nearby, skiers had slowed, no doubt to avoid colliding with me. One of them called down that he would bring me my poles. My one loose ski had navigated itself a considerable distance away, however.

"Are you sure you're okay?" Steve asked.

"I'm sore, is all...bruised up. But I didn't break any bones or anything."

A snowmobile roared up the mountain toward me. A man from the ski patrol, wearing a signature red suit and white plus sign, disembarked. "You all right, miss? We saw you fall."

"I was lucky, though. I'm okay."

A second patrolman on skis had headed down to collect my prodigal ski. He grabbed it and did a remarkably rapid herringbone to return. "What happened?"

"I'm not sure. The binding on one of my skis released while I was making a turn."

"Who the hell set these bindings for you?" the patrolman asked as he examined the ski in his hand.

"A guy at the ski store in Crestview. Two months ago."

"You didn't try to reset them yourself? Or get anyone else to work on 'em?"

"No. Why?"

"Look for yourself. The screws on this one are all sheared off. In all my ten-plus years of ski patrol, I've never seen something like that happen on impact."

"So...somebody tampered with my skis? Deliberately?"

He shrugged. "Sure looks that way to me."

Steve and I stared at each other in shock. "This thing is just never going to end, is it?" I murmured. I wasn't expecting an answer, and he didn't give me one.

Chapter 21

The patrolman gave me a ride down to the lodge on the snowmobile, while Steve skied down after us. At the lodge, Steve took off his skis; he told me he'd lost all enthusiasm for skiing today.

We walked into the lodge, Steve insisting upon buying me a cup of hot chocolate. My body was already aching so badly that I just wanted a hot *bath*, but I lacked the energy to argue with him. When we'd gotten through the line at the register, Steve said, "Look who's here," and pointed with his chin at Wendell Barton. We tromped across the room toward him in our awkward boots. He greeted us warmly, but did a double take at my face, which confirmed my suspicions that I looked as bad as I felt.

"Wendell," Steve said, "Erin and I need transportation back to the inn."

Wendell glanced again at me, then returned his attention to Steve. "So soon? What's wrong?"

"I took a nasty spill, and my skis are wrecked," I explained.

"After someone tampered with her bindings," Steve growled.

"You're kidding, I hope," Wendell replied.

"No, and I'm going to wring the neck of whoever did this to her."

Wendell put his hand on my arm. "Erin, I'll go talk to one of my salesmen, and you can go pick out a new pair of skis and bindings for yourself from the ski shop. All right?"

"Thanks, but fancy skis are wasted on me. I've skied my final run for the season, if not for all time."

He held my gaze with what appeared to be genuine concern. "At the very least, give me your damaged skis and let me get my repair people to fix them for you."

"We first have to take her one ski to the police. It's evidence," Steve interjected.

"I guess that's true, come to think of it." Wendell shook his head in disgust. "This is an outrage! I can't believe my people are being victimized like this! Right under my nose!"

Wendell considers me one of his "people." Ugh.

He patted me on the back—a marginal improvement over patting me on the head like a poodle. "Well, the least I can do is take you both home myself."

"Thanks." I still didn't trust Wendell; in fact, I considered him the prime suspect. But surely it was safe to accept a ride with him; after all, what could he do? Shove us both out of his BMW and then run over us? "Where's Audrey?"

"She, Mikara, and Ben are on the slopes," Wendell replied. "Ironically, I don't ski myself. Audrey and I are hooking up again in an hour, and I'll be sure to tell her what happened to you then. Don't worry." He gestured for us to follow as he strode toward the exit.

As we reached the parking lot, Wendell plucked his cell phone out of its special compartment in his parka and dialed. Moments later, he said into it: "Sheriff Mackey, this is Wendell Barton. Erin Gilbert's skis were tampered with and she took a nasty spill. It had to have been done while the skis were on my property at the inn. Meet her there, pronto." He hung up.

I glanced at Steve to share my dismay, then said to Wendell, "Wasn't that rather abrupt?"

"Yeah, but I don't suffer fools gladly." He held the door for us.

About thirty minutes later, Steve and I were standing in the mudroom, watching as Sheriff Mackey eyed the marks on my ski bindings. "This isn't real good proof," Mackey finally announced. "You could have done this yourself, for all I know."

"That's idiotic!" I cried, instantly losing my temper. "Are you seriously telling me that you think I hacked through the supports on my own binding, cranked up the setting on the other ski's binding, and then took to the slopes? Knowing that I was going to have a hellacious accident as a result? Why on earth would I want to do such a thing?"

"Some people will go to great lengths, including risking life and limb, to shift the blame off themselves."

"I don't believe this," Sullivan muttered.

"Who all would have had the opportunity to fiddle with your skis?" Mackey asked me.

"Anyone with access to the inn. They've been in the mudroom closet the past two weeks."

Mackey eyed Sullivan. "Did *you* do this?"

"No! Of course not!"

"Sheriff, have you made any progress whatsoever on the murder investigations?" I asked, not bothering to mask my contempt.

"Yes, as a matter of fact, I have," he fired back, "but I don't discuss evidence with my suspects!" He pivoted and stormed toward the door.

"Speaking of evidence," I cried, "don't you want to take my skis?"

He turned back and glared at me. "What good would that do? Fingerprints are useless. You just got through telling me the skis have been sitting out, unused, for two weeks. Anybody could have touched them. Might as well take this doorknob as evidence." He opened the door, then slammed it shut behind him.

After a bit of rest and a lengthy soak in the tub, not to mention a dose of acetaminophen on top of three ibuprofen, I felt better. The shipments of decorations for days one through five had arrived. There was nothing better than accessorizing rooms to lift my spirits after taking a nasty fall. The partridge in a pear tree design was absolutely stunning. Mikara's bedroom had definitely gotten the short shrift with the cross-stitched turtledove pillows. My four calling birds in the den made up for the understated pillows, however, and Steve's three French hens looked stunning.

Unfortunately, two of Steve's five wreaths were decidedly silver instead of gold. Sullivan was soon verbally sparring over the phone with the company that had sent them. He then left for UPS—or one of their competitors—taking the two silver rings with him.

Left alone, my thoughts turned to the turtledoves. Maybe I could do something with the lighting in Mikara's room to draw attention to the pillows. I gave a cursory knock on her door, surprised to hear a "Who is it?" She'd been so quiet, I'd assumed she wasn't home.

"It's Erin. I have the two pillows for your room for the inn's Christmas theme."

"Come in," she called. I entered. She was sitting in the middle of her neatly made bed. She'd been crying.

"I'm sorry," I said. "I didn't realize—"

"Don't mind me. I'm getting it back together. I just . . ." She let her voice fade.

"You're back from skiing early," I said. "You didn't hurt yourself, too, did you?"

"No. Ben and I both felt we had too much left undone to take a full day off. We came back after lunch. I'm sorry to hear about your accident, though. It's lucky you didn't break a leg."

"I was really lucky, all right. Thanks." Feeling more than a little embarrassed, I lifted the pillows in my hands. "I'm so sorry to have barged in on you. You're obviously upset. I really just wanted to drop off these pillows, and I'd thought your room was empty."

"That's okay." Mikara dabbed at her eyes with a tissue. "Every now and then the grief just overtakes me. When I'm least expecting it. Now poor Cameron is dead, too. I just . . . I can't believe this is happening, that everything is falling apart. It's like the Goodwin estate is suddenly at the epicenter of an earthquake. I'm missing my sister horribly. It's all so strange."

"Strange?" *That isn't the word I'd use; "cruel" or "evil" or "horrifying" would be more appropriate.*

She glanced at me, then quickly averted her gaze. "Erin, I'm glad you're here. I . . . need to talk to someone. I just can't keep trying to hide this. And now there's a second victim." She sank her head into her hands. "Maybe I'm responsible."

"What are you talking about?" I waited for a few seconds. Mikara rocked herself slightly and said nothing. "Responsible for what?"

She finally collected herself enough to meet my gaze. "Last week, I found an envelope addressed to Angie hidden in the post of the handrail."

"What handrail?"

"The one for the bridge over the creek. Right where Angie was killed."

"I don't understand. How could you find—"

"Henry had a hidden compartment built into the side of the left post. He used to keep a spare key to the back door in there. It was a secret place. When we were dating, he and I used it to pass little love notes back and forth. I was feeling...sad and nostalgic, and so I opened it up a couple of days after Angie died." Mikara reached behind her into the top drawer of her nightstand. "That's where I found this."

She handed me a business-size envelope. Angie's name was written on the front in block letters. I opened it and stared at its contents. "Money."

"Quite a lot of it, at least by Angie's and my standards. That's twenty fifty-dollar bills."

"Does anyone other than Henry know about your old hiding place?"

"Angie did, for one. She watched me open the compartment in the post dozens of times."

"You're thinking it's a bribe? A payment from Henry so that she would give the inn a passing grade?"

She pursed her lips. "It's not like there's a ton of other explanations. The string of Christmas lights you hung would have wrapped right around that particular post. It's disguised to look like a solid six-by-six, but it's actually separate boards. You can lift up the top and then pry off the front part of the post. Angie might have been out there, unwrapping the lights so she could open the secret compartment when the killer stumbled upon her."

"Maybe so," I said, my mind racing. "Who built that bridge? Do you know?"

"Ben Orlin. About twelve years ago."

"So *he* knew about the hiding place, too."

"He must have. Maybe he knows that Henry keeps a spare set of keys in there, too."

"It's unusual to hide keys so far from a house. Homeowners usually hide them on a front or back porch."

Mikara shrugged. "The fence post is halfway between the house and the shed. We kept the padlock keys for the shed in there, too."

"This could have been a setup, Mikara. Maybe the killer wanted you to find the money, in order to make it look like your sister was getting paid under the table."

Mikara nodded slowly. "That's possible."

"You should tell—" I hesitated, wishing I could find an alternative name to suggest. Sheriff Mackey, in my estimation, was a man of huge ego and little brain. "Do you and Angie have a family lawyer?"

"No. Which just leaves Greg Mackey. And he'll probably find a way to 'lose' this cash." (She'd drawn air quotes around the word "lose.")

"Even so . . ."

Mikara shook her head sadly. "The problem is, Erin, it's *not* a setup. Angie *had* been taking bribes."

"She told you that herself?"

"No. I looked into her financial situation after finding the envelope full of money."

"You checked her bank balance?"

She nodded. "She'd deposited four thousand dollars just four days before she was killed. Which was, of course, *before* she flunked the inn's tap water and front steps."

I felt a surge of relief; Cameron wasn't even in town for that first large deposit. "That implies that she was accepting bribes to keep the inn from opening on Christmas

Eve," I said, thinking out loud. "Or else she earned the four thousand from those extra jobs she was taking on." *Although the thousand dollars hidden in a handrail post disproves that theory*, I silently argued.

Mikara nodded. "That's precisely what I kept telling myself. But... then Cameron was murdered, and it grew impossible to keep fooling myself..." Her voice faded. "I get the impression that Sheriff Mackey doesn't really want to solve my sister's murder," she began again. "Or rather, he only wants to solve it if he can pin it on someone from out of town. Or on Henry. As if, just because Henry sold the inn, he's capable of murdering a former friend in cold blood."

I gave her back the envelope, and she returned it to her drawer. I mulled her words in silence.

Our gazes met. "I know you've had a loss, too, Erin. I don't mean to sound like Angie's is the only death that mattered."

"Thank you, Mikara. But losing a sister is considerably harder than losing a friend you haven't seen in a decade. And I share your concerns about the quality of the investigation."

"About Greg Mackey, you mean?"

I nodded. "Maybe someone at Angie's bank could verify if the deposit was made in cash, and, if so, in what denominations. Is there anyone at the bank you know well enough to ask for details?"

"Maybe. One of the tellers is a friend."

"As Angie's lone family member, you're probably entitled to ask questions about her account."

"That may be true, but I don't really want to raise suspicions about Angie's activities."

I glanced at the drawer that held the cash. "So what are you going to do?"

She rose and crossed over to the window. Her view, I remembered, was of the path to the footbridge where Angie had died. "I know I *should* turn it in as evidence to Sheriff Mackey. But I can't help but think, if anything, that would only turn me into the next potential victim. What if Mackey himself is in on it? What if there was a ring of townies involved with . . . I don't know . . . cover-ups and bribes at the ski resort? I mean, when you've already killed twice, what's a third murder, compared to keeping your secret safe?"

"You're going to stay quiet?" I asked. "Keep the money in a drawer?"

She gritted her teeth. "If that's what it takes to keep myself out of the morgue."

"What if we both go talk to this teller friend of yours? At least that way, you'll have a witness."

She hesitated. "Can we go right this second, Erin? Before I have the chance to change my mind?"

Mikara and I met the teller at the small deli where Mikara assured me the woman always went for lunch at precisely this time. The teller, Susan, was a plump middle-aged woman. We took seats across from her. She and Mikara exchanged some pleasantries, then Mikara jumped in and asked if Angie had been depositing a lot of cash right before she died.

"Yep. In fifty-dollar bills," Susan replied, setting aside her ham and cheese on rye. Then she added in a conspiratorial tone, "And wouldn't you know, that dashing young man who was just killed...Cameron Baker? *He* had opened a private account at the bank and had been withdrawing a lot of fifties!"

"But..." I stammered, "he only arrived in town the day before Angie was killed. You're saying he withdrew a thousand dollars the same day Angie was killed? Right after he opened the account?"

Susan squirmed in her seat and made a face. "Actually, he withdrew money *four* times. Two thousand twice a couple of weeks ago, then again a week after that, and finally a thousand on the Friday before Angie was killed. I remember stuff like that."

I was speechless. Cameron had to have been in town off and on before the meeting when we saw each other for the first time in all those years. Then again, this time frame wasn't really all that hard to fathom; he'd worked for Wendell for years. I knew he'd been focused lately on a different project back east, but it was reasonable that he'd periodically traveled into Snowcap to see his boss.

Even so, Cameron was now looking more and more guilty of a white-collar crime, at the very least. Would he have been so foolhardy as to open a bank account in the same small town where he was bribing its citizens, though? Maybe, I answered myself. Cameron's biggest fault had been his arrogance; he might have assumed nobody from a small town was smart enough to follow his money trail. And that, if they did catch on to him, a few thousand dollars in bribes was irrelevant.

"Has Greg Mackey asked you about any of this?" Mikara asked.

"Hell, no," Susan snorted. "His election to town sheriff was bought and paid for by Wendell Barton. You know that! Everybody knows that!"

"We've just verified my worst fears, Erin," Mikara said once we'd returned to my van. "I was right. Angie was taking bribes. But I don't see how it could have been Cameron who was making the payoffs. His boss, Wendell Barton, wants the inn to open on time to protect his investment."

"Unless he actually doesn't," I muttered, deep in thought.

"What do you mean?"

I started the engine, but allowed it to idle. "For all we know, Wendell could have been talking out of both sides of his mouth all along. Maybe he doesn't really *want* the inn to be a success. Maybe he'd be better off with the inn in forfeiture, so he can then buy it at a reduced price and become the sole owner, like he's wanted all along."

"So he could plow it down and put up yet more condos, you mean?"

"Exactly. And so maybe, if Cameron truly was the middleman who was giving your sister bribes, the payments might have been to *flunk* the inn's inspections."

Audrey was waiting for me when we returned, worried that I'd developed symptoms of a concussion and had gone to the hospital. The three of us made and ate a quick lunch, but Mikara was withdrawn, obviously still saddened by what we'd learned. She picked at her turkey sandwich and said she was going back to her old house for a while.

I gave Audrey a brief rundown on what Mikara and the bank teller had told me. Audrey listened patiently, then said, "I know you're deeply suspicious of Wendell, and much as I hate this aspect to his personality, he openly admits to bribing public officials, under various legal guises. Frankly, it would be just like him to turn a blind eye while Cameron handed out cash under the table . . . or inside a secret compartment of a fence post. But, Erin, the bribes might have nothing whatsoever to do with the murders. And, meanwhile, you're overlooking *Ben's* behavior."

"What behavior? And why would he kill Angie or Cameron?"

"I don't know his motives, but I've been watching him carefully for the past several days. For one thing, I'm certain that Ben resents having this place converted to an inn much more deeply than he lets on. I've seen a look of sheer hatred on his face, when he thinks nobody is watching. Usually it's after someone's asked him to make an alteration."

"Okay, but—"

"Let me finish. If nothing else, he has a misplaced sense of entitlement regarding this house. You've heard how he keeps talking about his family building this place." She hesitated. "And here's something else that's just a little odd. A couple of times, en route to the wine cellar, I've found him rooting around in the same old plywood box in the basement."

"A plywood box?"

"I suspect he's looking for evidence, or something that incriminates himself."

"Can you show me the box?" I asked.

"If it's still down there."

She led the way into the unfinished basement, a dark, dank space. Three rows of a half dozen metal posts supported the first story. The ceiling and walls were concrete, illuminated by three simple overhead light fixtures.

We located the plain plywood box and opened it. I rummaged through its contents: old, inexpensive toys—wooden cars, miniature trains, a spinning top, a small bat, ball, and glove, and some child-size tools. "This is certainly nothing worth killing for," I said.

"Nor is it anything worth being so secretive about. He doesn't have any children. So you've got to wonder what his interest is in some old toys."

"Maybe he was looking to see if there were things he could give to charity." Yet I didn't actually believe my own words, and added, "I have to admit, there's something a tad . . . creepy about this. You didn't happen to find a child's sled named 'Rosebud,' did you?"

We both jumped at the sound of footsteps on the staircase. I hadn't realized we'd left the door ajar. It was Henry. "What are you two doing down here?" he asked as he approached, his voice sounding idly curious.

"We were searching for more Christmas decorations," I lied. "Such as eleven pipers piping."

He chuckled a little when he spotted the box at our feet. "That brings back memories."

"Were these old toys yours?"

"No, they were Ben's, as a matter of fact."

"He kept toys in your house?" Audrey asked.

"That's right. Even though Ben was exactly my age, and he and his dad were over here all the time, his father didn't want Ben to play with my stuff. So he brought that box of Ben's toys to the basement and insisted Ben play down here all by himself."

"Why?" I asked, appalled.

Henry shook his head. "I don't know. His dad was a real craftsman. Hell of a carpenter. But when it came to fatherhood, he was kind of a bastard."

"Did Ben blame you? Did he think you'd told his dad you didn't want him to play with your toys, I mean?"

"No. I don't think so. We were kind of friends at school, but then had sort of an unspoken agreement to act like total strangers after hours. To avoid any hassles from his father. But, you know how things go," he added and grimaced slightly. "After a while, you fall in with a crowd that's just . . . easier somehow, you know? Both of us did. By the time we graduated high school, we were pretty much strangers . . . just like we'd pretended to be as kids."

Chapter 22

Ben came down the stairs a moment later and flinched when he spotted us with his open toy box by our feet. Beneath the scruffy four-day beard, his cheeks turned rose-petal red. "I thought maybe I'd accidentally left the lights on when I was down here earlier." He glanced at the furnace and added, "I changed the filter on the furnace. Trying to keep our carbon footprint under control." Clearly embarrassed at our having discovered that he'd kept his shabby childhood toys here, he shifted his weight and stepped back toward the stairs, as if eager to turn and run.

"Look what the ladies found," Henry said with a smile, gesturing at the box. "These are your old toys. Remember?"

"Yeah, you know, I noticed these down here last week. I, uh, looked through 'em to see if there was maybe something worth selling on eBay, but it's nothing but junk. And not very much junk, even at that. A couple of toy trucks."

I was still so shaken by the image of a young boy forced to entertain himself with such meager playthings inside this cold, hard space that I felt like crying. I glanced at Audrey. She, too, looked immensely sad.

Oblivious, Henry chuckled. "No kidding. I don't know what you found to keep yourself occupied all those hours when you were a kid."

"Well, I had some old comic books, too. Must've taken those with me. I'll bet *those* would've been worth something nowadays."

"Oh, jeez," Henry said, striking his forehead with the heel of his hand. "That stack of comic books were yours, after all! When we were in eighth grade, something like that, my dad gave me a batch of *Spider-Man*s and *Fantastic Four*s that he found down here. I tried to tell him they were probably yours, but he said he'd already asked your dad about them." He shook his head. "I just read 'em once and tossed 'em. How dumb can you get."

"They weren't dumb," Ben retorted. "They were classics!"

Henry's eyes widened. "No, I meant it was stupid of me to throw them out. I should've stuck them in my backpack and brought them to you at school."

"Yeah. No problem. Well, now you can just toss out my ratty toys, as well."

He pivoted and headed back upstairs.

Henry watched him go, then said quietly to us, "Man. I think I really ticked him off. But it's not like there's anything I can do about things that happened thirty years ago."

"I hope you remembered to give him the dollar-an-hour raise you promised him the other day," I said.

"No kidding," Henry replied. "I guess we invaded his private space down here."

Audrey arched an eyebrow when our eyes met. As she had suggested earlier, Ben's recent behavior could, indeed, be considered suspicious. But although he and Ben had some painful baggage in their past relationship, there was no immediate, obvious connection between that and Angie's or Cam's deaths.

For that matter, Mikara also had a large axe to grind with Henry. Maybe, in the dark, Cameron could have been mistaken for Henry. They were roughly the same height and build.

"Henry?" Chiffon called down from the top of the stairs. Suddenly the basement was Grand Central. If nothing else, this was a good reminder that, because the door to the basement opened off the central hallway, we needed to install a door lock before the inn opened.

"Yeah?"

"Is there an official meeting in the basement that I'm unaware of?" she asked.

I stifled a smile. If this were a TV sitcom, everyone in the entire house would traipse down those stairs and join us, and the last person would manage to lock the door after himself.

"No. I'll be right up." He rolled his eyes, and my hunch was that he was having second thoughts about dating her.

He caught me looking at him. "I'm starting to feel hemmed in," he acknowledged in a low voice, giving both Audrey and me a sheepish smile. "Just like always."

"Like always?" I snapped. "You got engaged to Mikara of your own free will, didn't you?"

"Yeah. And I really loved her. But there were always prettier girls out there, and in the end, I realized it was better for both of us to just make a clean break, before we said vows that I knew full well I was never going to keep."

"Too bad you didn't realize that *before* you popped the question," Audrey muttered.

"Yeah. Timing's everything."

Chiffon was waiting for Henry when we came upstairs. She promptly clutched his arm with both hands and shot me a don't-touch-my-guy glare. "Ben looked really upset when he came upstairs. What were you guys talking about?"

"It was really no big deal," Henry replied, shaking loose from Chiffon. "I'm going to grab something to drink. Can I get anyone else anything?"

"I'd like a diet cola," Chiffon said. "Thanks, honey."

Audrey and I said, "No, thanks," in unison.

"I've got a meeting with my producer at the Snowcap studio," Audrey said. "I'd better go get ready." She gave me a smile, then stopped to admire our partridge-and-pear-tree display on the large, square coffee table. "Erin. With all the excitement of your ski accident this morning, I forgot to tell you how much I love this. It's absolutely *gorgeous!*"

"Thanks, Audrey," I exclaimed. She headed upstairs.

In order to escape Chiffon's company myself, I was about to claim to need more pain medication when she touched my arm and peered into my eyes. "Erin, I have to tell you something that's going to be a major shocker."

"Oh? What?"

"I was examining your skis just now, and—"

"Why were you examining my skis?"

"I'd noticed that the binding on one was broken. Then Henry told me that Audrey told *him* you'd had an accident on the slope. Point is, I'm something of an expert at skis, and someone tampered with both of your bindings. There are file marks on one ski where the fasteners were sheared off. Your other release was set so high that it wouldn't have come free. Your ski was practically fused to your boot."

"The guys on the ski rescue patrol already told me that, Chiffon."

"But . . . you realize what happened, don't you?"

I spread my arms. "Somebody wanted me out of the way and tampered with my skis."

"No, Erin. Somebody wanted *me* out of the way, and got our skis mixed up."

"But that—"

She held up a hand to stop me. "I've been thinking about this, and I'm all but positive. You ski so slowly that you couldn't have gotten hurt all that badly. I'm a way better skier than you are, and I ski much faster. If *my* ski had come loose in the middle of one of my runs, I could easily have broken my neck."

She paused for air. "Furthermore, most of the time, my skis were at my condo. Just this past weekend, I happened to bring them here and I left them in the mudroom, along with yours. That has to be when it happened. See what I mean?"

Not really, I thought, but I lacked the energy to ask her to explain. "That's an interesting theory, Chiffon, but for one thing, I haven't skied in two weeks, so we don't know when the skis were messed with." I wasn't about to tell her that this was the second attempt on my life; I'd never told her about the eggnog. "Plus, frankly, this isn't the first time I've gotten caught up in a murder investigation. I've had a horrible propensity for finding dead bodies ever since I moved to Colorado. Maybe I was a coroner in a previous life."

"Irregardless, Erin, *I'm* the celebrity. *I'm* the skier. My fame makes *me* the target for all kinds of things."

You're also a drama queen who wants to constantly put yourself in the spotlight.

"The more I think about it, the more certain I am that this attempt was meant for me."

"That's possible, but I'm highly skeptical."

"I'm calling my publicist," Chiffon said, just as Henry dutifully returned to the hallway with her glass of diet cola. She waved at him to set it on the coffee table. "Something's come up," she said to him by way of explanation. A moment later she cried, "Richard!" into the phone; she must have had the poor guy's number on speed dial. "The most terrible thing has happened! There was an attempt on my life!" She drew a breath, as if to add dramatic tension. "It was made at the hand of some maniac!"

Henry slid her glass next to the pear tree and gave me a

quick what's-up gesture. I whispered, "She thinks whoever tampered with my ski bindings accidentally chose the wrong pair...that *her* skis were supposed to be booby-trapped."

Henry rolled his eyes, but Chiffon grabbed his arm as if for support during her terrifying ordeal.

"I'll be in my room if anyone needs me," I said and headed for the staircase. Chiffon blathered away to her publicist about the sabotaged bindings, which, "fortunately, thanks to the good Lord above, accidentally wound up being on the wrong pair of skis."

I thought back to Mackey's accusations. Chiffon could have tampered with my skis and concocted this story in advance, to make herself look innocent. Granted, I couldn't think of any plausible motive for her to kill Cameron, let alone Angie, but that didn't mean she was innocent. Chiffon seemed to be jealous of all women and to compulsively crave attention. Her troubles could run a lot deeper than that. Maybe Angie had once done something unforgivable in Chiffon's eyes. Furthermore, Chiffon's dinner date with Cameron might have gone nothing like she'd described it yesterday. Something could have happened then that led her to make Cameron a second victim.

Later that afternoon, Steve and I cuddled together on our bed, while he told me his very dull story of how long it had taken him to ship the silver wreaths back, due to crowds and logistics troubles; I told him my relatively riveting story of my conversations with the bank teller,

Henry, Ben, and finally, Chiffon, followed by my suspicions regarding the latter.

Steve furrowed his brow. "I do have to admit that Chiffon tends to come on really strong to me whenever you're not around."

"She does?"

"'Fraid so."

"Apparently I'm going to have to stop leaving you alone so often," I muttered.

He gave me a sexy grin. "I'm all for that. Chiffon is nothing in comparison to you."

At that, our bedroom door was flung open and Chiffon barged into the room unannounced. "Oh, oops," she said with an edge to her voice. "I didn't know you were here. I was just having fun, trying to follow your course of the Twelve Days of Christmas."

"We've only gotten days one through five done," Steve said. "More like days four-and-three-fifths, even."

"You know, I *thought* there were more than three golden rings!" she exclaimed. She noticed my unhappy expression and said, "I should leave. 'Scuse the interruption." She tiptoed out and ever so slowly shut the door behind her.

I sat there seething, certain that she'd had her ear pressed to our door, eavesdropping on our private conversation.

"Think she heard us?" Sullivan asked.

"Yep."

He gave me a mischievous grin. "If you're right about her being a serial killer, we know who her next victim will be. Been nice knowing you, Gilbert."

"Oh, are you planning on kicking the bucket soon, Sullivan?" I retorted. "You're equally likely to be in her crosshairs. Chiffon was rebuked at the party by Cameron shortly before *he* was killed. Now you've rebuked her, too."

"True. Feels like we're in the cast of *Ten Little Indians*."

I walked over to the window, wondering if the police crime-scene tape was still enclosing the sleigh. Not only was there no crime-scene tape, there was no sleigh; the police must have hauled it away as evidence while we were skiing, and I'd been too distracted to notice.

Just as I was about to turn away, I gasped at the sight of a man standing on the sidewalk, staring up at me. He turned away, but as he trotted past the lamppost, I recognized him. It was Ben Orlin.

Chapter 23

*Gingerbread houses are a fun
seasonal activity that combines
baking with arts and crafts. And,
because they're edible, unlike most
art projects, you don't have to store
them indefinitely.*

—Audrey Munroe

Domestic Bliss

I awoke at four-thirty from a bad dream about
being unable to keep up with Cameron in a tor-
rential storm, and couldn't get back to sleep.
At five A.M., I got up and went downstairs. The
kitchen was illuminated and the air was
scented with a sweet, spicy aroma. At first I
wondered if maybe Chiffon had managed to
hire Alfonso, the pastry chef, after all. But when
I entered the kitchen, I saw only Audrey, peering into the oven while the kitchen timer
buzzed.

"Morning, Audrey. You're baking molasses
cookies?" I guessed from the aroma.

"More elaborate than that," she said with a
smile.

I glanced at the counters next to the oven.

She had bags of different types of candies along with her icing paraphernalia at the ready. The dead give-away as to what she was baking, though, was that she had cut sides-of-house patterns from cardboard. Gingerbread! She removed a pair of cookie sheets from the oven.

"Oh, good for you. You're making a gingerbread house. Is this for a segment on your show?"

She nodded. "Once I practice up a bit. I'll present the how-to for the average baker-slash-hobbyist. I've also got a pair of experts scheduled who'll share ideas for the high-end gingerbread builders. They've con-structed full Victorian towns out of gingerbread, candy, and frosting. One of them built a five-car train, pulling up to Santa's workshop."

I glanced at a pair of thin pieces of wood, one inch wide by two feet long, on the countertop. "What are you using the wood trim for? Railroad tracks?"

"No. For now, I'm merely getting myself up to speed so that I can show how to bake simple, basic rectangu-lar houses. The pieces of wood are gauges I use to keep the gingerbread a uniform thickness. I use my longest rolling pin and roll the dough directly onto the sheet, keeping the wooden slats pressed against op-posite sides of the sheet." Her cookie sheets, I noted, were open at three sides.

"Clever."

"It took some experimenting. I had to learn to put

the cookie sheet and the wood slats on a damp cloth so they don't slide so easily on the counter."

"So the dough is rolled out to a perfectly uniform thickness—the thickness of the boards minus the cookie sheet," I concluded.

"It still rises a bit unevenly as it bakes, but the beauty of plaster walls is their texture and unevenness. Same thing with gingerbread."

"Sullivan and I should use your method to build our miniature models of our clients' homes."

"Which is precisely what I'll make next. Once I've completed this practice house, that is; I'll be making a model of the Snowcap Inn for my TV segment." She leaned toward me and whispered, "Mine will be a lot cuter than Chiffon's original."

"I don't doubt that for a moment." The only part of Chiffon's design that I'd liked—the sleigh—had been hauled away as evidence. My spirits sagged. I needed a quick diversion. "You use a thick cardboard pattern to cut out the dough before it goes into the oven, I see."

"Right. But I still need to do some trimming and fine-tuning," she replied. "It's best to do that while the gingerbread is still warm."

While I watched, she cut out a semicircle window in the attic. "I like to use Life Savers to make colored glass for the windows. I just melt them on waxed paper, and fasten that to the inside walls behind the window cutouts."

"That'll be adorable. I just hope it doesn't give Chiffon any ideas. Before we know it, she'll be fastening colored plastic wrap to our windows."

Audrey had no comment, absorbed as she was in cutting out a second semicircle window in the opposite wall. I glanced at her recipe card and asked, "How do you actually fasten the sides together?"

"With frosting. I pipe it on just like a thick bead of glue from a glue gun. But first, I put all of the pieces together for a trial assembly. To make sure everything fits before I turn off the oven, et cetera. And, since you're here, you can help support the sides now while I check everything."

I dutifully supported the outsides of the walls while she made some minor adjustments here and there, including carefully shaving off the occasional rough spot on an edge. Then she held the two slanted A-frame roof pieces on top.

"Looks good," she said.

"You're being too modest. It's adorable! It's going to be the perfect witch's cottage from 'Hansel and Gretel.'"

"You can let the sides lie flat again now."

I did so gladly, relieved that they hadn't crumbled in my hands. "I have to admit, I've never been all that much into baking," I remarked. "I don't think I could do this."

"Oh, sure you could, if you wanted to." Audrey grinned at me. "The success of a gingerbread house is really contingent on the icing. You just have to use the icing bags with the right tips. I find it's easier to lay the pieces out flat and decorate them first, and then assemble them. I use toothpicks a lot to help correct errors in my frosting designs. Sometimes I use a wet paintbrush and paint the dyed frosting on." She started to expertly decorate the front of her house even as we spoke. I mused to myself that, once Mikara realized how good Audrey was at this sort of thing, Mikara would beg *her* to serve as the breakfast/pastry chef for the inn.

"Where did you get the gingerbread recipe?"

"Oh, just online. There are a ton of sites with recipes and construction tips. I got a great suggestion from one . . . to cover ice-cream cones in dark green frosting to look like fir trees. And to use the sections of graham crackers as shutters. I'm also going to build a snowman out of marshmallows . . . with pretzel sticks for arms."

"And with peppercorns as its eyes and its semicircle smile?" I asked. "Ooh, and an orange sprinkle for its nose!"

"Is that your way of volunteering to help me?" Audrey asked.

"Sure. As long as I don't have to appear on your television show, or do any of the actual baking or frosting."

"Don't worry. I'll have the sides all ready to go in another twenty minutes, tops. I'm just going to have you hold them together while the frosting solidifies."

I grimaced. "Gee, Audrey. Are you sure my degree from Parsons School for Design is enough training for me to hold gingerbread walls steady?"

"Yes, and in the meantime, I'll let you look through the jar of sprinkles for the snowman's orange nose," Audrey retorted, without a hint of irony.

Chapter 24

Steve joined Audrey and me in the kitchen while we were putting the final touches on her gingerbread house. Although she'd done everything else herself, Audrey had eventually ceded control of the marshmallow snowman to me. When our work was complete, I sat down next to Steve at the kitchen table. He paused from eating his wheat flakes long enough to whisper in my ear that the snowman was his favorite design element, which, however silly, made me happy.

"I meant to ask you last night," Audrey said to me,

bringing her steaming cup of coffee to the table, "what did Sheriff Mackey have to say about your skis?"

"He postulated that I could have booby-trapped them myself, and then he asked Steve if *he'd* done it. He didn't even take the skis in as evidence."

Audrey rolled her eyes. "Erin, you and I need to put our heads together and solve this case ourselves."

"You're right," I replied casually. "Mackey couldn't solve a simple math equation."

"Excellent!" Audrey cried. "Let's start today!"

"Seriously?"

Beside me, Steve stopped eating mid-bite.

"Of course," she went on. "You've done this before. You *always* get the culprit. You're an unstoppable force. If you ever get bored with interior design, you should consider advertising your skills in criminal investigations. You should be a paid professional." She paused. "A professional *sleuth*, that is."

I glanced at Steve, who clearly did not appreciate Audrey's little motivational speech. "Since you two are deputizing each other, what do you want *me* to do?" Steve snapped. "Act as your muscle?"

"Excellent suggestion," Audrey replied. "Dress in solid black and wear shades at all times. You can lurk behind us everywhere we go."

Steve glowered into his bowl and resumed eating, spooning up the cereal with a vengeance. Despite his negative reaction, I was quickly warming to the idea of poking into Snowcap's past with Audrey. Maybe both Ben's and Mikara's hostility toward Henry were linked to Angie's murder, and Cam had uncovered a murder clue that cost him his life.

"Actually, Steve," I said gently, "the inspector's scheduled to come out tomorrow morning to reexamine the wheelchair ramp. Could you double-check the specs against Ben's work to make sure it will pass this time?"

He shifted his angry eyes to me. "In other words, you want me to do your work while you go off and play amateur detective with Audrey?"

"Just for a couple of hours this afternoon."

"You nearly broke your neck skiing, thanks to the killer still running around loose! Tell you what, *you* stay here, treat the ramp measurements like we're trying to pass a NASA inspection for a space launch, and *I'll* go try and catch a killer with Audrey."

"You're trying to protect Erin. That's sweet," Audrey said, patting Steve's hand. "She's really got her hands full this morning, so she deserves to get out of the house this afternoon. She's covering a wall in cloth, and we—"

"Wait," Steve said and turned toward me. "We already painted the accent wall in our bedroom. You're not applying the ten lords a-leaping toile fabric as if it were wallpaper, are you?" Although his brow was furrowed, he sounded more curious than anything else.

"No, I'm making panels," I answered. "Ben's making the frames for me. Then I'm going to hang them like large pictures. They should each come out to be about five feet tall and three or four feet wide. I hope to get four male dancers in one frame and three dancers each in two of the frames, but the fabric is sixty inches wide to start with. I just know that two frames with five dancers apiece won't work. I might even have to do five frames with two leaping lords each."

"So you're putting sections of fabric into picture frames? Under glass?" Audrey asked.

"No. I'll wrap the fabric around the frame, and staple it to the back side."

"Well, getting back to our plans for the day," she said, returning her attention to Steve, "all I had in mind for Erin and me this afternoon was to do some research under the guise of Christmas shopping downtown."

"Research while shopping?" Steve rose and brought his cereal bowl to the sink.

"Precisely," she replied. "We'll casually ask some shop owners about their relationships with our associates at the inn. This is strictly women's work, Steve."

Steve grimaced. "It doesn't sound like anything I'd be much help with. I will say that."

Whereas it sounds like a perfect afternoon to me. Gossip and shopping? Woo-hoo!

"When is Ben supposed to build these frames for you?" Steve asked me.

I glanced at the clock and cursed to myself. I'd somehow lost an hour in the process of building a marshmallow snowman and holding up gingerbread walls. "Five minutes from now. I really wanted to have figured out my precise dimensions by then."

"I'll give you a hand," he said.

I grabbed a pair of large T-squares, and he helped me unfurl the fabric in the central hall, where there was plenty of floor space.

"These frames are going on the wall across from our bed?" he asked.

"Right." He knew that already, which meant he had an objection, but I didn't want to hear it; I was busy trying to picture the finished wall hangings. We'd already painted that wall in our bedroom a complementary gray-blue, and I'd managed to match one of the pattern's accent colors to that exact hue.

Audrey, curious to see the fabric herself, had followed us and said with a smile, "These are scenes from *The Nutcracker Suite*, right?"

"Yeah."

"That's wonderful! Doubly appropriate for Christmas! Now you've got the typical holiday ballet, *plus* the ten lords a-leaping."

"Which makes it doubly seasonal, though," I said. "I wanted to be sure to attach the fabric on easily movable frames. Come May or June, Mikara can remove them, or we could replace the fabric with something summery. Or Steve and I could come back and switch them out every season, which would be good for our job security."

"Erin, for the time being," Steve interjected, "we're just concentrating on pulling off the Twelve Days theme and opening the doors Christmas Eve without any more fatalities."

That afternoon, Audrey and I parked in the lot just out-side of town, then walked toward Main Street. I was struck once again by how truly lovely this mountain town was. Truth be told, I sympathized with the Snowcap natives. I could easily imagine how frustrating it must have felt to have this pretty, cozy community change so rapidly and so drastically.

"Let's begin by discussing our game plan," Audrey said, "over a hot toddy." She gestured at the pub across the street.

I shivered from a chill unrelated to the brisk wintry breeze. "I'm up for the hot toddy, but let's go someplace else. I went there with Cameron. The night that Angie was killed."

Audrey ushered me toward a second bar. My mood had darkened. Here I'd been treating this afternoon like it was just another happy little excursion with Audrey, but all the while, two people were dead. I was also being inconsiderate to Steve; my fabric panels had taken longer to construct than I'd anticipated, so I'd selfishly allowed him to add hanging the panels in our bedroom to his to-do list. Not to mention preparing for tomorrow's building inspection.

With a purposefulness that I didn't share, Audrey entered the old-time bar—mahogany wainscot paneling and forest green walls extending up to the hammered-copper ceiling—strode across the room, and claimed a booth. Never having been here, I stopped just inside the door to study a display of a dozen black-and-white photographs of Snowcap Village.

The oldest photo had been taken eighty years ago; downtown had consisted of five wood buildings with an Old West flavor to them. I was startled to spot a second picture of what must have been three generations of Goodwin and Orlin men. According to the card below the picture, it had been taken nearly forty years ago in front of "the Goodwin estate." Two elderly gentlemen were centered in the foreground, flanked by younger-looking men who, judging by strong family resemblances, could only be their sons. Two five- or six-year-old boys, one beaming and one frowning, were standing in front of their fathers. I didn't need to refer to the caption to know that the happy boy was Henry Goodwin and the sad one was Ben Orlin.

As I slid into the seat across from Audrey, she said, "I ordered us both hot cocoas with a shot of schnapps."

"Sounds good."

"We need to know what caused the extreme bad will that could give someone a motive for two murders," Audrey told me with the same matter-of-fact tone she'd used to inform me of our drink order.

"One obvious source of bad feelings is Wendell Barton buying the mountain and the inn. But for someone to actually take another person's life . . . the offense has to be deeply personal. Personal enough that the killer felt that his or her life was destroyed by the victim . . . or *would* be destroyed in the future, if the victim continued to live."

"Which is why Wendell makes such a weak suspect," Audrey said. "He's King of the Hill. He didn't even *know* Angie Woolf. Neither Angie nor Cameron had the ability to destroy Wendell's life."

I held my tongue, but in fact, I suspected Angie or Cameron might have easily possessed some piece of evidence of wrongdoings on Wendell's part that could have knocked him clear off his mountain. "For now," I said, "we should concentrate on looking into Angie's past. She grew up with Mikara, Henry, and Ben. She might have done something hurtful to one of them a long time ago."

We paused as a waitress delivered our drinks. "I learned that Ben's father blamed Ben for Henry's teenage pranks involving the town's nativity scenes," I then told Audrey. "And last night, I saw him staring up at Steve's and my window from the front lawn."

"He was staring at your window?!"

"Yes, and it creeped me out, but maybe he's an insomniac and just happened to be looking up at the house, or at Chiffon's horrible decorations." I took a sip of my spiked hot chocolate, which was delicious.

"Maybe Ben and Angie used to date in high school," Audrey suggested, "or there was some other tempestuous personal history between them. But even if there was, we still have to wonder why Cameron was also killed. Could he have witnessed something?"

"No, he was with me all evening. If he'd seen something suspicious earlier that afternoon, he'd have told me or the authorities about it."

"Unless Cameron was keeping quiet to protect you. Maybe he caught Ben in the act of tampering with your skis, for example, and tried to stop him, but Ben overpowered him."

"I'd hate to think that Ben had any reason to want to kill me."

"*Somebody* did," Audrey stated.

"I'm starting to like Chiffon's theory suddenly... that my skis were merely mistaken for hers." I sighed and muttered, "Although it's pretty unlikely my eggnog would have been mistaken for hers."

"There was friction between Angie and Mikara due to Mikara accepting the job at the inn," Audrey said. "We know Mikara used to work at the art gallery. That's a perfect place to investigate while pretending to be shopping."

Twenty minutes later, we were studying the artwork in the two-room gallery. We were the only patrons, although a family of four was leaving as we entered.

"Oh, look, Audrey!" I said, pointing at a small, framed oil painting. "This is the perfect picture for the kitchen! See that woman carrying a pail? She could easily be a milkmaid. Now I won't have to decoupage the tray."

"Wonderful! We'll be able to charge the purchase to the inn, even," Audrey replied, grinning at me.

The word "purchase" drew the immediate attention of one of the two sixtyish women behind the counter. She approached us, smiling, and said, "You're Audrey Munroe, from the *Domestic Bliss* show. I'm one of your biggest fans! I made us get a TiVo, just so I would never miss your show."

"Oh, thank you! You've totally made my day!"

"I'm Mildred, and this is my sister, Carol."

At her name being mentioned, the second owner, a dyed blonde, rounded the counter to join us.

"Nice to meet you both," Audrey said. "This is Erin. She's an absolutely brilliant interior designer."

"Audrey's flattering me, of course. It's nice to meet you, Mildred and Carol."

"I'm sure a little extra praise is welcome these days,"

Carol replied. "Mildred and I are well aware of all the terrible times you've been having at the Goodwin house."

"I understand Mikara used to work here, before she came to the inn," Audrey said before I could reply. "So you must have known her sister, Angie, too."

"Yes," they both said in unison.

"Poor thing," Mildred added. "She'd pulled herself back together after her divorce."

"Let's not gossip with our customers," Carol scolded. "So were you just looking for the one painting today?"

"Oh, no, not necessarily," Audrey said. "We might need lots and lots of pieces!"

Audrey proceeded to explain about the milkmaids, and I added that, technically, I was now down to looking only for drummers, although I thought I'd check for Steve's sake to see if they had any particularly eye-catching ballerinas for the library. I'd checked his notes earlier today and knew he'd only purchased six lady dancers so far.

"Has your gallery been here since before the resort opened?" I asked.

"Yes," Mildred said. "We're hanging in there. All of us business owners incorrectly assumed our profits would go up with the influx of yuppie skiers." Her eyes widened and she hastened to add, "No offense, Erin."

"None taken. I'm certainly a young, urban professional, but my skiing days might already be history."

"She took a nasty spill yesterday," Audrey explained. "Erin and I are always anxious to support the local businesses. It's unfortunate that so many of the original owners in Snowcap apparently didn't do well after the ski resort opened."

"For what it's worth," I added, "my business partner and I try to buy from local merchants whenever possible." I glanced in the back room and saw stacks of paintings leaning against the wall. "Is there any chance you might have some pictures of drummers?"

"We have at least one," Carol said. "I remember getting in an acrylic depicting a little drummer boy."

"I'd also like to buy some blown glass for my bedroom," Audrey said. "Did you know the Woolf sisters well?" Not a particularly deft segue, I mused to myself.

"Oh, yes," Mildred replied. "They grew up just down the block from us. We used to say that those two were going to be best friends for their entire lives. Which is why I think it was all the more heartbreaking that *Angie* wound up being the reason that Mikara's and Henry's wedding was cancelled."

Chapter 25

Did Angie and Henry have an affair?" Audrey asked.

"That's what *I've* always suspected," Carol said, exchanging glances with Mildred. "Mikara never said that directly, though. But it was pretty much implied."

"Personally," Mildred interjected, "I don't think those two actually slept together. I always figured it was just Angie being Angie, acting like she knew better than Mikara about who she should marry, and then—"

"And then *Angie* was the one who wound up marrying a good-for-nothing drunkard and bully," Carol scoffed.

"So," Mildred continued, "when Angie's hubby was out of town on a fishing trip, she set out to prove to her sister that Henry was incapable of being faithful."

"Angie and Henry went either all the way or just part of the way," Carol said, "but, in any case, Angie made a point of being seen all about the town on Henry's arm." She indicated Mildred with her chin. "We spotted 'em ourselves at the church bazaar. They were being all kissy-face at a fund-raiser in the morning, just in case Mikara missed hearing about Angie and Henry's escapades the night before."

"Such as how she'd been sitting in his lap at a corner table at The Nines," Mildred added bitterly.

"That couldn't have sat well with Angie's husband when he got back into town," I said.

"I'm sure it didn't," Mildred agreed. "But that marriage was on the skids from the time it started."

"They got married because Angie was pregnant," Carol explained. "But she lost the baby."

"Angie told me a couple of years ago that she thinks it was her depression over that loss that led her to have a fling with Henry," Mildred said. "Although she still claims she really only had Mikara's best interests in mind."

"Maybe that's the truth, too," Carol said. "She's gone now. I'd like to think the best of her."

"Oh, absolutely. The poor thing. Angie claimed she sincerely wanted to protect Mikara from marrying the wrong man . . . from making the same mistake she'd made." Mildred sighed. "She dropped Henry immediately after he and Mikara broke up. I guess Angie truly felt she'd only acted on her sister's behalf. At the time."

For the first time since Audrey and I first opened the floodgates of the Snowcap Rumor Mill, the gallery owners paused.

"How long was it till Angie and Mikara became close again?" Audrey asked.

"Three, four years later?" Carol said tentatively, looking to Mildred, who nodded.

"Their mother had gotten breast cancer around that time," Mildred continued. "She died two years later. Both girls moved back home and took turns caring for her. They vowed to set their differences aside for the mom's sake."

"And managed the feat admirably," Carol chimed in.

"Right. I think their whole ordeal kept them too preoccupied to object when Wendell opened the ski resort, even though our town changed so dramatically."

"Till they also lost the house they'd grown up in, that is." Carol grimaced and shook her head.

"When Wendell bought it and tore it down?" I asked.

Mildred nodded. "He bought up all the houses near the base of the mountain, where he wanted to put his condos. And *that* was when Angie and Mikara started fighting again."

"Mikara and Angie were the last holdouts," Carol added, "but Wendell just built right around their property. It looked god-awful, seeing their little bungalow on its quarter-acre lot, surrounded on all sides by three-story condos. Then Angie caved."

"According to Mikara," Mildred countered. "I'm not so sure Mikara wasn't the first to actually decide to take the money."

"It's hard to say. Mikara took the job at the inn, which paid better than Mildred and I could. She claimed she needed the money because Angie's too-low settlement with Wendell had made it impossible for her to move out. She couldn't afford the rent on a one-bedroom place, and the rent on the two-bedroom apartment they shared kept skyrocketing. Once Mikara took the job at the inn, Angie said she'd never forgive her for joining forces with the enemy."

"Or words to that effect," Mildred muttered.

"Do you think Mikara could have killed her own sister?"

Carol answered "No," just as Mildred said, "Never."

"They were going to reconcile again eventually," Mildred said. "Angie and Mikara were different sides of the same coin."

Carol was nodding. "Mikara didn't hesitate to make amends with her sister when their mom was dying, and they'd each leave chicken soup and such for the other when one of them was sick, even when they were at each other's throats otherwise."

"Family ties are strong," Mildred said, nodding in synchronization with her sister.

"If anything, I think Henry was even angrier at Angie than Mikara was," Carol said. "She showed the whole town what an ass he was."

"Yet he was elected mayor," I pointed out.

"His competition was a former socialite from Denver who lived in Bartonville. That's what we locals call the condo development." Carol paused, then said, "No offense," to Audrey.

"None taken. Contrary to what you might have heard, Wendell and I are not an item. We're just casually dating. Plus, I'm well aware of how badly he's alienated the townspeople. The man can be quite the horse's derriere."

Mildred chuckled, and Carol said, "No kidding," under her breath.

"Aren't you suspicious about Mikara's guilt, considering that Angie died on Henry's property?" Audrey asked. "And that she'd argued with Mikara about starting work there?"

"That's made me suspect Henry," Mildred said, "but not Mikara. We've known Mikara her whole life. She's not a killer." Carol nodded.

"I have to say," Audrey interjected, "I really like Henry. As far as I can tell, he seems like a nice person. Maybe he hides a Mr. Hyde–like monster, but he seems compassionate and thoughtful to me. Although maybe I'd feel differently if I'd lived here and known him from when he was just a boy."

"Not necessarily," Mildred said. "He's a charming man and can be both thoughtful and compassionate. Yet, other times, he's so self-serving that he forgets about everyone else's feelings."

The bell above the door jingled as two women entered the store. Mildred went over to greet them. Carol snorted. "Listen to us, gossiping away, like we had nothing better to do."

I would have loved to hear what else Carol and Mildred had to say, but the new customers made it impossible for us to continue our private conversation. "Can you show me that painting of the drummer boy?" I asked Carol.

En route to the back room, Audrey selected a lovely indigo hand-blown glass vase, which delayed us for a few minutes. To my delight, though, not only was the drummer boy painting charming, but we also found an affecting photograph of three uniformed members of a drum line, shrouded in shadows as if marching bravely out of the darkness. Plus, I found a whimsical contemporary sculpture of a drummer made from recycled parts of a clock, which allowed me to cross off the Energizer Bunny from the bottom of my list—a desperation item I knew I could find at a toy store if push came to shove. I'd found five of my twelve drummers in one store!

Audrey praised the photograph, then said, "I suppose these boys are actually in a high-school marching band." Then she turned to Carol and said, "Angie used to date Ben Orlin in high school, right?"

Carol laughed. "Who told you that?"

Audrey looked at me for help, but I gestured with my chin for her to go ahead. She'd wandered onto a limb, and she was going to have to find her own way back.

"It was just a general impression I got from everyone's interactions, I guess," Audrey said, admirably bailing herself out. "Why? Was I mistaken?"

"Ben is gay."

"He is?" I asked, surprised.

"Yes, although he's never been flamboyant or outspoken about it," Carol replied. "I think he's pretty much decided to never search for a life partner. You know, his dad used to actively keep him away from boys his age. In my opinion, Ben's never come to terms with his homosexuality." Carol forced a smile. "Shall I ring you up, or do you want to look for turtledoves and such?"

"Just the drummers and the one milkmaid," I replied. "Thanks."

"The art glass will have to be on a separate tab," Audrey said.

The three of us returned to the front room. As if thinking aloud, Carol muttered, "That Angie sure used to tease Ben mercilessly. She called him 'Ben-Gay,' like the muscle-ache cream. Some people are just so narrow-minded."

Audrey and I carried our purchases toward the parking lot. We were silent for a minute or two, privately mulling what we'd just heard. Ben, Henry, and Mikara all had reasons to kill Angie. While the gallery owners felt their former employee was incapable of killing her own sister, Mikara had good reason for bottled rage. Angie could easily have pushed her over the top the night of the murder by engaging her in a bitter argument about Henry. Mikara could have spotted Angie by the bridge and stuck on Ben's boots to disguise her tracks in the snow.

As for one of the suspects also killing Cameron, he made enemies easily with his arrogant bossiness. He could have said the wrong thing about Angie's death and made the killer panic.

"I have to tell you, Erin," Audrey said, jarring me from my reverie, "this business of ferreting out a killer isn't as fun in actuality as it is in theory."

"I could have told you as much." In truth, I *had* told her that, more than once.

"The shopping part was enjoyable, though. In between hearing those depressing stories from the past. We might not have gotten anywhere as far as ruling out any suspects, but at least we have one milkmaid and five drummers. I'll bet we can find a retro store someplace that sells Ringo bobble-head dolls."

I laughed. "And Ringo will blend in so perfectly with religious little-drummer-boy scenes."

"Which reminds me, Erin. There is that wonderful—" She broke off as she gazed straight ahead of us. "Oh, look!" She smiled. "Here comes Wendell."

Wendell Barton was indeed heading in our direction, but he seemed to be absorbed in his own world. His own *hostile* world. His fists and jaw were clenched, his brow was furrowed, and he had a purposeful stride, oblivious to his surroundings.

"Hi, Wendell," Audrey said as he drew close.

He stopped and looked at us in surprise. "Audrey. Hello."

"You look like you're on your way to wring somebody's neck," Audrey said.

He was clearly embarrassed at her catching him in this mood. He tried to force a smile. The effect was more of a grimace than anything else. "No, I'm...sorry. I was just..." He gave her a peck on the cheek, although, again, in his unpleasant mood, it seemed artificial and almost obligatory—as though he was bussing the cheek of his difficult cousin.

"As the expression goes," Audrey said, "are you trying to

drain the swamp, and finding yourself up to your elbows in alligators?"

"Yeah, that's a good way of summing it up." Wendell sighed. He finally shifted his vision to me and said, "Hi, Erin."

"Good afternoon, Wendell."

"I don't know where my head is. I almost brushed right past you lovely ladies." He shook his head. "There's no excuse for that. I apologize."

"What's wrong?" Audrey asked.

He rubbed his forehead, looking truly pained. "You don't want to know, Audrey. Trust me."

"Sure I do." She gave me a little glance. "Erin and I aren't in a rush. We could take a quick coffee break and chat for a while."

"Oh, that's all right..." Despite his demurral, Wendell's eyes had lit up at Audrey's suggestion.

"Sometimes it helps immeasurably to see one's troubles from a different perspective." Audrey was slipping into her TV personality—the advice-giving domestic goddess role.

Wendell glanced at me and seemed to lose enthusiasm for the coffee break idea. "Thanks for the offer. I've just got...business troubles. Like the saying goes: It's a dog-eat-dog world out here. I always knew that. And yet...the truth is, even after all these years of running my own company, it never fails to take me by surprise when *I'm* the one getting bitten."

Chapter 26

I'm sorry to hear that you're having a tough time, my dear," Audrey told Wendell. "Where are you heading? Are we making you late for a meeting?"

"No, thank god. I've had quite enough meetings for one day." His smile was starting to look more sincere. "Actually, I was heading downtown in general . . . hoping to clear my head and maybe do some Christmas shopping, if the spirit moved me."

"I'm almost always in the shopping spirit," Audrey said cheerfully. She turned toward me. "And you are, too, right, Erin?"

"Absolutely, but then, I shop for furnishings and accessories for a living."

"That's true," Audrey said with a chuckle. "Your *not* wanting to shop would be the equivalent of a writer getting writer's block."

"Or of your getting camera-shy," Wendell returned to Audrey, just as I was about to say the same thing. That was a little icky; I'd hate to start discovering commonalities at this point. Despite what we'd learned from the gallery owners, Wendell Barton was still a prime suspect in my mind. His underhanded relationship with Sheriff Mackey alone made me deeply uncomfortable. Especially while watching him flirt with my beloved friend.

"Erin and I were about to go back to the inn," Audrey said. "Are you sure things are okay with you?"

Wendell made sad puppy-dog eyes at her, which instantaneously repulsed me. "If I said no and that I'd like your company, would you spend the rest of the day with me?"

"Actually, Audrey," I said, intent at preventing her from saying yes, "I need your help. Steve and I should really get your approval on our Christmas décor in the twelve rooms. We're nearly finished." No way was I leaving Audrey alone with Wendell if I had any say in the matter. At least not when he struck me as having an unhealthy dose of anger simmering.

Audrey arched her brow as she looked at me—not a good thing—but said, "Well, there goes that idea, Wendell. I'll call you soon, though."

"That's fine, dear." Audrey and Wendell gave each other an affectionate hug, which made me cringe. It hit me that Steve, when he'd watched me with Cam, must have felt even worse than I did now, seeing Audrey and Wendell together—seemingly charmed by a man we suspected of murder.

Wendell continued downtown alone. As we neared Audrey's car, she said, "I know you think he might be a murderer, Erin, but you're wrong. I'm a better judge of character than you are. For one thing, I've been around longer than you have. And for another, I've been around *him* much longer than you have."

"But he has a lot riding on the inn, Audrey. You heard him yourself just now—he's got 'business troubles,' and he's probably referring to the inn."

"All the more reason he wouldn't want his right-hand man to die. Cameron took care of things for him."

I shook my head. "But they'd been arguing. You saw that for yourself during our fancy lunch. They could have had a complete rift, for all we know."

Audrey unlocked her car and, as if her glass vase were made of plastic, tossed her bag onto the backseat. I carefully set my bags by my feet as I slipped into the passenger side. She got behind the wheel and donned her sunglasses. Her lips remained in a firm line the entire time.

"I've obviously upset you, Audrey, and I'm sorry. We'll let it drop... until I uncover some evidence that indicates he's guilty."

"Thank you," she replied. "I guess."

I should have said *unless* instead of *until*.

Her face was still set in a scowl by the time we'd pulled into traffic. The tension between us was palpable.

Using the only tension breaker that came to mind, I sang out cheerfully, " 'On the first day of Christmas—'"

To my relief, Audrey laughed.

Henry and Mikara were in the kitchen, making lasagna for dinner when we arrived. We were showing them our purchases when Steve joined us. After a minute or two of chitchat, I asked how the leaping-lords wall hangings looked.

He made a wavering gesture with his hand. "They're in our room, but we didn't actually get them installed."

"Why not?"

"Ben had some other jobs to handle that took precedence." Sullivan wasn't quite meeting my eyes. Something was up. "So I told him I'd hang the panels myself. Then I couldn't find the recharger for the battery in my drill."

"There's a drill in the garage," Mikara said.

Ignoring her, I said to Sullivan, "But Ben and I spent a lot of time making those panels this morning. They were ready to be hung when I left." He furrowed his brow. *He's making excuses, probably because he doesn't like my leaping-lords design.* I had a vague recollection of feeling guilty about making Sullivan do my work for me, but now I bristled at the possibility that he didn't think my work was up to snuff. "It would have only taken Ben another fifteen minutes to finish the job completely."

Sullivan shrugged. "And it'll just take me fifteen minutes to hang the panels tomorrow morning. Once I get a drill with a good battery."

"I'm pretty sure the battery's charged up and ready to go," Henry said. "And I've got some small drill bits out there, too, that you can borrow. They're in a plastic container, hanging from the Peg-Board."

"I'll go get them now, and we can finish the wall hangings tonight. I want to start crossing things off my list." I started to head for the door.

"I'll go with you," Steve said, "and we can talk some more about this list of yours."

We donned our coats in the mudroom. He held the outer door for me. As I brushed past him, I said, "You're joining me so that you can tell me privately you hate my leaping lords, right?"

"There's nothing wrong with the lords themselves. But we're going to have to hang them somewhere else. They don't work in our bedroom."

"What do you mean, they 'don't work'? Are they not leaping high enough?" I sniped. "Are they suddenly not pointing their toes?"

"I like the fabric you picked out, but the room is out of harmony, no matter where we hang the panels."

"But... they were going to really pop against the blue-gray color I painted the wall."

"Yeah, that's another thing I wanted to discuss. When I saw the panels weren't right for that wall, the paint wasn't right, either. I repainted it aubergine, like we'd originally discussed."

I whirled around to face him, although it had grown so dark that I couldn't see his features. "Please tell me you're kidding! That you didn't just arbitrarily overrule me on my room design and paint my wall eggplant!"

He shook his head. "There was nothing arbitrary about it, Gilbert! The fabric panels are wrong for that room. I asked Ben his opinion, and he agreed with me."

I marched over to the garage door keypad, distracted and annoyed, unable to remember the combination. "Oh, well, then, the panels *must* be all wrong then, if the *builder* doesn't care for the *fabric*."

"Speaking of fabric, the aubergine makes the comforter look like it was woven from pure, twenty-four karat gold strands."

"So the bedspread now looks as hard as a chunk of metal?" I cursed in silence, wondering if the combination could have been a four-letter word.

"You forgot to ask Henry for the combination to open the garage door, didn't you?" Steve asked.

"I didn't think I needed to ask, because they told it to us when we first started, and you programmed it into your cell phone." That memory brought back another one. "And I remember the code was a mnemonic for Henry's name." I keyed in the number equivalent for H-A-N-K, just as Steve looked it up on his phone and read out the digits to me. "Never mind," I said as the door opened. The bright overhead light automatically came on as well.

"You don't need to get crabby," Steve snapped while we waited for the rumbling door to open fully. "It's not my fault the panels don't look good."

"They were *my* panels, and you might have been wrong about them! But now that you've painted the wall a completely different color, they're guaranteed not to look good!"

"I've got more than ten years of experience working in this field, Gilbert, and I'm telling you right—"

"Just because you're four years older than me, Sullivan, and have been at this for four years longer, doesn't mean you've always got better judgment than I do!"

"Did you lean the panels against the wall before you left? Or pin the fabric up to see how it looked in the room before you made the panels?"

"Well...no," I admitted. In retrospect, my not temporarily fastening the fabric to the wall had been a horrendous oversight. The fabric had arrived the morning we'd discovered Cam's body, though; I hadn't been in my right mind. "I'm not saying that I'm necessarily right. Just that *you're* wrong."

I spotted the battery-powered drill resting on two pegs and started to head toward it.

"Wait here. *I'll* get the drill." He brushed past me.

"What? Now you don't trust me with a carpentry tool?"

"With Mackey dogging you, I'd rather not have your fingerprints on it. Even if I'm *wrong* about your damned panels."

"You're bound to be a bigger suspect in Cam's murder than I am."

A heel print in the center of the two-port garage, between Mikara's banged-up silver sedan and Henry's red pickup, had captured my attention, distracting me from Sullivan. I walked over to it and crouched down for a closer look. A muddy imprint had been made by a man's very expensive shoe.

"Erin?" Sullivan sounded worried. He must have assumed I'd stormed back to the house, or fainted the instant his back was turned.

"Over here," I replied. "Do you own a pair of Gucci loafers?"

"No, but if you're thinking about Christmas presents, I wear a size eleven." He rounded the front of the pickup to join me.

"This is a shoeprint from a Gucci heel. I've noticed that both Cameron and Wendell wear Guccis frequently. But why would either of them have been in Henry's garage?"

"Beats me." He, too, studied the mark on the concrete floor. "Maybe Henry owns a pair of really nice shoes. But, even if he *doesn't*, he sometimes leaves the garage door open. All this means is that Cam or Wendell might have been looking around in the garage."

"And that Cameron might have been in here shortly before he was killed. His car was parked right next to the garage that night."

"Enough said. Let's take a look around to see if we can spot anything that might have drawn Cameron's or Wendell's attention. Or that proves Cameron was in here." He strode over to the controls next to the side door and pressed the button, lowering the garage door. "I'm closing this so nobody can look out the window and see us rummaging around."

Our hunt for generic evidence was probably a wild-goose chase, but then Mackey and his men were so inept they probably hadn't thought to search this space. I watched the door descend, blocking our view of the illuminated windows in the house. "We were supposedly just retrieving the drill. They'll think it's strange of us to close ourselves up in here."

"I'm sure they'll assume we had a sudden urge for privacy," he said. "After *they* see how bad those fabric panels look in our bedroom, I mean. That's when they'll realize we must be out here arguing about where to hang your leaping lords."

"Such a comedian," I snapped. "You'd better switch on the overhead, or the light will time out in a couple of minutes."

"Good point." He returned to the side door to operate the push button for the interior light. He hesitated and muttered, "That's odd." He turned the doorknob and opened the door. "Apparently Henry not only leaves the garage door up a lot of the time, but he also leaves the side door unlocked."

"He must assume nobody could find anything worth stealing within this mess."

The back and sides of the garage were jam-packed with useless odds and ends—lawn chairs with rotted webbing, rusted pipe fittings, old warped boards, mildewed sports equipment, and so on. It would have been optimistic to term our search "a needle in a haystack"; we didn't even know if there was a needle to be found. Rationalizing that the heel print was pointing toward the middle of the back wall, that's where we started. We then each worked our way toward the front along opposite walls.

A few minutes later, after we'd both made it about a third of the way along the side walls, Steve said, "Jeez." I immediately stopped rifling through a musty box of old paperbacks and joined him. He shoved aside a piece of plywood and lifted out a brown leather satchel. "Does this look familiar?" he asked.

"Yeah. I'm pretty sure I saw that in Cameron's car when we went out for dinner. In any case, it certainly doesn't belong out here. For one thing, it isn't covered in grime."

Steve carefully set the case on the hood of Henry's pickup truck and removed a stack of loose papers from the main compartment—twenty or so sheets.

"Give me half of them to look at," I said.

"No. You aren't wearing gloves. I am."

"Well, then spread them out on the hood, so I can read without actually touching them."

Steve followed my instructions and laid out half a dozen pages for me to examine. After just a minute of rapid reading, I cried, "Oh, my god! These are copies of letters Cameron sent to some company in Denver. Cameron was planning to purchase the inn himself after it failed! And here's a printout of a series of e-mails." I skimmed it in silence, then said, "Cameron describes how he would ensure the inn's failure by bribing the building inspector. He wanted to prevent the Snowcap Inn from opening till after ski season, when lodging rates drop exponentially. *Then* he planned to bribe the restaurant inspectors so that the kitchen couldn't operate."

"Jeez," Sullivan said. "That's even worse than what I'd suspected he was up to."

"I don't believe it. Cameron wouldn't do this. And it's just too convenient. The briefcase . . . his plans all spelled out like this. Someone must have forged his signature and made him the fall guy."

Steve was reading a paper in his hands. "Sounds like the ultimate goal would be to raze the entire Goodwin estate and erect hundreds of condos in its place. Cameron planned—" Steve paused. "If this is authentic, within the next five years Cameron intended to build a second resort in direct competition with Wendell's. He was sinking millions into buying up all that property on the southern face of the mountain."

Mikara had predicted that would happen all along— that this irreplaceable historical building, the Goodwin estate, was going to get flattened in favor of condos. "Wendell was probably backing the venture," I said. "Cameron could have been acting on Wendell's behalf, just like always."

"Maybe." Steve's skepticism was evident in his voice. And for good reason; I was grasping at straws. The letter had plainly stated that Cameron, not Wendell, would be the new owner of the inn and its surrounding acreage.

He reached into a second compartment and removed four or five sheets of graph paper. They were crudely drawn maps of the town and the existing resort, with the new resort and new condo development sketched in. In spite of myself, I recognized Cameron's handwriting. I glanced back at Sullivan, who was glaring at a sheet of paper in his hand.

"What's that you're reading?"

"Nothing. Just something that caught my eye." He hastily stuck it behind the other sheets of paper as he started to put everything back into the satchel.

"Why did it catch your eye?"

"The name 'Audrey Munroe' in the text leapt out at me."

"Let me read it."

He turned his shoulder to prevent me from taking the briefcase. "Just let it go, Erin."

"Steve, for heaven's sake! Now you've got me imagining things like pornographic pictures of myself!"

He sighed, pulled out the sheet of paper, and set it down on the hood of the truck so I could read it for myself. "I tried to warn you about him. Guys like Cameron don't bother to keep up the same façade they use on women when they're talking to other men."

My initial reaction was shock. In response to an e-mail from Wendell asking what he could do "to get this damned Goodwin guy to cave," Cameron had written:

No prob, W. If HG wants two "unbiased" copartners, get him some brainless bimbo. Snowcap's full of them. Tell HG you want to get a third partner from Crestview. I've got the perfect candidate. One of my ex-g's is living with Audrey Munroe. She's wealthy and busy with artsy-fartsy stuff and charity crap, and does a local *Martha Stewart Show* knockoff. Watch it a couple of times to get the drop on her. My ex-g has always been putty in my hands. *And* Audrey's a divorcée in her sixties. Putty in *your* hands!

Wendell had written in reply: "Perfect! We can double-date! When it comes to fixing a deal, you're pure genius!" Then Wendell had asked for contact information for Audrey.

My head was reeling. "Why would Cameron have printed out these e-mails in the first place? This has to be fake. It doesn't make any sense."

"Maybe you're right," Steve said, putting the e-mail printout into the satchel and clicking the clasp shut.

Despite my protests, the reality was sinking in. "Damn it! Cam often printed his e-mails when he was in college; he liked to always keep a paper trail. He didn't care a rat's ass about me or our memories. He just wanted to get his hands on this property. So he could raze the entire place. He could have been killed over a blackmail scheme that went bad. The killer could have stolen the briefcase from Cameron and threatened to reveal its contents unless Cam paid up. Or maybe Cam was late getting back from his date with Chiffon, and Wendell got his hands on Cam's briefcase in the meantime. He saw that Cam was double-crossing him. So Wendell lost his head and killed Cameron."

"Let's let Mackey deal with this," Steve said.

"You might as well have suggested we hand this over to Bozo the Clown." I felt overwhelmed. "I wish we'd never found the damned briefcase. Mackey's just going to twist things around to make it look like we planted it here."

"Maybe the killer *did* plant it here, assuming the sheriff and his men would search the garage. Does the wording sound like Cameron's?"

The question brought back a memory of meeting Cameron for the very first time. Three girlfriends and I had decided to try our hands at darts in a Manhattan pub one afternoon. We spotted Cameron across the room and agreed that he was the most spectacular-looking man we'd ever seen. Our conversation immediately turned to whether or not he was gay, but before I could cast my vote, he smiled at me and crossed the room. He asked if I was a student at Columbia, and I'd said no, Parsons. He rejoined: "Ah. The artsy-fartsy school."

Irked, I blew him off with a sharp reply. As I started to turn away, Cameron made a strange noise and clutched at his throat, alarming me; I remembered thinking at the time that something must have gotten lodged in his windpipe. He managed what appeared to be a painful breath, grabbed my hand, and said in a raspy voice, "I'm eating my words, and they were so bad, I'm choking on them. Forgive me, or I swear to you, I'll drop dead on this very spot."

The remark had been so corny that I'd laughed. Now the memory made me inexorably sad. My first love had been a horrible man. Never again would I be able to remember our good times without having them tainted by that realization.

I replied to Steve, "Yeah, it sounds just like him." I rubbed my forehead, wishing I could rub away my thoughts. "I think he schemed to get me and Audrey involved in the inn, in order to convince Henry to sell it to Wendell. Meanwhile, Cam was contriving to buy up the second half of the mountain himself. All so that he could make a big profit. Regardless of how many people he was stabbing in the back."

Chapter 27

Steve got the nonemergency number for the sheriff's office from information. "What's the name of that deputy?" he asked me as he waited for someone to answer.

"Penderson."

He nodded and said into the phone, "Could I speak to Deputy Penderson, please?" After listening to the dispatcher's response, he winced and said, "Fine, thanks." A few moments later, he was telling Mackey the gist of our discovery.

After hanging up, he said, "Mackey says we should stay put, and he'll be right out."

"He makes such a terrific authority figure." I tried to count to ten to quash my mounting resentment.

Sullivan dragged both hands through his hair, in a doubly strong tell for how great his own frustrations were. "At the party, Cameron told me that he was cooking up a venture of his own and was finally ready to be *The Man* himself."

"Meaning he was going to split from Wendell. And when Audrey and I ran into Wendell this afternoon, he was talking about his having been betrayed—saying business was a dog-eat-dog world, and so forth. He could have been pretending to have found out only just then about the extent of what Cameron had in the works. To make himself look innocent of Cameron's murder three nights ago."

"Cameron was a really fit guy. I don't see how Wendell could have overpowered him," Steve said.

"I think whoever killed him had to have caught Cameron by surprise . . . shoved him, so that he wound up facedown in the sleigh. Once he was down . . . and badly injured, he'd be unable to run into the house for help."

"Unless it was Chiffon, who'd lured him into the sleigh for some foreplay that went seriously afoul. But, yeah, Mikara, Ben, or Henry are all tall enough to have pushed him so that he could have toppled into the sleigh. And Wendell's burly enough."

The fact that I was spending a chunk of my evening closed up in a garage discussing the murder of my ex with my lover hit me. "We're never going to get past this, are we, Sullivan?" I said, suddenly feeling so crushed I could barely breathe.

"Get past Cameron's murder? Of course we are!"

"No, I mean all of it. Our clients getting us involved in murder cases. I had never known a single murder victim until you and I wound up vying over our room designs three years ago. It's like we've been cursed ever since."

"You feel cursed?"

"Yes! Don't you?"

"Quite the opposite." He was using his soft, sexy voice, but my sense of despair had taken root too deeply for me to snap out of this.

"I thought we'd broken the streak when we got together romantically, but now things are worse than ever. We've got a moron running this investigation. We could both wind up in prison for murders that we didn't commit, and we'll have to bribe our jailers just so we can pass each other notes through the bars of our tiny cells."

He caressed my arm. "Will these notes be love letters or design tips for sprucing up our tiny cells?"

"I'm serious, Sullivan. I can't take it anymore!"

"We'll get through this, Gilbert. Mackey's going to have to turn the investigation over to the state, or to whatever larger department governs local sheriffs. He's clearly in over his head."

"Yeah, but now it's a matter of how much damage he's already done. It might be so severe that whatever evidence might once have—"

The garage door began its noisy ascent, startling us both. Steve put his arm around my shoulders protectively, and we watched to see who'd operated the keypad.

"What are you two doing out here?" Mikara asked. Her vision dropped to the satchel that was still in Sullivan's hand.

He squared his shoulders and stepped back from me. "We were just talking," he said. "We found Henry's drill. . . ."

"We also found Cameron Baker's briefcase," I said, realizing there was no way to explain this away. "Sheriff Mackey's coming to pick it up."

"Cameron left his briefcase in the garage?" she asked, sounding baffled. "Is it . . . Did you learn who killed my sister? Can I see what's inside?"

Steve shook his head. "The sheriff told us to stay here and not discuss the contents with anyone. I'm sorry."

"But you must have read Cameron's papers . . . and felt they were important enough to turn over to the sheriff."

"We had to," I replied. "Cameron's the second victim. His briefcase is evidence."

She gritted her teeth. "Evidence that might reveal who killed my sister!"

Headlights appeared in the driveway. "Here comes Sheriff Mackey," I said.

Mikara turned and watched as Mackey emerged from the driver side. He'd come alone. "Evenin', Mikara. I'm afraid I've got to talk to the decorators in private, so—"

"I'll do anything I can to help the investigation," she interrupted. "Including leaving the garage and not saying a word to anybody. All I ask, Greg, is once you arrest my sister's killer, you'll tell me immediately."

"You'll be the first to know. I swear."

With a grim expression, she gave a final long glance at

the briefcase, then turned and went back to the house without another word.

Sheriff Mackey watched her go, then walked up to us with a swagger in his step. "Did you tell her anything about what's in the briefcase?" he asked me with an accusatory glare.

"Just that we found it and it belonged to Cameron."

"Damn it!" He eyed Steve. "Didn't I tell you to keep your yaps shut?!"

"She opened the garage door and saw me holding the thing," Steve said. "What was I supposed to say?"

"That it was yours. Period."

"We'd been in the garage for over twenty minutes," Steve explained. "She wanted to know why. The instant she saw you heading toward us, she'd have figured out that the briefcase wasn't mine."

Mackey grimaced and shook his head as if we'd made an unfathomably stupid mistake. "So, you conveniently found the victim's briefcase. In the Goodwin estate garage. Is that right?"

"We came out here to borrow Henry's drill. I spotted Cameron's footprint right there," I said as patiently as I possibly could, pointing at the grimy marking. "There was no obvious reason for him to have been in Henry's garage, so we were suspicious. We found Cameron's leather portfolio wedged behind a sheet of plywood, behind those studs." I pointed again.

"And right away, you knew it was evidence in the murder investigation."

"With all due respect, Sheriff Mackey," Steve interrupted, "when a new-looking leather satchel is discovered completely hidden behind a board in a garage, it's pretty obvious that someone put it there deliberately."

"You think?" he mocked.

"Yes, *we* do," I declared. *Unlike yourself.* "Maybe Cameron's papers were stolen, and he was being blackmailed with the threat that his big, self-serving plans would be divulged, and thereby ruined. Or maybe Wendell Barton found out about his right-hand man double-crossing him and hid the evidence out here till he could destroy it. Or maybe Cameron had a partner and was meeting with him or her, they fought, and he wound up dead."

"Give me the briefcase," Mackey barked at Steve, who promptly held it out to him. Mackey, who, like Steve, was wearing leather gloves, yanked the case from Steve's grasp. He opened it and looked in the compartments. "Is this everything?"

"As far as we know," Steve replied.

"The two of you figure this is the part when you give the hick sheriff the crucial piece of evidence that he couldn't *possibly* have found on his own, right?" Mackey's face was red and his right hand was balled into a fist. His features were so tight with anger that a vein on his forehead bulged. "Isn't that how things happen with you and the Crestview police all the time?"

"What are you—"

Mackey cut me off. "I got a call from a Crestview detective today. A Detective O'Reilly. Seems he wanted to know if I could maybe use some help."

"That was nice of him," I said feebly, not knowing what else to say.

"*Nice* is hardly what I'd call it. You're covering your asses! Things aren't quite working out the way you'd like, so you're hoping to get assistance from someone you've already got buffaloed!"

"Oh, my god," I groaned. "No, that is not what I'm doing. I want to see whoever killed Cameron and Angie get brought to justice. And you seem dead set on assuming only an outsider could have committed the crime."

"You think I'm this hick sheriff from the mountains." Mackey puffed out his chest. "Well, missy, just 'cuz this town is named Snowcap doesn't mean you can pull a snow job on me."

He pointed at me as he spoke, his finger an inch away from my face. It took every ounce of self-restraint I had to refrain from biting it.

"Let me make this clear. *This* hick sheriff is going to bring you down! I'm going to get the state police to look into every one of those other murders you and your friends on the police force managed to hang on other people! Your Bonnie-and-Clyde reign has come to an end!"

He pivoted and stormed out of the garage.

I gaped at the sheriff's retreating form till he'd disappeared into the inky blackness, then looked at Steve. He put his arms around me. Over the sound of Mackey's revving engine as he drove off, Steve told me, "It's going to be all right, Erin. We'll hire a lawyer and do whatever we have to do in order to stop this craziness, but we'll weather this storm. I promise."

Chapter 28

The next morning, drawn by the aroma of bacon, I strode into the kitchen with my mouth watering. Chiffon was sitting at the table, sobbing into a tissue. Henry was leaning back against the counter, a pasty pallor to his features. Preferring to be a hungry coward over becoming trapped into listening to a tale of woe, I promptly whirled around and tried to leave.

"It's all right, Erin," Chiffon said through her sniffles. "Don't let us delay your breakfast."

"No, you're not. I'm not hungry. I really had no reason to enter the kitchen. It was just force of habit."

"Let me get you a cup of coffee," Henry said.

"No, thanks. That's okay," I said. "I truly didn't mean to interrupt, and I'm just going to head back upstairs and finish accessorizing the bedrooms on the second floor."

Ignoring me, Henry filled a mug with coffee, adding an ample amount of milk, just the way I liked. "Here you go, Erin." He handed it to me. "I'll leave you two alone now. Again, I'm sorry, Chiffon, but this really is for the best for both of us." He strode toward the mudroom.

"You son of a bitch!" Chiffon screamed at him. She sprang to her feet and hurled the box of tissues at him, striking him on the shoulder. It bounced off of him and fell to the floor. He didn't as much as break stride as he let himself out the door.

Chiffon dashed to the counter and snatched up the pitcher that I'd only recently procured.

"Oh, my god! Not the milkmaid pitcher!" I blindly deposited my coffee mug on the nearest flat surface and raced toward Chiffon.

"That bastard!" Chiffon ignored me and started to charge after Henry, waving the ceramic pitcher in one hand.

"You don't want to hit him with a pitcher!" I got both of my hands around the pitcher, but she'd break the handle off if she didn't let go. "Use the frying pan," I cried, pointing with my chin at the stove behind her.

Now if Chiffon bludgeoned Henry with the skillet, I was probably an accessory to assault and battery. But my frying pan suggestion *did* make her relinquish her grip on the glorious pitcher. Housing eight milkmaids inside a single kitchen wasn't a simple feat, and the pitcher was easily my very favorite milkmaid of all.

Still sobbing, Chiffon managed an indignant "But this pan has bacon in it!" as she picked up the frying pan. She set it back down on the burner in disgust. "I'm a vegetarian!"

That was news to me; last night she'd eaten a healthy serving of lasagna with ground beef. "You won't be able to catch him before he gets into his car, regardless."

"No thanks to you!" she retorted, not altogether inaccurately. She stomped her foot. "I should have known this was coming when I saw him slip his car keys into his pocket first thing this morning. The man's a slime bucket!"

"Didn't you tell me not all that long ago that you two weren't anything serious?"

"Yeah. We weren't. And we still *aren't*. But that doesn't mean *he* can break up with *me*!" She swiped at her cheeks with both her sleeves.

"I'm sorry, Chiffon." (I hoped she didn't notice how tightly I was hugging the pitcher to my chest.) "I agree that he really should have at least made it sound like the breakup was your idea." A dose of basic child psychology seemed to be in order. "Which I'm sure it really *was*, if you think about it."

"Well, yeah, it *was*," she said, sniffing. "Sort of."

"You now own almost a third of his house. By this time next year, you'll be able to come and go at will, but Henry will be officially through with his role here."

"Serves him right. This house is too nice for him. He's got the biggest ego and the tiniest aura of anybody I've ever met. There's only room for himself in his world." She stuck her lower lip out and glanced again at the skillet. "I'm really going to miss his pancakes, though. He used to put Mickey Mouse ears on them for me." She started crying again.

"It's hard to build a relationship around pancakes." From the corner of my eye, I spotted Sullivan starting to enter the kitchen, but he assessed the situation and managed to beat a hasty retreat with greater success than I had just a minute or two earlier.

"Yeah, I know. I was trying to write a love song for Henry as a Christmas present, but the pancakes weren't even enough to build three or four stanzas around. Let alone a lasting relationship. Men always seem to dump me," she whined. "It's the story of my life."

"Chiffon, you're only twenty-two. Your life story has barely begun to be written."

She widened her eyes and muttered, "I can use *that* in a lyric."

Hoping she would focus on songwriting and I could safely put down the pitcher, I glanced at the counter. I'd sloshed quite a bit of my coffee, which I no longer wanted. "I really need to go get some work done. Steve and I are starting to get down to the wire as far as decorating for Christmas." The inn's opening was less than a week away.

Chiffon's eyes were starting to overflow again. "For an old guy, Henry was great in the sack."

"Again, not really the stuff of a love ballad." I gingerly set down the pitcher, calculating that I'd clean up the coffee spill from the granite countertop later, but I didn't want to continue this conversation for another moment.

"What's wrong with me, Erin? I realize that I'm too emotional, but that's the place where I get my art from! I can't be all stiff and professional and yet—"

Blessedly, my cell phone started to ring. I snatched it up. The screen indicated it was Steve—and I was already undyingly grateful. I feigned grave concern and announced: "Oh, jeez. I'm sorry, Chiffon, but this is a client, and it could be an emergency. Take care." I strode purposefully through the double doors, saying into the phone, "Yes, this is Erin Gilbert."

"I had a sudden idea to have breakfast out this morning," Steve said with a smile in his voice. "Care to join me?"

"Absolutely." Aware that Chiffon could still hear me, I added, "I'll leave right away. I'll bring my partner, and we'll look into that immediately. I'm so glad you called."

"Yeah. Me, too. We'll have to go someplace that serves pancakes. They're good for relationships, I hear."

I managed to stifle a laugh as I started to climb the stairs. Mikara was heading out of her bedroom and gave me a friendly wave, which I returned. She turned toward the kitchen. I felt a pang of guilt and said, "Okay, bye," into the phone. Mikara's sister had been killed, and here I was, leaving her to face Chiffon's sob story alone. Not to mention my spilled coffee. I was only marginally better than Henry; he'd done a dump-and-run, but I'd done a spill-and-run. Neither of us had the decency to clean up our own messes.

I doubled back. Already, Mikara's voice had risen to a shout. "Well, of *course* he dumped you!" she cried.

"What?! You didn't have enough evidence that he's a serial dater? You never heard how he gave me the heave-ho the week before our wedding?!"

"I wasn't looking for marriage, though," Chiffon replied. "Besides, I'm *fun*!"

"Not right now, you're not. I'm sure you stopped being fun for Henry just as soon as you started expecting him to behave like you were his significant other. Any idiot could see he was only dating you to keep you from selling out to Wendell."

"So what? I was only dating him till something better came along. And then you went and distracted me."

"Excuse me," I muttered and walked directly between them toward the sink. I grabbed my coffee cup, plus the pitcher for good measure.

"I did?" Mikara asked. "How did *I* distract *you*?"

"*You're* the one who brought Alfonso here for the interview. That was my dream come true! I was so close!"

"You wanted to hook up with *Alfonso*?" Mikara asked in dismay. "But you aren't even sure if the man's straight or *gay*."

I wrung out the sponge and headed toward the coffee spill, keeping a grip on my pitcher, all the while.

"No, I didn't want to hook up with him! I wanted him to name a dessert after me!"

"The Lemon Chiffon Walters Pie?" I couldn't help but interject.

She shrugged, at least having the humility to blush a little. "I know it's shallow of me, okay? But I didn't choose my name. My parents did that. And so, yes, I wanted a world-famous pastry chef to name a dessert after me, at the inn that I own. And I can't bake for beans, so it's not like I can manage a recipe on my own."

"That's pathetic," Mikara said. She lifted her chin in greeting as Audrey and Steve both appeared in the doorway.

"So?" Chiffon whined. "Plenty of much smaller celebrities than me have hamburgers and sandwiches named after them. And it's not like any of *their* first names is 'Cheese.' Or 'Turkey.'"

Audrey looked puzzled and said, "I missed the first half of this conversation. But is there anything I can do to help?"

"Henry broke up with Chiffon," Mikara said gruffly, "and it turns out she wanted Chef Alfonso, who has already decided *not* to relocate to Snowcap, by the way, to name a lemon chiffon pie after her."

"It's been my dream as long as I can remember." Chiffon sniffled.

"Good heavens, Chiffon," Audrey said with a smile. "That's something I actually *can* help you with. I make a wonderful chiffon pie. I'll teach the recipe to our new cook, whoever Mikara hires, and we'll put it on the menu."

Steve and I grabbed a bagel downtown for breakfast, but we ate on the run. The inspector was scheduled to arrive between the hours of nine and noon to examine the handicapped-access ramp, and I was determined not to leave Ben alone with him this time. Both Chiffon's and Henry's vehicles were gone by the time we got back, and Steve had to meet with a metalworker for his eleven pipers design.

It was chilly outside. Making a Thermos of cocoa for myself, I put on my ski clothes, with mukluks replacing the ski boots, and took a seat on the wrought-iron bench by the back door.

Ben gave me a bemused smile as he walked past me. "You know what they say about a watched pot never boiling, don't you?"

"Pardon?"

"You're waiting on the inspector. Probably, he won't come till you give up and go back inside."

"True. But it's nice and brisk outside, at least. I enjoy the feeling of a slight chill on my face, as long as I'm wearing warm clothing."

He gave me a half smile. "I'm kind of that way, too." His breath formed little cloud puffs of condensation.

"I brought along a second mug, in case you'd like to share my hot chocolate." I lifted the large Thermos to show him that I had plenty.

He hesitated. "Well, okay. Guess that won't harm my schedule too much."

I poured him a cup, which he accepted with a quick "Thanks."

"What's on the agenda for today? The ramp looks to me like it'll sail through." (Plus, Sullivan told me that he'd gotten a separate copy of the guidelines straight from the inspection office yesterday and had determined that the inn's ramp was within specifications.) I patted the seat beside me, and he grudgingly obliged me.

Ben glanced at the access ramp. "It does look nice. I like the wood a lot better than the concrete."

"So do I. It shows your excellent craftsmanship, as always."

He gave me a small smile, then stared straight ahead. "Tasty hot chocolate," he muttered after the tiniest of sips.

Snippets of my previous conversation concerning Ben returned to me; if what the gallery owners had said about him was true, he was probably lonely. "Do you ever think about leaving Snowcap Village? Of getting a fresh start someplace new?"

"It crosses my mind from time to time." He shrugged. "But I want to keep the Orlin Builders business going. I owe my dad's memory that much."

"Are you hoping to pass the business down to another family member when you retire, then? Do you have any siblings?"

"I see you've already ruled out that I'll ever have a kid of my own." He snorted and gave his head a rueful shake. "You've obviously heard the rumors about me."

"You're right, and I apologize." He gave me no reply, and I added gently, "Some gay couples adopt."

"Yeah. But I'm not half of a couple, now am I?" he snapped.

"That doesn't mean you won't *ever* be."

He mustered a smile. "I guess that's true. Now that my parents have passed away, I don't have anybody else's reputation to worry about but my own. Have *you* met any gay men up here you can fix me up with, by any chance?"

"No. But I know several in Crestview, if you ever change your mind and decide to leave."

He glanced behind him at the back door. "I just don't think I could ever stand to leave this place."

"Meaning Snowcap, or the Goodwin estate itself?"

"Goodwin," he said sadly.

Meaning *Goodwin* himself? I put some things together— Ben's behavior when Henry was reminiscing about their old times, the father's determination to separate his son from Henry, and Ben's odd slip of the tongue a few days ago, saying: "Tell that to Henry," about his being indispensible, when he'd meant to say Cameron.

"Forgive me for bringing up such a personal subject, but I've gotten the impression that you care truly deeply for Henry."

He winced, and our gazes met for just a moment. There was anguish in his eyes, and I knew at once that I'd hit upon a truth that he'd kept hidden for years. Ben was in love with a straight man. Talk about the hopeless situation.

"Henry's leaving town himself next year," I said.

"Maybe he'll change his mind," Ben said sadly. He snorted. "And his sexual orientation." He took a gulp of chocolate that had to still be uncomfortably hot, then set his mug down. "Thanks for the cocoa, but the handrails still need sanding."

For some reason, it dawned on me then that Wendell's accusations about Ben tipping off the inspectors were true, even though the contents of Cameron's briefcase had already revealed that Cam's fury toward Ben had been an act; both men had wanted to delay the inn from opening. "I guess Henry is more likely to stay in town if the inn never manages to open under its new ownership."

Ben pivoted and stared at me in surprise. "I put my heart and soul into this place, Erin! I always have. I never would have let so much as a loose nail get by me."

"No, but you've made certain that the inspectors were fully up on their codes . . . and aware of minute violations."

He held my gaze for a moment, then averted his eyes in a taciturn admission of guilt. "Have you told Henry about this?"

"No. Did you kill Cameron? Or Angie?"

"No. I'd swear to that on a stack of Bibles."

"Do you know who did?"

He said, "No," but his hesitation spoke volumes.

"But you're afraid that Henry's guilty."

"I'm scared he is, yeah."

I waited out his silence.

"Angie was taking bribes from Cameron. Henry had a big grudge against her. He has a bad temper. I figured maybe Cameron saw Angie's murder, or claimed he did, and Henry got desperate and killed again. But I could be way off base."

"Okay, so . . . why were you staring up at my window the other night?"

He spread his arms. "I wasn't paying attention to whose window it was. I couldn't sleep and went for a walk. I live just a mile and a half from here."

"Why didn't you wave, then, when you saw me at the window? Why run off, like you had something to hide?"

"I don't know, Erin. I guess I didn't want to be seen, staring at the house. All right?!" The muscles in his jaw were working, and he was once again glaring at me. "But the way you keep poking into things, you'd better watch yourself, or you could be the next victim."

Chapter 29

I watched through the kitchen window as Ben shook the inspector's hand. The wheelchair access ramp had passed. Barring an explosion of the septic system, which was about the only thing yet to fail on us, the town could no longer block us from opening on Christmas Eve.

A floorboard creaked behind me, and I turned around. It was Steve, who asked, "How's the inspection going?"

"Finished. The ramp passed with flying colors."

"Why do you look so down, then?"

I clicked my tongue, now wishing I'd feigned a bit of

cheerfulness. "Ben said some things to me that bothered me. It turns out, he's been carrying a torch for Henry for thirty years or so, and he told me I should watch myself or I could wind up the next victim."

"Ben threatened you?"

"It was either a threat or a warning. I couldn't tell. I don't trust anyone in this town anymore."

"Neither do I." He paused. "Let's go home to Crestview," Steve said gently as he walked up to me. "We can come up for the day a couple of times later on in the week. We're just twenty or so man-hours from being finished."

"Which means ten to twelve woman-hours, tops."

Steve chuckled and caressed my cheek. I kissed the palm of his hand. He gazed into my eyes. "Erin, all I know is—"

The door to the mudroom opened, and Ben interrupted our romantic moment. "Great news. We passed the inspection."

"I'm glad," I said.

"As far as the town's concerned," Ben continued, "we'll be ready to open next week as scheduled."

"Excellent for all of us," Steve said, glowering at Ben. "Tempers are getting short from stress."

Before Ben could reply, there was a noise in the mudroom, and we all stared at the door. A moment later, Henry staggered through the door, gasping for air. His face was red and damp with perspiration. He kicked the door shut with his heel, then bent down and grasped his knees, physically exhausted to the point of collapse.

"Henry," Ben cried. "What's wrong?"

Henry was still struggling to get his breath too much to speak. He held up a hand and, a few seconds later, managed to say, "I'm fine. Just not used to running."

"Why were you running?" Steve asked.

"I hid my pickup truck in a buddy's garage," he said in staccato bursts through his gasps for air. "Nearly bumped into Chiffon downtown. Ran all the way back here."

"Why?" Ben asked.

Henry made a "duh" face at Ben, but I'd been about to ask why myself. "So that Chiffon can't take a sledgehammer to my truck. Obviously." He caught his breath enough to make his way to the kitchen table. He slumped into one of the slat-back chairs and shook his head. "I'm getting too old for this kind of stuff."

On *that* point, we were in agreement. Ben, meanwhile, got Henry a glass of water and set it on the table in front of him. Henry took a couple of gulps without acknowledging Ben's kindness. "Sounds paranoid, I know, but trust me," Henry declared. "Underneath that blond-bimbo bubbly exterior, Chiffon is vindictive as hell."

"Seriously?" Ben asked.

"Yeah. Turns out, last year, she filled her ex-boyfriend's convertible with manure."

"I'll bet she didn't shovel the manure herself," Ben remarked. "She probably hired a day laborer for the job. Yet I can't even hire a drywall installer willing to work on the Goodwin property."

Henry popped a couple of Tic Tacs into his mouth. He looked at me. "Do you know where Audrey and Wendell are?"

"Audrey's at the TV station. I haven't seen Wendell

since she and I ran into him in the village yesterday afternoon."

He crunched his breath mints as if they were peanuts. "We're going to have to round them up. Considering the potential for disaster with Chiffon, I need to call an emergency board meeting. We need to discuss how we're going to proceed."

Steve rubbed his forehead. "This really doesn't concern Erin and me."

In spite of myself, I was getting deeply annoyed with Henry. "Chiffon's a board member, too," I pointed out. "Maybe if you treat her like an adult, she'll act like one. Maybe this story of the manure in the convertible isn't accurate. Or maybe her ex-boyfriend damaged her car first, and she was retaliating."

"*Or*, maybe I sold thirty percent of my family's house to a crazy young chick," Henry fired back. "And a two-time murderer."

"Yeah, that's possible," Ben said, and I detected a bit of a hopeful lilt to his voice that struck me as inappropriate. Henry glared at him, and he added quickly, "I got some good news for you, though. The access ramp passed. We're good to go—no future inspections."

Henry sat up. His natural rate of breathing had returned and he seemed to have recuperated from his overexertion. "That's great, Ben. Thank God *you*, at least, have been on my side all along. I don't know what I'd've done without you."

"No problem." Ben averted his eyes. "I just have some last little things to take care of in the garage. For one thing, I wanted to fix that busted lock on the door."

"Great," Henry said, rising. "'Preciate it." Shifting his attention to me, he said, "So, anyway, Erin, could you call Audrey for me and mention that I need to talk to her privately? I don't want to spring this trouble with me and Chiffon on Wendell till I know where Audrey's coming from."

"Audrey already knows you dumped Chiffon," I said. "She came into the kitchen just after you'd left, when Chiffon was still in tears. The way gossip spreads in this town, everyone will know by nightfall."

"Yeah, probably," Henry acknowledged. "The thing is, though, Chiffon's turning out to be such a nut job really put a monkey wrench in my plans. Wendell's now got the controlling vote. But there's no way in hell I'm going to let him get sole control of my property. He and I both know the land this house is occupying is worth much more than the house itself."

"Actually," Steve interjected, "it looks like it was Cameron Baker, not Wendell, who had plans to raze this house in favor of a batch of condos."

Henry paled. "What are you talking about?"

Steve hesitated and looked at me. I said, "Steve and I found a set of plans and papers, partially in Cameron's handwriting, that outlined his personal plan to build a second ski resort in competition with Wendell's. In the blueprints, he'd built condos right where the inn is located."

"Cripes! I knew that guy was a sleazebag from the minute I saw him," Henry grumbled. He glanced at me. "No offense, Erin."

"The man's dead. It hardly matters now what people's

first impressions of him were." Unless that's what led to his being *murdered*, I added silently, wondering if Henry was only acting—pretending to be hearing all of this for the first time.

Henry jumped at a noise in the mudroom. Without looking back, he sprang to his feet. "Damn it!" he said in a half whisper. "That's bound to be Chiffon! She's hunting me down!" He snatched up his coat from the counter where he'd tossed it.

"Are you sure it isn't just Audrey?" I asked. "She should be finishing up at the studio right about now."

"I'm not taking the risk to wait and find out. Don't tell her I was here." He started to head toward the front door.

"No! I haven't been asked to lie like this since I was in high school! You're mayor of this town, and you can't stand up to a twenty-two-year-old you broke up with after all of two weeks?"

He stopped in the double doors to the main hall, his coat unfastened. He turned toward me. "When you put it that way, I sound ridiculous."

"How *else* would you have me phrase this?" I retorted.

"That I'm trying to avoid a chick who's completely off her rocker."

He winced as someone approached the window in the back door, then he sagged with relief. "Mikara," he said as she entered the kitchen. "I was afraid you were Chiffon."

Mikara winced at Henry's words, and an instant later, Chiffon walked up behind her.

"Trying to avoid me, Henry?" she asked, her arms akimbo.

"We arrived at the same time," Mikara explained, setting down two bags of groceries.

"Are there more groceries I can bring in?" Steve asked.

"No, that's everything," Mikara replied. "Thanks, though."

"I asked you a question," Chiffon said to Henry. "You've got your coat on. Where's your truck?"

"I left it at a friend's house. I had visions of you filling its bed with manure."

"Because *you're* such a chickenshit, you mean?" Chiffon asked matter-of-factly.

Henry scanned our faces, as if hoping one of us would jump in and take his side. Apparently he didn't know about the sisterhood that forms instinctively when a woman's been unfairly dumped; Mikara and I weren't *about* to defend him. Steve, meanwhile, had managed to affect a glassy-eyed, lost-in-thought-and-not-really-listening facial expression.

Henry shrugged. "I just heard a rumor, is all."

"Straight from a gossip magazine, no doubt. Get a grip! You're really not important enough to me to go through that kind of effort. Hard as I'm sure that is for you and your enormous ego to believe." She snorted. "I'd be happier if we never saw each other again."

"So why are you here?" he asked.

"I left some of my stuff in your bedroom." She pulled an empty plastic grocery bag out of her coat pocket to show him that she'd planned ahead. "Is that all right? Do you want to send Erin along to play watchdog to make sure I don't rip those awesome flannel shirts of yours to shreds?"

"No, Chiffon," he said sheepishly. "That's fine. We'll wait here."

She sneered at him. "Thank you. That's really courageous of you."

She brushed past him and pushed through the saloon-like double doors. Nobody spoke. I rose and wordlessly helped Mikara put away the groceries. After the sound of Chiffon's high heels had faded, Mikara said, "Honestly, Henry. That was an embarrassment just to *witness*. She's half your age, and yet *you're* the one who's acting completely immature."

"You haven't experienced her mood swings like I have," Henry retorted in an angry whisper. "I'm telling you, that girl is schizophrenic. She can turn on a dime!"

"If you say so," Mikara muttered, filling the teakettle and putting it on the burner. She grabbed the cast-iron skillet and carried it over to the sink, muttering, "You're lucky she didn't crack you over the head with this thing."

"I'm going to go see if I can help Ben with that lock in the garage door," Henry said.

I felt a pang for poor Ben. He was going to feel tortured by Henry's proximity and would never, I was sure, admit his feelings.

Henry started to head through the mudroom, then said, "Oh, good. Audrey's back. I need to ask her opinion about the board meeting tonight."

Mikara glanced at me as Henry headed outside to talk to Audrey. "What board meeting?"

"He's scheduling an emergency meeting to discuss how his breaking up with Chiffon might affect ownership at the inn."

"He should have thought of that before, for heaven's sake. He does this all the time. He breaks up with a woman, hides, assumes all hell's going to break loose, and creates even more problems for himself."

"I think he regrets his lack of foresight now."

"Erin?" Steve said, finally emerging from his conversational coma, "we need to hang those shelves of yours in the master bedroom. Once Chiffon's gone, that is."

"Right. In any case, I haven't gotten much of anything done this morning."

"You deserve to take a break now and then," Mikara said.

"We're pretty much done anyway," Steve said. "In fact, Erin and I might want to head back to Crestview this evening, then come back early Friday to finish up for the party."

"Party?" I asked.

Mikara gave Steve a sharp look. "Did you forget to tell your partner about the second housewarming party?"

Steve winced. "Henry and Chiffon decided on that back when you and Audrey were out shopping the other day. We decided on the date for the party to show off Audrey's Twelve Days theme. It's this Friday. Mikara told Audrey, so *she* knows."

I heard Chiffon's footfalls descending the stairs just as Audrey came inside. "There's a housewarming party here on Friday?" I asked Audrey immediately.

"You didn't tell Erin?" Audrey said to Steve.

"Neither did *you*."

"Now we'll *have* to stay for the meeting tonight," I said

a bit testily to Steve. "We should finish up everything before we leave town, in any case."

"Or we can finish everything Friday afternoon, before the party," Steve countered. "We'll have to come back up then anyway."

He had a point, but so did I, and I had already won this particular argument by virtue of his having forgotten to tell me that the party had been scheduled.

Chiffon returned to the kitchen, her eyes puffy once more. She'd obviously started crying again once she was alone and had probably been trying to gather herself. Her grocery bag was now partially full.

"I'm going to get back to work," Steve said, brushing past Chiffon as he made a hasty exit.

"Where's Henry?" Chiffon asked.

"Ben's giving him a ride to get his truck," Audrey replied. "He seems to think your breakup is going to cause severe problems as far as your being a co-owner of the inn. He's wrong about that, isn't he?"

"Of course he's wrong! That's ridiculous! He isn't even a co-owner—you and Wendell are, and I've got nothing against either of you. We all share the goal of making Snowcap Inn a successful venture. What the hell is Henry's problem?"

"He does seem to have some strange ideas about women," Audrey remarked.

"He thinks we should all be as unemotional as *he* is," Mikara said. "As if emotions equal craziness."

"So he acted like this to you, too?" Chiffon asked her, perking up a little.

"Absolutely. Been there, done that. Of course . . . in *my*

case, we were engaged to be married, so I had a lot of cause to be emotional. *You've* been together for all of two weeks."

"They were important weeks, though." Chiffon sniffed. "Two people were murdered. And somebody tried to tamper with my skis and kill me. You get extra close to a person when you're facing life and death together."

"I haven't forgotten about Angie and Cameron," Mikara snapped, "considering the first victim was my only *sister*." She dried the now clean skillet and put it away, banging the cabinet door shut. "One of these days you need to figure out that *everyone's* the star of their own story, Chiffon."

"Meaning what?" Chiffon asked, jutting her lip out defiantly.

"Meaning you're not half as important as you think you are."

"Oh, yeah? Well…neither are you! And neither is Henry…*Bad*win. Or Henry Bad*loss*, more like it."

"Go home, Chiffon," Mikara said, shaking her head.

"*You* can't tell *me* what to do!" Nevertheless, Chiffon turned and stomped through the door.

"That was harsh," Audrey said to Mikara. "She's just a kid. And she's been treated unfairly by the man she was dating."

"I realize that, Audrey. But I'm sick and tired of indulging in her egotistical fantasies, including naming a pie after her."

"She plunked down a lot of money to own a part of this inn," Audrey interposed. "The place hasn't even opened yet. With the power struggle between Henry and Wendell, and now this breakup nonsense between Henry and Chiffon, the friction among management is going to sink us before we're even off the ground."

Mikara sighed. "You're right, Audrey," she said grudgingly. "When I accepted this job, I promised Henry I'd help him out. Next time I see Chiffon, which sounds like it's going to be at tonight's meeting, I'll apologize."

"Thank you," Audrey said, touching Mikara's arm. "That's big of you, and it will make a difference to her. And, you know, Chiffon truly is a draw for the inn. She makes it cool for the young professionals with all kinds of discretionary spending to stay at a B-and-B. That's an important demographic. If only Henry hadn't been so damned stupid as to date her as a means to manipulate her vote, things would be nicely balanced."

Audrey started cleaning the kitchen, and I helped her. Mikara, meanwhile, started reading a copy of yesterday's *Denver Post* that someone must have bought downtown. I ran through my to-do list and realized that Sullivan and I were down to just three bedrooms to decorate for our Twelve Days. After that, we needed to do a final inspection of all the rooms for any last-minute details, then we were done. If we could both work efficiently, we might be able to finish today, head home, and return on Friday like Steve had suggested. *No sense in cutting my nose off to spite my lover.*

Audrey stood transfixed, staring out the window above the sink. "That's odd," she muttered. "Now, why would Chiffon be carrying a stepladder toward the shed?"

Mikara rushed beside Audrey and peered out. "She has

to be carrying the ladder *back* to the shed. Oh, God! That's a spray can in her other hand!"

"Let's hope she was just touching up the paint on the cardboard M-and-M's," I offered hopefully, though I knew full well that Chiffon's it's-all-about-me mentality would never allow her to focus on something so wholesome when her feelings had recently been injured.

Mikara bolted toward the front door and I followed, while Audrey dashed to the back door, probably to try to speak with Chiffon.

Mikara trotted halfway down the walkway, then turned to look at the gingerbread façade. She grabbed her head in shock and glared at the house. I whirled around and looked at the still-wet red paint graffiti. Mikara's face contorted and she cried, "Look what that spoiled little princess painted on our house!"

Chapter 30

Chiffon had painted in enormous block letters that "Henry G" was a crude term for part of the male anatomy.

Hoping to inject some humor, I said, "She's got really legible print, for using a spray can freehand."

"This isn't funny, Erin!"

"Maybe not, but it *is* the best thing she possibly could have done for us. Now we can take down that idiotic façade."

Mikara was having none of my very rational response. She balled her fists and started to march toward the driveway. Chiffon's cute little powder blue Prius was heading toward us.

Mikara broke into a run, determined to block her exit. Chiffon stepped on the accelerator, and for a terrible moment, I thought I was going to be witness to a hideous collision.

"Let her go!" I hollered to Mikara, racing toward her for all I was worth. I grabbed the back of her blouse, but by then she had pulled up short anyway. Chiffon flew past us, barreling onto the street without slowing, let alone stopping, for possible traffic.

"You idiot maniac!" Mikara screamed at her, shaking her fist in fury. "You're never setting foot in this house again!" She was panting in rage as Chiffon drove away.

For my part, I was immensely grateful that there was no squeal of brakes, followed by a crash. "Seriously, Mikara, it's *just* graffiti," I said as we watched Chiffon's car disappear down the hill.

"I know that! This house is historical! It represents all of what's good and solid and decent about the old Snowcap! And that little twerp is the epitome of what's gone wrong with this town!"

"She *didn't* mark up the house itself, though. She ruined her tacky Masonite gingerbread!"

Audrey was trotting toward us but stopped to examine the house. "Oh, my!" she cried. She turned back to us as we made our way up the front walk. She beamed at us. "Hallelujah! We get to take down the god-awful gingerbread!"

Several minutes later, when Henry arrived home, he threw a dozen "I told you so's" at all of us, then settled into the task of moving tonight's meeting up to five-thirty, in the hopes that Chiffon would miss it entirely.

He kept grumbling about wanting Chiffon to be arrested. Ben, however, pointed out that the inn would be much better served by taking down the Masonite board immediately than by having the graffiti on display for another hour or two, while the sheriff investigated and the townspeople came by to see for themselves what was causing yet another fuss. Ben said he would store the offensive boards in the garage so that Henry could show them to Sheriff Mackey later. Sure enough, in less than two hours, Ben had restored the inn's beautiful siding, which lifted my mood considerably.

At around four o'clock that afternoon, the doorbell rang. Steve and I were checking the paint job in Audrey's room. He grinned at me. "I know what this is. Meet me in our bedroom." He trotted downstairs to get the front door.

Much as I'd have liked to think that he was about to present me with something so intensely romantic that the privacy of our bedroom was required, I knew he was strictly in work mode; we were moving the ten lords a-leaping from our bedroom into Audrey's. (He'd sung: "Six crows Erin's eating..." while, instead of the panels, we placed a lovely oak highboy against the aubergine accent wall.) I sat on the Queen Anne bench at the foot of our bed and waited for him.

A minute later, Steve entered our room, exclaimed, "Tah-dah!" and presented me with a long, skinny package. He sat next to me and proceeded to open a second, larger box.

"What's this?"

"It's the eleven pipers piping." Steve handed me his pocketknife.

"It's heavy...but I'm surprised you can fit eleven pipers into one long box like this." I started to open it. "Wait. Didn't we agree on eleven candlestick holders?"

"Yeah, but eleven separate candles didn't feel right to me."

Concerned, I met his gaze. "So you put them all together into one candelabra? Isn't that going to be sort of *Phantom of the Opera*-ish?"

"Reserve your judgment till you at least look at it, okay?"

I worked my way through the protective packaging and removed the bronze sculpture/candelabra. The base was three feet long and loosely resembled a flute, or rather, a flute that had been adapted into a candlestick holder, with eleven holders projecting from the holes in the flute. The middle candleholder was the tallest at six inches, with each of the surrounding holders progressively shorter; the ones at both ends were only an inch tall. "So there are ten finger holes, plus one blow hole for the flautist?"

"Which have all been converted into candleholders."

"You realize your 'piper' had to have twelve fingers? He'd need two thumbs to hold onto this instrument."

He shrugged. "Artistic license. Did you notice my eleven pipers?"

The tiny figurines were molded into the front side of each of the candleholders. I grinned as I studied them. "They're cute."

"Some of them could probably have used a little more detail," Steve said, peering over my shoulder.

"The four littlest ones on the ends are a bit generic. But the seven bigger ones on the taller candleholders all look great."

Steve smiled and unpacked eleven cream-colored, elegant, tapered candles and put them in place while I stared at his creation. By the time he'd inserted the eleventh candle I decided I liked it very much.

"Were you going to put this on our mantelpiece?"

"Originally. But I think we should center it on the wall over the bed. Ben is going to build us an eight-inch-deep shelf this afternoon." He knelt on the edge of the king-sized bed and held the candelabra against the wall so I could get a feel for how it would look there. "You've got to imagine this with the candles lit. And a crackling fire in the fireplace directly opposite."

"Yes. It will work wonderfully," I told him honestly.

He grinned at me. "Thanks."

"So now you've got one thirty-six-by-eight-inch shelf to install, while I finally hang the leaping-lords panels. Then I've got to hang two pictures depicting four drummers, and tactfully distribute eight drummer figurines in Henry's bedroom. Which, by the way, makes me feel a bit like the Easter bunny, hiding drummer boys instead of eggs."

Steve crossed his arms and arched an eyebrow. "Looks

like this time my man-hours were more efficient than your woman-hours."

"That's only because I've been a slacker this past week."

"My point exactly."

I was on the verge of suggesting that we engage in some truly enjoyable slacking together, but I heard heavy footsteps ascending the staircase and correctly guessed that this would be Ben, reporting for duty. He leaned in the doorway and knocked on the lintel. "I got that shelf ready to install."

"Excellent," Steve replied.

"I'm going to go creatively place my dozen drummers in . . ." I let my voice fade as my imagination wandered. "A dozen drummers. A dozen eggs. Damn! Why didn't I think of this before! I could have had a dozen Fabergé-egglike creations made up for this! The interior of each one could have revealed a different drummer figurine. That would have been fantastic!"

"And it would have blown our entire budget on one room," Sullivan replied.

"Oh, and *then* some, but it would have been amazing!"

"Next time we get a twelve-plus room mansion to decorate for Christmas, using a limitless budget, you'll be ready."

"I will, indeed. And you'll already have a premade mold for a bronze candlestick holder."

With one small, square painting of a drummer boy, one long photograph of three drummers emerging from the mist and the dark background, and eight figurines to blend in with the existing décor and accessories, this was a design challenge. Because of the relatively small, short dimensions of the pictures, I had to spatially treat them more like figurines than wall hangings. I had to move personal effects, accessories, lamps, and paintings accordingly to achieve visual balance and harmony in the room. This was more an art than a science, and I had plenty of false starts.

I knew I would need to place one figurine on each of the two nightstands. I was thrown off guard, though, when I discovered a five-by-seven picture frame facedown, pushed off to the side on the left nightstand. I flipped it over and saw to my dismay that it was a photograph of a much younger Angie Woolf and Henry embracing.

This photograph being here was so odd that I didn't know what to do with it, and, frankly, I didn't feel fond enough of Henry at the moment to ask him. Mikara had hired her maid-service staff to begin work on December 23, one day before the inn's grand opening gala on Christmas Eve. Till then, she was responsible for dropping off fresh linens to our rooms. She would come in here eventually and would be hurt at seeing this picture next to Henry's bed. I immediately suspected Chiffon of planting it here, but then, she wouldn't have had access to such an old photograph. It had to have been taken in high school, before Chiffon was even born.

While I was still staring at the picture, Ben did his usual knock on the open doorway. "Need my help with anything?" he asked.

Could Ben have put it here to cause trouble? I wondered. I showed him the photograph. "You wouldn't know anything about this picture, would you?"

He came closer and smiled wryly. "That's from our senior prom. It was in the yearbook. Angie and Henry were chosen as king and queen." He glanced around. "You found that in here?"

"On the nightstand, lying facedown. I guess I'll keep it there and work around it."

"I guess," Ben replied, taking a long, sad look at the image before handing it back to me. I returned it, faceup, to its place on the nightstand. "If you don't need me for—"

"Give me just a minute. Let me just set out my drummers at random so I can get an idea of what's left to be done." I arranged the final three drummers on Henry's large mahogany dresser. "I might want to duplicate Sullivan's design of putting objects on a small shelf. It works with the three of them here on the dresser, but the balance of the twelve within the one room might be wrong."

I glanced back at Ben for his opinion, but he was staring at the photograph with sad eyes.

Ultimately, I liked having the three drummers on the dresser and was pleased with how nicely all twelve blended in. When five-thirty rolled around, Wendell, Audrey, Mikara, Steve, and I took seats around the fireplace in the main hall. I deliberately positioned my chair so I could gaze at the breathtaking gilded partridge in the pear tree. Henry held court, marching back and forth across the hearth, chomping down Tic Tacs as he enumerated the reasons why we should back his decision to return Chiffon's money and allow himself to be a thirty-percent owner.

"No," Wendell said firmly the instant Henry had stopped talking. "There's no way that's ever going to happen." I heard a noise in the kitchen as Wendell continued. "If you want to discuss Audrey and me assuming Chiffon's shares of the inn, that's one thing. But, Henry, you are not going to buy her out."

Chiffon burst through the double doors, leaving them flapping in her wake. "I heard that! Nobody is buying me out! This place is almost one-third mine, and it's going to stay that way!"

"You can't be here," Mikara declared, pointing at Chiffon. "You have no right to ever set foot inside this place again after what you did this morning!"

"Oh, puh-shaw. I got a little emotional." She flicked her wrist in Mikara's direction. "I'm an artist. That sort of thing goes with the territory. Get over yourself."

"*I'm* not the one who has to do that. *You* are!"

"But I already *am* over myself." She looked at Henry. "And I'm over you, too. You're older than my dad, for God's sake. It's all behind us now, so let's just move on. You already got your revenge by taking down my gingerbread display. We're even."

"For one thing, it's not that easy," Henry said, "and for another, I don't believe you. You'll be doing real damage to my house the very next time you're off your meds. I'm writing you a check and buying you out."

Chiffon narrowed her eyes. "First of all, my 'meds' are for my allergies. To dust and all sorts of furry animals.

And, second, if you try to give me a check, I'll rip it up. And, by the way, my lawyer is from Hollywood! He's used to dealing with all kinds of important people. Famous people, with lots of fans. He'll run right over you in court."

"Just like you nearly ran me over with your car!" Mikara snarled.

"Get serious. You'd have had time to jump out of my way," Chiffon said. "Besides, I was crying. I could barely see. It's amazing you've reached your age when you don't even know not to step in front of a car of a woman who's just been jilted!"

"Reached my *age*?! How—"

"This is all beside the point!" Henry interrupted. "One of the owners of this establishment painted dirty words on the front of the house! That *owner* thereby forfeits all ownership rights!"

"Says who? Our contract doesn't say anything about forfeiting our rights and voiding our contracts because of a minor bit of damage to a Christmas display. I checked!"

"No matter what happens," Mikara announced, "the Lemon Chiffon Walters Pie will be served at this inn over my dead body!"

The front door banged open and footsteps resounded in the hall, causing us all to turn to stare at the door. Sheriff Mackey and two deputies barged into the room.

"Wendell Barton," Mackey stated with a bravura that indicated he felt this was his finest moment, "you're under arrest for the murder of Cameron Baker."

Chapter 31

Looking shocked, Chiffon dropped into the nearest chair—a hand-carved bergère upholstered in a gold-and-cream-striped silk that was positioned opposite Wendell's. Mikara scooted over to distance herself from Chiffon.

Wendell gaped at the sheriff. "What do you mean I'm under arrest! This is ridiculous, Greg! Is this some kind of a joke?"

"Go ahead, Deputy Penderson," Mackey said, pointing with his chin, "cuff him and read him his rights."

Penderson took a step toward Wendell. "No!" Wendell

cried at Mackey. Penderson hesitated. "There's been a big mistake. If you want to talk to me about some false information that implicates me, you can call my lawyer. Once I'm done with this meeting, I'll come in, and we'll get everything straightened out."

Steve and I glanced at each other. I felt both shocked at the situation and annoyed at Mackey. Even if he was arresting the right person, there was no chance he had gotten the airtight evidence he would need. The case against Wendell would get dismissed, and he'd go scot-free. Come to think of it, maybe allowing Wendell to get away with murder was Mackey's ultimate intention.

I scanned everyone's faces. Audrey was glaring at Mackey and had a white-knuckle grip on the arms of her chair. Mikara, too, looked angry. Her eyes, however, were focused on Wendell; she must have believed that he'd killed her sister. There was a peevish wrinkle forming between Chiffon's perfectly plucked eyebrows. Knowing her need for attention, she was surely livid that Mackey and Wendell had stolen her limelight. Henry had taken a seat on the hearth, leaning back a little against the stone. He was pale and looking down at his lap, stunned.

"You're not writing the rules, here, Barton," Mackey declared. "I'm the law in this town." *And we've somehow blundered into a spaghetti western.*

Penderson was still hanging back, but moved behind Wendell's leather club chair. "Mr. Barton, sir? Could you please stand up and put your hands behind your back so I can put these on?" He opened one of the handcuffs.

"No! You're not putting those damned things on me! This is stupid! I didn't kill anybody!"

"We have plenty of proof that that's not the truth," Mackey said with a snort.

"What proof?!" Wendell asked.

I gave Audrey a quick glance; she was still glaring at Mackey.

"Documents written by the victim himself. They were in Miss Gilbert's possession till recently."

All eyes turned toward me. "They *weren't* in my possession. Steve and I found them in the garage. We turned them over to the sheriff's office immediately."

Mackey said to Wendell, "Plus, your receptionist is on record claiming that you recently shouted at her, 'I'd like to raise Cameron Baker from the dead just so I could kill him again!'"

"But I didn't mean *I* killed him in the first place," Wendell sputtered. "Only that I was mad enough to kill him, considering that he was already dead. Which isn't really a crime." He spread his arms in frustration, and Penderson snapped the cuff on his right arm. "Hey!" Wendell yelled, "Get this thing off me!" The deputy kept a grip on the other end of his handcuffs. Wendell leaned away from him and eyed Henry. "Henry, *you're* the mayor, for God's sake!" He pointed with his free hand at the sheriff. "Fire him!"

"I can't!" Henry said. "Like me, he's an elected official, and he's only doing his job, albeit in his usual moronic style."

"Stand up and put your other arm behind your back," Penderson said. Wendell responded by holding his left arm out as far away from the deputy as possible.

"Wendell," Audrey said, "you're not helping yourself.

Let the deputy put the handcuff on your other wrist. Give me the name of your lawyer, and let me call him."

Wendell grimaced, then grumbled, "Fine. Someone has to act like an adult here." He rose and put his hands behind his back but glared defiantly at Mackey all the while. "You'd better hire a lawyer yourself, Greg, because I guarantee you, I'm going to be filing false-arrest charges."

While Penderson consulted with a pocket guide and started Mirandizing Wendell, Audrey grabbed a pen and pad. Wendell gave her the name and contact information for his lawyer in Denver. As Penderson and Mackey led Wendell away, Audrey called after them, "Sheriff Mackey, whatever popularity you might gain with this arrest will backfire, once word gets out that you arrested the wrong person."

"And you can forget receiving any more financial support for your reelection campaign from me," Wendell added. "A dead deer would make a better sheriff than you!"

Audrey began to dial her cell phone. "Stop talking, Wendell. I'll meet you at the jail. And I'll see to it that your lawyer's there, too, even if I have to fetch him myself."

"Thanks, hon," Wendell called over his shoulder as the two lawmen dragged him out the front door. Henry, meanwhile, rose and began to pace once again in front of the fireplace.

Audrey wandered into the kitchen with her phone; she was speaking directly with Wendell's lawyer. Sullivan gave my hand a squeeze. I still believed Wendell was guilty of both murders, and I knew that Steve agreed. My one source of nagging doubt, though, was that Audrey obviously believed Wendell was innocent. Then again, Mikara had remarked that women's judgment gets impaired by love. Maybe Audrey cared more for Wendell than she was admitting, even to herself, and she wasn't seeing him clearly.

"So, does this mean the meeting's over?" Chiffon asked. "Because if *not*, I call for a ruling of the remaining board members. All in favor of Chiffon Walters retaining her ownership shares of the Snowcap Inn, raise your hand." She raised her hand, scanned the room (in which only we nonboard members sat), and said, "Motion carries."

"For God's sake," Henry muttered, dragging his hand across his features and looking truly exhausted, "I just... don't have the energy for this." He looked at Chiffon. "Okay, fine. I'm dropping this thing for the time being. If you pull one more stunt like that, though, I'm dragging you to court, and I guarantee you will get the boot, no matter *how* many famous clients your California lawyer represents."

"Fair enough," Chiffon chirped.

"I'm not kidding," Henry said, jabbing his finger in her direction. "This is your last warning. You behave like a crazy, vindictive ex-girlfriend again, and I'll burn this place to the ground before I let you own so much as a toilet here."

Chiffon scowled at him. "You made your point already. I'm just trying to live up to my fans' expectations anyway."

Henry rolled his eyes but held his tongue.

"In the meantime, Henry," Mikara said pointedly, "your majority owner has just been hauled off to jail for murder. They're probably going to determine that he killed my sister. It's always possible that his girlfriend, a second owner of the inn, aided and abetted."

"Hey!" I shouted and leapt to my feet. "That is not even remotely possible!"

"My point is simply this: Henry now has to figure out how to handle a much more serious situation than a part owner's idiotic behavior with a can of spray paint."

Audrey returned to the room. She was fastening the buttons of her white wool coat. "I'm heading to the jail now. Wendell's lawyer is on his way in from Denver. For the record, not only am I completely innocent, but so is Wendell. The real problem here is that Snowcap Village elected a donkey's ass as sheriff." She looked at me. "And that there was circumstantial evidence that was misleading." She shifted her gaze to Henry. "I move that we adjourn this meeting."

"Seconded," Chiffon said.

"Meeting adjourned," Henry said.

Audrey continued, "This will get resolved soon, and I recommend that the inn take no action. Until that time, everyone's response to questions from the media needs to be 'no comment.'" She turned.

"Audrey?" Steve asked. "Would you like me to go with you?"

"No, but thank you, Steve," she replied with a sincere smile, then left.

"Well," Mikara said, rising, "I must say that this was the least dull business meeting I've ever attended."

"Before everyone heads off and does their own thing," Chiffon said, "could I please just mention that I really think the Lemon Chiffon Walters Pie would be a big seller? Just 'cuz everyone's ticked off at me doesn't mean we have to drop a good marketing idea, does it?"

"Yes," Mikara and Henry said in unison. Steve and I stayed mute, but we had no say in the inn's menu anyway.

Chiffon's face fell. She gathered herself, rose, and left without another word.

"Cripes," Henry grumbled. "I hope she isn't about to paint a big yellow pie on the front of the house."

"She's not that stupid," I said. "I think Chiffon lives her whole life with an image of herself on MTV, and acts accordingly."

"Erin's right," Steve said.

"That's what makes Chiffon absolutely insufferable, in my opinion," Mikara said. "So, on that note," she glanced at her watch, "I'm going into town to have dinner with friends."

We said good-bye to Mikara, and she, too, left the house. Henry sank into Wendell's leather chair and seemed to be lost in thought. "Do you have dinner plans?" I asked.

"I'm not hungry." He muttered, "It really was low of me to dump her and dash out of the kitchen this morning."

"It's always hard to break up with someone," Steve said. He seemed to be studiously avoiding my gaze, and my heart started pounding. That was just basic paranoia on my part, I assured myself; no way was Steve on the verge of breaking up with me.

Henry rose. "I need to apologize to Chiffon. To tell her

that I'll do my best to convince Mikara that we can put her damned pie on the inn's menu. Once we *get* a menu."

"You're going to Chiffon's house right now?" I asked in surprise.

Staring into space, Henry didn't acknowledge my question.

Uh-oh. Henry was now enticed by Chiffon simply because he enjoyed the chase. The best chance of opening the inn on time would be to leave things as they were between those two. "You might be better off e-mailing Chiffon, just so nothing gets misinterpreted, you know?" I said. In the corner of my vision, I could see Steve trying to resist a smile.

"Maybe so." Henry popped a breath mint into his mouth. "But I'd feel better doing this in person."

"In that case, good luck. But... shouldn't we take into account that this is a bed-and-breakfast inn? Wouldn't it make more sense to put some kind of lemon chiffon pastry on the menu? Or lemon chiffon yogurt?"

Henry grinned. "Hey! I like that idea!" He hopped to his feet. "Now I definitely need to go tell Chiffon about this in person. Have a nice evening, you two." He left.

Steve shook his head as the back door clicked shut behind Henry. "Somewhere there's a definition of 'glutton for punishment' with Henry's picture beside it."

"And there's a picture of Chiffon next to the definition of 'camera hound.'"

Steve chuckled and stretched in his seat. "We should try to scrounge up something for dinner."

"I suppose so. There's some leftover chicken in the fridge. I'd be fine with a Caesar salad."

"Me, too."

There was a palpable tension in the room. It felt as though we were having this trivial conversation just to hear ourselves talk. Our eyes met. "What do you think, Steve? Is this mess finally over? Could Wendell have killed both Angie and Cam, regardless of what Audrey thinks?"

Steve gazed at the fire, which was starting to die out. "Yeah, Erin. I think that Wendell was paying both Angie and the sheriff to do what he wanted, and that Angie wasn't playing by his rules. Ultimately, neither was Mackey. So I think Wendell killed Cameron for betraying him."

"I hope you're right. I mean ... you must be. I've suspected him from the start." It's just that Audrey was so seldom wrong about people. Trying to snap myself out of a sinking mood, I said with a forced smile, "I think this is the first time we've been alone here since we arrived."

"Yeah. We should celebrate." His voice was oddly flat.

"You don't sound all that enthused," I remarked.

"I am." He gave me an apologetic smile. "Sorry. I was concocting a plan in my head. That's all."

"A plan?"

"Absolutely. For our celebration. For having the place to ourselves. And for finishing our job ahead of time, and in Gilbert and Sullivan Designs typical unparalleled style."

"You mean Sullivan and Gilbert Designs."

"Right. Isn't that what I said?"

"No, you said my name first."

"I'm not really listening to myself." Once again, he

seemed to be avoiding my eyes, and he was making me a little nervous.

Now that I thought about it, *he* was the one who was acting strangely nervous. I could have sworn his hand shook a little as he raked it through his hair.

"I'm going to run to the store and get a bottle of chilled champagne. I'll be back in a few minutes."

"Okay. I'll make dinner."

He searched my eyes. "Actually, Erin, just in case Henry comes storming home in a few minutes, raving about Chiffon's being nuts, how about champagne in our room first... dinner later."

Oh, my god. Although jumping out of my skin, I nodded. "That sounds wonderful," I managed to say with a resemblance of calmness. Steve pivoted and left. My knees were shaking and it was all I could do to grab two champagne flutes and head up the stairs.

Unless I'd grown completely delusional, Steve was about to propose to me.

Chapter 32

Bombarded by emotions, I climbed the stairs to our bedroom. I was scared half to death at the thought of Steve popping the question—and even more scared at the possibility that he had no intention of doing any such thing. The memory of our first meeting three years ago raced through my brain. He had been belligerent, sure that I'd deliberately named my business "Designs by Gilbert" and located myself two blocks down from him on the same street in order to trick potential "Sullivan Designs" customers into coming to me. I'd thought he was a detestable, arrogant jerk.

Several months ago, when our love felt impervious, we'd teased each other about our first impressions. I'd found out that he'd felt much the same way about me — that I'd been haughty, the hot new designer from New York who was going to sweep onto his turf and show him, the hick designer from Colorado, what true style was all about.

I shut the bedroom door behind me, feeling more panicked than ever. The same insecurities that had brought out the worst in me back then still weighed me down, and Sullivan had his own burdens, as well. We'd risen above them for the last several months. Why were we fooling ourselves into thinking Wendell Barton's arrest meant we were free to move forward? Maybe the only lesson to be learned here was that we weren't in control of our own lives, not even our love for each other.

How arrogant to think we could keep our love alive when our very presence seemed to draw forth such murderous hatred in the people who surrounded us. Ours was a relationship that had been doomed from the start! The way our luck had gone so far, when we were saying our vows at the altar, an earthquake would strike the church, and the falling shards of stained glass would take out the priest and half of the wedding party!

Then again, if I were ever to relay these fears to Steve, he would smile and say: *Then let's elope*. The simple truth was that I was hopelessly in love with the guy. If I *had* to be on a rudderless boat, he was the man I wanted to be sitting beside.

We'd intentionally made our own bedroom wildly ro-
mantic. *We might as well take full advantage of that ourselves during our final night up here.* I set down the
champagne flutes on the oak highboy and changed into
my nicest negligee (also my *only* negligee, but then, I had
to pay a fortune for the wardrobe I wore when making
pitches to clients. Nightgowns received the short shrift).

I got a fire going, still somewhat regretting our decision
to stick with the existing wood-burning fireplace. However, the gas lines would have cost a fortune to run and
would have driven up the heating bill. Still, a romantic fire
at the flip of a switch would have been sumptuous. I
turned on the CD player, not remembering what CD we'd
left in there, and grimaced when I realized it was *The
Nutcracker Suite*. Surely I could find something more romantic than that in the small rack we'd incorporated into
our built-ins alongside the bed.

Someone knocked on the door. Sullivan was back already? He must have grabbed a bottle at a dead run. I
hadn't even had time to refresh my makeup.

"Come in," I said, battling yet another attack of nerves.
The door opened, and Mikara stood there, looking as startled to see me as I was to see her. "Mikara. You're back."

"I thought you and Steve had left. His van's gone."

"He's out getting champagne, actually. To celebrate
the near completion of our assignment here."

"You must have thought I was him."

"Yeah, and it's one of my more embarrassing moments,
actually." Imagining my having arranged myself in a
highly suggestive pose, I added, "It could have been a lot
worse, though, I suppose."

I'd said that jokingly, but she seemed highly distracted and didn't react. Her hands were gripping a set of folded linens so tightly that her knuckles were white. She was studying the room as if committing it to memory.

"What happened to your dinner with friends tonight?" I asked.

"Cancelled. I barely got out of the driveway before my friend Carol called me. My other friend, Mildred, has that awful flu virus that's going around."

"I'm sorry to hear that."

"We had an interesting little conversation on the phone, though."

"Oh? What about?"

No reply.

"You must be relieved that an arrest was made." I scooted back against the headboard, dearly wishing I hadn't changed into such a risqué nightgown.

Mikara said nothing, now staring at the unlit candles above the bed.

Growing more uncomfortable by the moment, I offered, "Those are the eleven miniature pipers piping."

"That my true love gave to me," she said, harshly.

"Uh, thanks for bringing up the linens." I hoped she'd take the hint and leave.

She shifted her gaze to the fireplace and dropped the linens on the bench at the foot of the bed. She clicked her tongue. "That's not much of a fire you built."

"Fires are not my forte."

"I'll get it going for you."

"No, Mikara. But thanks. Steve can do it."

"It's no bother." She started jabbing at the logs with the

poker. She was mostly just holding the sharp point of the poker in the flame, though her every movement seemed to be filled with venom.

My heart rate started to increase. Could Audrey have been right all along about Wendell's innocence? Surely Mikara would never have killed her own sister; her grief after Angie's death had struck me as sincere. And what possible motive would she have had to kill Cameron?

In fact, Mikara as the murderer didn't make any sense. My imagination was running away with me again, making me afraid of her for no good reason. I'd been through too many incidents in which I was forced to confront a killer on my own; I'd become paranoid. "You're getting that poker overheated," I said.

She removed the sharp point from the flames. "I can see why Barton killed Cam, but I don't know why he'd also kill my sister," Mikara said, staring at the poker in her hand.

"Your sister was a smart woman. It must have been because Angie was turning the tables on Cameron or Wendell . . . blackmailing the man who had bribed her."

"As if money matters to anybody when you're faced with your life coming to nothing." A tear was running down her cheek. "With your hopes and dreams turning to ashes."

Okay. This conversation was heading straight to hell. Paranoid or not, I lifted the bronze eleven-pipers candelabra off the shelf. Mikara was acting and sounding wacky, and, worse, she wasn't putting down the poker. I rose, keeping my defensive weapon behind my back as I covertly yanked the candles from the holders and stashed them on the bed.

Where was my cell phone? I glanced around the room. Damn it! I'd left it downstairs in my purse. "Mikara, I don't mean to be rude, but I forgot that I needed to make—"

"Everything was all finally going to turn out fine for me. For once it was going to be about me, not my damned little sister, who everyone always doted on, who always had everything so much easier than me. Sure, she had her loser husband, but I was going to be married to the prince—to Henry Goodwin. Cinderella rising from the ashes."

Oh, God. Not again! I'm going to have to fight for my life with a killer!

"You had to rub that all in my face, didn't you, Erin? You *had* to set the photograph of Henry and Angie on Henry's nightstand!"

"It wasn't me! I found that photo already there, face-down. Where would I even find an old photo like that?"

"My damned classmates made him the prom king, and her the *queen*, even though she was just a sophomore! She wasn't even eligible, except as his date! That's why she plotted to have him ask her, you know. My own sister, my own classmates did that! Humiliated me! And yet, years later, I almost won him anyway. Except she stabbed me in the back and slept with him before our wedding."

"But...didn't all of that take place a decade ago?"

"Our parents left *her* the house in their will! I'm sure they did that because they'd thought I'd be Mrs. Henry

Goodwin, way back when they had the papers drawn up. And then my whole town got wrecked, by people like you. Angie was going to take it all away from me. She sent that chair full of poisonous spiders herself! She was trying to kill me! I had no choice. It was her or me. She didn't realize I had that kind of strength in me. That she couldn't tromp all over me anymore. And *you* underestimated me, too."

"How?"

"By snooping around Mildred and Carol, and thinking I wouldn't find out till you had me arrested! And, on top of that, you just *had* to taunt me with the photograph, didn't you?"

"I did not! I found it on the nightstand, and I left it there! Maybe Henry put it there. In any case, I've been on your side all along!"

Mikara's crazy! I should have realized that clear back when we first met. She must have planted the bones by the front steps, just to stir up misery. And she probably splattered hamburger blood on my folder. And poisoned my eggnog.

She shook her head. "Henry would never have hurt me that way. Did you put the picture there as some kind of a sick joke? Did you get a good laugh at my expense?"

"No! If it wasn't Henry, it was Chiffon. She went upstairs when we were all in the kitchen. *She* must have brought the picture into the house this morning. When she came here to get her things from Henry's room."

I saw a flicker of surprise dawn on her features. She realized she'd accused me for no reason. Still, she took a step toward me with the hot poker.

I backed up against the wall and gripped the candelabra as though it were a baseball bat. "Mikara. You can't get away with this. Steve will be back any moment. Run away. Leave town. Start a new life."

"I can't! This town was my only home. You and your kind stole it all away from me!" She shook her head, her eyes wild. "You had it in for me at the start. That's why I tried to poison you. And I wanted Chiffon to break her neck skiing so she'd keep her claws off Henry. How was I supposed to know you two had identical skis? It's all gone to pieces. Carol and Mildred knew how much I hated Angie. How I'd vowed I'd die before I'd see anyone plow this house down, after what those bastards did to mine."

"They never told me anything of the sort, Mikara," I argued automatically, even though I knew I was wasting my breath.

"You just *had* to poke your nose into things. Talk to my friends. To my old boss. You had no right!"

In a flash, Mikara swung the hot poker at me. I anticipated the move and blocked the poker as if parrying with a sword. She seemed surprised by the solidness of the bronze piece in my hands.

I swung at her face. She dodged the blow, but tripped and fell to her knees, losing her grip on the poker. I tried to race to the door, but my feet were suddenly yanked out from under me. I fell flat on the floor, realizing too late that I'd tried to run across the red-and-green throw rug. Mikara had pulled it right out from under me.

My breath was knocked out. Mikara had me by the hair before I could even suck in a single breath. I automatically pressed both of her hands down to ease the pressure on my scalp.

"You're about to have an accident down three flights of stairs," she snarled at me. She dragged me from the room by my hair.

"No! Stop! I didn't do anything to you!"

"Cameron would never have come here in the first place if it weren't for you! I didn't want to kill him. But he needed to die. He was going to plow under Henry's house, *my* house, just like Wendell did to my childhood home! I was going to be left with nothing!"

"Stop! Please!" The pain was excruciating.

"You easterners come to Colorado and you think you can just take it over! You and all your superior airs."

This all felt so surreal. I was crying from the pain, hooking the banisters with my feet. I dug my nails into her wrist and hand. She loosened her grip on my hair.

"You ruined my life!" she screamed at me. "You ruined my hometown!"

"I did not! I barely even know you!"

Mikara stopped, unable to drag me closer to the stairs without tumbling down them herself.

She let go and tried to move behind me. Before she could, I broke off a fistful of sharp holly leaves from the garland and slashed at her eyes.

Mikara yelped in pain, but recovered. She started to strangle me. She was just too strong. Everything was going gray.

I was dimly aware of a noise below us. Was that the back door opening? "Help!" I cried with my last remains of air in my lungs.

"Erin?" It was Audrey's voice.

Mikara hesitated, startled. I thrust the heel of my hand into her chin with all my might. She was staggered by the blow. I grabbed onto the banister, then thrust-kicked her square in the chest.

Mikara gasped, lost her balance, and tumbled head over heels down the stairs.

I sat up, gripping the railing, feeling severely battered. Although she was lying still on the second-floor landing, I heard Mikara groan. She was alive, though knocked unconscious.

"Erin! Good Lord! What the hell just happened!" Audrey yelled. "Is *Mikara* the killer?"

"Yeah. She tried to kill *me*, too."

Steve bolted into the central hall and raced toward Audrey. He dropped the bottle of champagne onto the leather club chair. He looked up at me. "Good God! Erin? What's going on? Are you okay?"

"I'll be fine." My neck and scalp were throbbing and my limbs hurt, but that was nothing compared to Mikara's injuries.

"Mikara tried to kill Erin," Audrey cried. "I'll call nine-one-one."

Steve charged past Mikara without a second glance and raced up the stairs two at a time. He sat down beside me and gently took me in his arms.

I pulled Steve closer as, below us, Mikara appeared to regain consciousness and moaned, "Henry? Henry?" She moved, shifting her position on the hardwood floor at the base of the stairs. "Ow! My head! My leg!"

"Don't move!" Audrey shouted at her, grabbing the

champagne bottle by its neck and lowering the cell phone in her other hand. "You stay put, or I'll club you!"

Mikara began to whimper. "I need to go to sleep now. Don't tell Henry. Please. He mustn't ever know that I still love him."

Chapter 33

When hosting large Christmas parties, focus on making your guests relax and take the night off from their seasonal to-do list. A festive, convivial mood is automatically in the air, so you're already halfway to a great party!

—Audrey Munroe

Domestic Bliss

One week later, on Christmas Eve morning, Steve dropped me off at my house. He was going to pick me up in a couple of hours to drive me up to Snowcap for the big Christmas Eve party to celebrate the inn's grand opening. (The open house on Friday had, of course, been canceled.) My muscles and neck were still aching; my body sported various bruises. Hildi pranced over to me the moment I'd entered from the foyer. I stroked her soft fur for a few seconds, and was surprised to smell the aroma of fresh-baked cookies and to hear the rustling of paper from the kitchen.

Indeed, to my surprise, Audrey was still here in Crestview. After Mikara's arrest, and Wendell's subsequent release, Audrey had accompanied

Steve and me back home, but she'd continued to plan for the party at the inn from afar. She'd also decorated her house more since last night, although she'd ultimately deserted her blue, purple, and silver idea and reused the ornaments from Christmases past.

I said hello, and she gave me a perky: "Good morning!" She was individually wrapping homemade sugar cookies in red or green foil and then securing a candy cane with a shiny silver bow.

"The Christmas decorations look great," I told her honestly. "I'm sorry that I was never able to get going on the purple, blue, and sometimes silver ornaments."

She gave me an easy smile and a shrug. "Next year."

"I assumed you'd be staying at Wendell's house or in one of his condos last night. Shouldn't you be up in Snowcap by now, staging tonight's party?"

"There's plenty of time. I'm leaving in another hour or two. I'm putting the party favors together now."

"For, like, a hundred guests? Couldn't you have hired someone to do that?"

"Of course, if I'd wanted to. But this gave me something to do these past couple of days."

"In addition to decorating the entire house," I said, still feeling a pang of guilt, although I knew full well that Audrey would have been angry if, under the circumstances, I'd felt obligated to go ahead and make purple and blue wreaths and centerpieces for her. "If it was me who was hosting an enormous party ninety-plus minutes away, I'd be panicking by now."

"Oh, everything's pretty much already done, Erin. I checked with Henry. The rental company delivered the extra chairs yesterday. It's already a picture-perfect setting for a Christmas party." With a wistful lilt to her voice, she said, "The house itself nestled in among the evergreens with all that pristine powder snow...you can't get more evocative than that. The inn's decorations are absolutely stunning, thanks to you and Steve." She went back to her busywork; she'd laid out her star-shaped cookies atop pieces of foil in rows of five. "I just need to get there in time to set the mood and light a few scented candles, put some appropriate music on the sound system, set the dimmers for each room, and put the first basket of party favors near the front door."

"*And* make sure the caterers and bartenders aren't going to flake out at the last minute." With my chin, I pointed at her task at hand. "Can I help you with that?"

"No, thanks. I'm almost finished, and I honestly enjoy doing things like this." She gestured at the kitchen stool. "Have a seat, Erin."

I didn't argue. I felt a sharp pain from my bruised leg while easing myself into the seat.

"Even if neither the caterers nor the bartenders show up, we'll be fine." She put a group of five completed cookie-candy-cane bundles into a pretty wicker basket. "When it comes to food and drink for parties, I've always got a Plan B. In this case, it's a gourmet pizza place that delivers, including on Christmas Eve, and they are happy to do a crosscut on their pizzas to produce bite-sized pieces. The inn's wine cellar is well stocked. We're in good shape."

"Except if that were really to happen, you *also* wouldn't have a serving staff."

She paused in her work and looked up at me. "You know, Erin, that has actually happened to me a couple of times over the years, and it's really not all that terrible. Shortly after the guests arrive, I make a big show of kicking my shoes off and suggest that everyone do the same, and I announce that the party's officially turned into self-serve. In actuality, there's always a percentage of guests who feel more comfortable when they're able to lend a hand anyway. Next thing you know, someone's running around with platters of pizzas or heated pot stickers, and someone else is mixing drinks or pouring wine. All you have to do as hostess is make it clear that you're enjoying the company yourself. You simply set the right tone. You focus on making your guests feel comfortable and wanted. And you try to match up the introverts with the extroverts during your introductions. It couldn't be more simple."

"You've got hosting parties down to a fine art. But, in all honesty, Audrey, that just doesn't sound easy to me."

"Maybe not in your current circumstances. I'm just really, really grateful that you and Steve are coming up tonight, despite everything."

I winced a little, truly wanting to be excused from that obligation. Truth be told, what I'd wanted the most for

Christmas was simply the opportunity to spend Christmas Eve at home with Steve and Hildi.

"Erin, your being there for the inn's opening gala means the world to me."

"You're playing me, aren't you," I stated.

"Like a fiddle. But I sincerely do need you there for emotional reasons that I'm not willing to delve into just now. So humor me, as a personal favor."

"But Audrey—"

"Erin, this is all I want from you for Christmas. Please."

"I'd just been thinking the same thing, in reverse."

"Lucky for me, then, that I said it first." She winked at me, and I knew that once again, she was going to win this argument. She pointed at the bag in the chair beside me. "Could you grab me some more candy canes? And then tie one to each cookie packet?"

Chapter 34

A light snow was falling as Sullivan and I made the drive up the mountains. The guests would be arriving shortly after us, thanks to my shameless procrastination.

I hadn't been back to the Snowcap Inn since my battle at the top of the stairs, five days before. Steve had promised me we'd leave the party no later than midnight, and that he'd drive us back down to Crestview. The traffic at that hour, he reminded me, would be light. We'd be home by one-thirty on Christmas morning.

Audrey had taken off about four hours earlier and probably had everything under control by now. Still enthused about being a part owner of the inn, she was saddened by my abhorrence of the place. Knowing her, however, she was also confident she could change my mind eventually. There seemed little point in explaining that I was already battling nightmares every time I fell asleep and that I didn't feel safe in Snowcap.

A couple of hours later, the party was in full swing. Audrey, Steve, and I had alternated taking guests on tours of the house, starting at the pear tree and zigzagging our way through the house till we reached the twelve drummers in the master bedroom. On each of my three turns as tour guide, my thoughts had been fully occupied with the task at hand, and I only felt myself growing anxious afterward, whenever I found myself standing at the top of the stairs.

Audrey's miniature ornaments echoing our theme were also a big hit. I was admiring the tree decorations up close when a woman's voice said, "Hello, Erin."

I turned and said, "Hi, Carol." I wondered if Mildred was here, too. "I was just thinking that I like Audrey's turtledoves better than the two pillows I got for your room."

"Oh, that's not my room. Didn't Henry tell you? That room's going to be the inn's overflow guest bedroom. I'm happy living with Mildred. I don't want to make this a live-in position."

"I'm out of the loop. All Henry told me was that the art gallery was going out of business, and you'd agreed to take over Mikara's role. Also that you were a brilliant manager."

"Yes, well . . . it's been all of two days so far."

"I'm sorry to hear about the gallery closing. I hate to see anything having to do with the arts go under."

"Me, too. But the fact is, Mildred and I were in the red all this past year. When we heard about Mikara's confession, well, Mildred threw up her hands. She said she'd been working by her side in that store all those years, and she was fed up. She announced she was going to retire and read books all day long. And finally take cello lessons."

"You weren't ready to retire yourself?"

"Not by a long shot. Then, wouldn't you know, Henry came into the gallery, only an hour or so after I'd put the 'Going Out of Business' sign in the window. He was desperate, and he offered to hire me on the spot. Frankly, I leapt at it. Not to brag, but I'm perfectly suited for this job. I'd been wanting to open a small B-and-B myself, but I hadn't the heart to desert Mildred and the gallery. I'd been green with envy when Mikara got this job. Now I'm managing the Snowcap Inn. Mildred's retiring and closing up the gallery for good the end of next month. And Mikara's in jail for her heinous, horrible crimes. Everything's as it should be." She smiled, but it started to fade a moment later. "Or rather, *almost* everything is." She was staring past my shoulder, and I turned and followed her gaze. Chiffon had latched onto Henry's arm.

"Those two are dating again?" I asked.

"No sensible person would bet on their union lasting beyond New Year's Eve."

Or beyond Christmas Eve, for that matter. I watched as the front door opened. "Oh. Ben's here. I'm going to say hi."

By the time I'd crossed the crowded central hall, Ben was chatting with Chiffon and Henry. I joined the trio, and we exchanged greetings, Chiffon's somewhat cool.

"I'd better go work the room," Chiffon said to Henry. "I'll look for you again in a few minutes." She gave his arm a squeeze, then headed toward a pair of elegantly dressed couples who were standing near the partridge in the pear tree.

"We're back together again," Henry explained, superfluously.

"I don't know what to say to that," Ben said.

"Yeah. Can't say as I blame you, with my track record," Henry replied.

"Did you hear *my* news?" Ben asked him.

"I heard what I'd hoped was a false rumor," Henry said. "It's not true, is it? You're really leaving Snowcap after all this time?"

"You *are*?" I asked, already happy for him.

"Yep. I rented a little house in Denver as of the first of the year . . . got hired by a first-rate contractor."

"Hate to see you go." Henry shook his head. "I don't know how they'll replace you."

"*They?*" Ben repeated.

"Wendell and company. Here at the inn."

"I'm sure they'll manage just fine," Ben snapped. "Anyway. I actually have other plans tonight. I just wanted to stop by. Season's greetings, Henry."

"Hey, you, too. Good luck to you." They shook hands,

then Henry said, "I'd better go work the room myself." He headed for a group of people standing at the opposite side of the room from Chiffon.

I gave Ben a hug and wished him a merry Christmas. I urged him not to hesitate to let us know if he was available to work on the occasional remodel job. He cast one last sad look in Henry's direction, then headed for the door.

As the night wore on, Audrey, as usual, was the perfect hostess, and Wendell was fully in his element. None of the people who'd booked rooms were from Colorado, a fact which gave Wendell the opportunity to pontificate on "champagne powder" and the wonders of "a Colorado Christmas." From my perspective, though, the conversation was tedious, and I was relieved when Wendell discovered that one of the couples had yet to go on what he'd termed "the official Twelve Days tour," and whisked them off.

Audrey escorted me to a quiet corner near the kitchen and asked in a low voice, "You're still not terribly fond of Wendell, are you?"

"What matters is that you like him, so I'll try not to be anything less than gracious when we're together."

"Have no fear, Erin. Wendell and I have had our fun, and there are no hard feelings, but he was never going to be the one to spend my golden years with me."

"Really?"

"You're trying hard not to sound relieved, but you can go right ahead and admit it."

"Okay, yes, I'm very relieved."

She pursed her lips. "You weren't actually worried that I'd fallen for him, were you?"

"We can't always control our feelings for people. Sometimes you can find yourself drawn to someone you don't even like."

"True, but that type of attraction never lasts for long." She searched my eyes and gave me a smile that struck me as maternal. "I don't mean to monopolize your time, though. Excuse me." She whirled around and headed through the kitchen doors. As I watched the doors wave back and forth in her wake, I wished once again that Henry hadn't insisted on keeping the stupid things; they'd forever reminded me of the saloon doors from *Gunsmoke*.

I was puzzled by her abrupt exit until I turned and saw Steve approach, wearing his coat. I returned his smile and said, "You're carrying my coat. No wonder Audrey fled the scene when she spotted you. You're ready to leave already."

"Actually, I wanted to get some air, so I thought we could take a quick stroll around the grounds first."

I hesitated. I had a sudden fear of seeing another body strangled with Christmas lights on the footbridge. Not giving me much choice in the matter, though, Steve helped me with my coat and ushered me toward the kitchen. We exchanged a few words of small talk with yet more guests in the kitchen, then slipped out the back door.

The chill air was invigorating, the stars were out, and the blanket of snow seemed to take on an ethereal glow. Directly ahead of us, the lights on the gazebo sparkled. Henry—or more likely Ben—had hooked up the speaker wires. One of my favorite carols—"O Holy Night"—was playing at a soft volume. "The gazebo looks really pretty," I said, happily lacing my fingers through his.

Steve gave my hand a squeeze as we crossed the yard. "It really does. You know, I barely set foot in the thing till this evening, when I came out to sweep the snow off the floorboards."

"That's the thing about most gazebos, especially in winter. They're seldom used. Most of them make you feel like you're on a ministage in the middle of somebody's backyard."

Despite my words, Steve was leading me right toward the gazebo. We climbed the three steps. I was starting to get suspicious, but said nothing. "I hung one last Christmas decoration here," Steve said. "I'll show it to you." He led me to the center of the octagonal floor and said, "It's kind of corny, I know, but look over your head."

I gave him a wry smile, still gazing into his eyes and not overhead. "*Mistletoe?* From *you*, Sullivan?" I looked up and was momentarily startled. A small gray-and-red toy rocket dangled from a thread. Suspended beside it was a pink balloon, shaped like a foot, with red and green ribbons tied around its big toe. I laughed. "Missile toe."

I lowered my eyes to look at him and gasped. He'd dropped to one knee. He was holding a blue Tiffany ring box. My eyes filled with tears.

"Before I met you, Erin, I was alone. Since then, there has always been somebody trying to take you away from me. You've told me more than once that the Fates are aligned against us. I can't believe that the Fates are that foolish, but in any case, my love for you is a stronger force.

Please say that you'll marry me. Allow me to be your husband for the rest of my life."

I hesitated, but only because I was too choked up to speak.

"Please say yes, Erin. I'll let you keep the missile. And the balloon."

My laughter mingled with my tears as I said, "Well, in *that* case, yes."

Steve slipped the stunning ring on my finger, and it fit perfectly. He stood up and swept me off my feet into his arms. Behind us, I heard cheers, and was now certain that Audrey had known about Steve's plan all along; it explained why she'd been so adamant about my coming up to the inn tonight.

Very soon, I intended to turn around and acknowledge Audrey and our fellow partyers, who were no doubt lined up along the windows, watching us embrace. But for this one moment, I was already with my entire world.

about the author

LESLIE CAINE was once taken hostage at gunpoint and finds that writing about crime is infinitely more enjoyable than taking part in them. Leslie is a certified interior decorator and lives in Colorado with her husband and a cocker spaniel.